LUCIFER'S ORIGINS

J.M. ERICKSON

The Prince: Lucifer's Origins

Editor: Sara at *Kirkus Editorial*
Senior Editor: Suzanne M. Owen

Cover design: Cathy Helms, Avalon Graphics, LLC
http://www.avalongraphics.org/

Publisher: J. M. Erickson
http://www.jmericksonindiewriter.net

Interior Formatting: eB Format
http://www.ebformat.com/

ISBN: 1-942708-06-8 (Soft Cover)
ISBN: 1-942708-07-0 (MOBI Format)
ISBN: 1-942708-08-7 (ePub Format)

Library of Congress Control Number: 2015904464

THE PRINCE: LUCIFER'S ORIGINS BOOK REVIEWS

"The Prince: Lucifer's Origins is a fast-paced, survivalist nail-biter, with a large helping of science fiction adventure, a dash of military action, and a pinch of coming-of-age drama." ***Self-Publishing Review***

"...a great science fiction tale with plenty of classical and religious references...Not only do I love this book, I love the idea of this book." **Ray Simmons,** *Readers' Favorite Reviews*

"The Prince is a compelling novel of action, survival, and stark morality, where the struggles range from unique and personal to galaxy-shaking." ***Self-Publishing Review***

"Erickson presents strong, talented women of varying ages who hold their own in what is still largely a patriarchal universe...there's plenty of action, intrigue and humanity to enjoy as well." **K.C. Finn,** *Readers' Favorite Reviews*

"Science fiction enthusiasts will no doubt find *The Prince* entertaining, and there are elements enough of other genres to draw a readership from a far larger crowd." ***Self-Publishing Review***

"The Prince: Lucifer's Origins, is a thought-provoking and intense read that's brimming with action, adventure and exploration." **Jack Magnus,** *Readers' Favorite Reviews*

"Various peoples, planets, societies, aliens, customs, and technologies populate the book, which creates a setting that feels viable and a depth that is palpable as the plot progresses." ***Self-Publishing Review***

"The characters created have such a depth to them that you could almost picture yourself walking on this journey right alongside them." **Kathryn Bennett,** *Readers' Favorite Reviews*

Other novels by this author:

Action/Adventure Thrillers

Albatross: Birds of Flight—Book One (Revised)
Raven: Birds of Flight—Book Two
Eagle: Birds of Flight—Book Three
Falcon: Birds of Flight—Book Four
Flight of the Black Swan

Action/Adventure Science Fiction

Future Prometheus I: Emergence & Evolution—Novellas I & II
Future Prometheus II: Revolution, Successions & Resurrections—Novellas III, IV & V
Intelligent Design: Revelations

LIST OF CHARACTERS

Prince Victor Venture IX—Twelve years old, one of many princes who are heir to the kingdom. He hoped that he had been forgotten so he could spend his time learning on the university planet, Pax. As a royal it's expected that he leave this learning society when he is eight years old, but he was left behind for an additional four years. His brother Prince Jason made room in his court for him so he could eventually take over Sagittarius Sector. While he was recovering from an operation to implant an AI symbiont in his frontal lobe, Victor received orders to leave Pax and go first to the Royal Academy and then to join Prince Jason in the Sagittarius Sector.

Sergeant Marcia Devin—Disillusioned and tired special operations expert and former captain, she and her team—Corporal Dias, Privates Ross, Athena, Mayer, and Nova and other specialists—are busted down in rank for not following orders to attack protesting citizens on Oceania. In what she expects will be her last assignment, her job is to escort Prince Victor from Pax to the Sagittarius Sector. Her orders and sources have indicated that this prince is somehow special. What is also evident is that the prince's eldest brother, Prince Ramsey of Capricorn Sector, wants him dead. Sergeant Devin and her team are there to make sure that doesn't happen.

Captain Regina Devin—Independent contractor and captain of the stealth ship *Nightfall*, she is four years younger than her cousin Marcia Devin. Their families lived together on an agricultural planet. While Marcia was conscripted into the royal forces, Regina and her family left before she too was pulled into service. While both women are very different, they are also very close and trust each other with their very lives.

Mary, the pilot—Fifteen-year-old, talented, skilled pilot of the *Nightfall*'s descent ships as well as ship mechanic, she was orphaned and has been taken under Captain Regina Devin's care. Prior to her metamorphosis, Mary was a loner, serious, not very expressive, and certainly not seen as happy. But once she's exposed to the forces of the planet Hell, she changes with more strength and powers than thought possible for a teenage pilot.

Theta—Xenon science officer of the *Nightfall*, he is one of three aliens serving under the command of Regina Devin. It is unusual for Xenons to spend time with hominids, as they tend to stay within their own territories with their own species. They see the kingdom and hominids as immature, and have in the past stepped in to quell internal struggles and interplanetary violence. Technologically more advanced, ancient creatures with six limbs, heavy structures, deep voices, and vast intellect, they know a great deal about hominids and Origins Sector.

Commander Jana Virgil—Once vice admiral of her battle group, she was busted down to commander and assigned an old heavy cruiser, *Rising Sun*, for her refusal to suppress riots and protesting on the planet Oceania. Skeptical and with only a few members of her crew loyal to her, her goal is to keep Prince Victor safe from his brother, Prince Ramsey, and even his father, King Talus, and to give him a chance to prove himself.

Hell—Third planet of a small, yellow star on the very edge of the known galaxy. Archaeological theories place this planet as the original birthplace of the hominid species of their worlds.

While the planet, located in Origins Sector, is actually named Earth, it is called Hell since its core and gravity have been altered, creating a harsh environment, hostile inhabitants, and a time-space distortion that is unpredictable; there are times when minutes experienced on Earth are experienced very differently farther away from the planet. Hours on Earth could be months or years on a ship orbiting the planet. This planet holds many secrets that, once unleashed, will change the known galaxy.

It must be considered that there is nothing more difficult to carry out, nor more doubtful of success, nor more dangerous to handle, than to initiate a new order of things. — Niccolò Machiavelli, *The Prince*

CHAPTER 1
PLANET MERIDIAN SIX

I'm not interested in preserving the status quo; I want to overthrow it. — Niccolò Machiavelli

Sergeant Marcia Devin opened the saloon door slowly at first, until she was sure there was no one on the other side. The poorly lit room was filled with exquisite aromas, noise, and overall good cheer from the patrons within the drinking establishment. It was a welcome sensation as her eyes adjusted from the bright sun to the darker room. The environment was in stark contrast to the bright, sandy road she had traversed to get here, even though she'd been dropped only meters from the door. The air-conditioning and cool breeze, in comparison to the still heated air outside, dried the sweat on her exposed skin within seconds. And while she was out of her royal guard uniform and full tactical gear, she was still sweaty from the one-piece battle dress uniform she wore. The plan was to be unobtrusive and draw only the attention of her guest, whom she was sure would recognize her.

All was good until the door closed behind Devin. Her vision was adjusting even though she could feel the patrons' eyes all over her. The noise level dropped off to the clinking of ice and drinks being placed on the table. Devin looked around and knew she was persona non grata. With very little in the way of weaponry, she could see that the number of antiroyal, antigovernment customers far outweighed those loyal to the royal family and kingdom.

"What do you want?" the barwoman said.

Not very inviting, Devin thought.

"I'm here to meet someone."

"Here? Do you know where you are, soldier?" a patron at the front of the bar said.

Devin had a sudden flashback to an earlier conversation she'd had with her team about the nature and place of the meeting. All had been opposed. Their logic both then and now was not without merit.

"I know where I am," Devin said. She walked defiantly toward the bar. The few people in her way moved aside as if she had some flesh-eating disease. The man who spoke to her looked uncomfortable, but she could see he would be the type to throw the first punch. She was sure the barwoman had one hand on her weapon—the only weapon allowed in the bar.

"She sure does know where she is," a young female voice from the other side of the bar sang out. Devin felt the corners of her mouth curl up. The voice was older than she remembered but the tone and the beautiful quality of it were unmistakable. Devin made sure to put both her hands on the bar as an indicator of being unarmed, respecting the planet's local customs about no weapons in the presence of food and drink. It took her just a moment to see the young woman approach. She wore her hair long in an elaborate braid and was dressed in a skintight two-piece outfit that displayed the smooth, pale skin of her midriff and too much cleavage for Devin's liking. Devin narrowed her eyes and frowned in disapproval. Her expression did not go unnoticed by the young woman.

"I haven't seen you in five years. You give me a day's notice of your arrival and I get that look? What's up with you, Marcia?" The tone, though firm, was not angry.

"I just think that a young woman with such a gift of

beauty doesn't need to flaunt it so much. I mean, really, Regina. What would your mother say?"

The woman rolled her eyes and the exchange elicited some laughter from the patrons. Their jocularity ceased when the young woman raised her hand up and made a tight fist. The room fell silent as a tomb. Devin found the response remarkable. The only time she saw that kind of response was when she was in the field with her team on some operation that required stealth.

"I see. This is a bit more than the usual bar," Devin said as she looked a bit closer at the faces and then boots the patrons wore. The male faces were either clean-shaven or had well-manicured facial hair. The women's hair was pulled back in tight buns while the intersex—those having both gender characteristics—had very short hair. Regardless of the length of their hair, they all appeared to be clean on a sandy, dirty planet. Their boots were all a dull black, the same dull black as her own. Devin was smiling as the woman came within three feet of her. Her crew was right. She had walked right into a trap.

"So. As I live and breathe. Captain Marcia Devin, royal guard, black ops specialist and questionable loyalty to king and crown. Well, have you and your team finally come to your senses and want to sign on the right side of history? Maybe fight for justice and equity rather than maintaining the status quo of those bastards?"

The woman folded her arms, which only enhanced her slender figure and her large breasts. Even though Devin was taller than her, the younger woman oozed her own authority and power.

"It's sergeant now. I was busted down several ranks for not following orders," Devin corrected. She was still not used to her drastic demotion.

The woman remained silent. The bar was still as if

waiting for a more accurate response.

"I'm fighting the enemy from the inside. More will be accomplished that way. But I may need to be more bold and come out from the shadows in this next move," Devin explained...

The woman's demeanor became serious and her eyes looked deep into Devins,' as if she was looking for the truth. After a brief moment, she sighed and leaned in to hug her. The embrace was not a surprise except that her grip was stronger than Devin expected.

"We have all missed you, Marcia. Your mother and father are after me all the time to see if I can find out what you're up to. And Mom is guilting me to death to drop my efforts, find you and get the hell out to the distant colonies."

Devin hugged her back and took in the strong smell of her younger cousin's perfume. It was a mixture of an ancient smell of something she remembered as cocoa bean and cinnamon.

"I missed you, too, Regina," was all Devin could say. A flood of memories overtook her for just a moment, of a simpler time when she and her family all lived together in a farming community. Warm winters and hot summers were filled with hard work, lots of playtime at night, drinking, driving, and sex. All great times. As Regina pulled away so did the memories of a time long gone. She'd been conscripted into the Royal Special Operations Team and Regina and the family had gone underground. She'd gone on to protection detail for the royal family and become disillusioned. Regina had joined the succession efforts to make a living and supported the Xenon invasion. After years of not seeing each other, a chance meeting several years ago had revealed more similarities than differences. Above all, they'd agreed that there would be loyalty to family first and foremost. Whenever one needed the other, all they had to do was ask. Regina, for her part, made far more requests than Devin did. This was the first favor Devin was going to ask. It was a big one.

"Everybody! This is my cousin—Marcia!"

The hostile crowd burst into shouts of joy and appreciation. Devin was surprised at the sudden turn of good cheer and the slapping on the back she received in addition to several thank-yous. Regina guided her through the crowd to the back of the bar. As the crowd thinned out in the back, she found herself sitting at a table where there were two pints waiting. The barwoman placed some kind of cooked meat and side dishes on the table just as Devin sat down.

"Thank you so much, Sergeant Devin. The money you sent built my business back up and I got my family tickets to get out of here. Thank you," the woman said with a strong hug and kiss on the lips.

Devin was surprised at how quickly the woman moved and receded before she could even respond. She looked at Regina, still in shock.

"That black operation you dialed us in on before the *Dauntless* showed up meant a cache of not only much needed medical supplies but precious metals, currency, and royal minted coins. My entire crew remembers that. That barwoman was my navigator for five years. I had to convince her to stay back here with her family and two children. She did, but she sent her girls and husband to the outer worlds for safety and she stays here as a base of operations. She likes both men and women, so if you're interested, she'll be more than happy to oblige," Regina said with a smirk. Devin was still taking it all in as she watched her thin cousin take a stab at her meat and pull a large piece off to eat. Devin took a moment to pull herself together before she spoke again. Even as Regina chewed her food and drank her ale, she continued talking throughout.

"Mom says that she's pissed at your dad for making her leave the core planets for the outer worlds. The good news is that my dad plans to get her and my brothers out next month. They'll be together soon. You ever think about bugging out and leaving the shit behind to be happy, Marcia? And it looks like you lost a lot of weight."

"Yeah. Lost some weight."

"No—you lost a lot of weight. I'd say it was the food, but I know your first officer there, Dias, can make animal waste taste good, so I know it's not that. Are you coming off of some spec ops or some miserable assignment?"

"Nope. I've asked for a protection detail for a prince on the planet Pax."

"That's the university planet. All the smart ones go there. I thought the royal family got their smarts from their cortical AIs? I hear they use real books and papers on that planet with all kinds of intergalactic news agencies from all sectors. Kind of a free-thinking place," Regina said all in one breath. Devin marveled at her speed of talking and her immediate ingestion of food and drink.

"Yup. He's different. My contact there got word this prince was to be rejoined with his family. He's different from them, from what I'm told. A possible new beginning. He needs help, though. My contact is convinced that this prince is perceived as too dangerous by his older brother, Prince Ramsey," Devin said in a low voice. Even though her immediate surroundings appeared friendly, she felt the need to keep her voice down and remain discreet.

"They all suck," Regina said aloud. "You ever really think about putting all of this cloak-and-dagger palace intrigue behind you? I'm ready to retire if you are. Half my crew will be happy to leave. Most lost their entire lands and families to the crown."

"I sure do think about leaving, but I need your help on this one. It may be the last one I do as a guard for king and crown," Devin said. It was easy to see that Regina's expression was that of total shock. She managed to swallow a large piece of meat and some kind of mashed material before she spoke next.

"Seriously?"

"Yes," Devin said. "The civilian protesting quelled on Oceania and her moons was enough for me."

The silence was palpable. The unfiltered images from two months ago, of the royal guards and infantry with heavy weapons and tractor vehicles, still hung in her head. Devin realized that she was looking down at her uneaten food. She'd stopped eating then with the sole exception of rations, the only thing she could keep down. She swam in her uniform even after Dias had taken it in herself.

"So it's the Oceania uprising that got to you. I hear they were looking for more rights to elect leaders. Three million citizens killed. Is that where you lost your commission?" Regina asked.

"My entire team did. Other commanders did as well. Even a vice admiral. Compared to four million killed, our lost commissions and ranks were nothing," Devin explained.

"Four million? The reports said three and a half."

"Three and a half million killed outright. Another half million from subsequent injuries. Scores more injured. And it wasn't over rights to vote. It was over food and water," Devin said.

"What!" Regina's voice carried and the patrons looked. She looked back at them and they continued to go about their business. "What do you mean, food and water?"

"I mean they wanted food and water, Regina. Just the basics that a local government should be able to provide. I was there."

"Are you bullshitting me? Were you part of the force to put them down?" Devin could see real fear in her cousin's eyes. It was obvious that she wanted her to say she was not.

"I was part of the force, but I refused to go." More silence filled the small table. Regina's eyes searched her, looking for clues.

"That's treason."

"Sure is. But Vice Fleet Admiral Jana Virgil of the Fifth Battle Group refused to engage her ship and her troops. That made it easy for all of us to stand together."

Regina's eyes widened in disbelief. If Devin hadn't been there to see the defiance of a direct royal order on a massive scale, she would never have believed. Devin went on to elaborate as her cousin's eyes and slackened mouth made it clear that she was having difficulty believing such a massive treasonous act.

"We arrived on day four of the protesting. The planetary forces and three battle groups had started their assault. We were ordered to take the eastern sectors and make sure any ships fleeing were destroyed—not captured or detained, but destroyed."

"No way!"

"Yes…Vice Admiral Virgil announced to her fleet that she had no intention of harming the very citizens she was sworn to protect. We did not engage. We didn't stop the slaughter. We let all ships that came in our sector fly by. Two of the five ships in her battle group had mutinies, which were put down by those loyal to Virgil."

"And you all got away with it? What the hell?"

Devin felt she was far away from her cousin as images of the horrors that had occurred below kept her awake at night. The admiral had not engaged, but she had allowed the hell to happen. Devin knew Virgil. She knew that it ate her up to sit and do nothing. Devin remembered what her cousin said after a moment of distraction.

"Well, we all were punished. Those who mutinied were advanced in rank. And those who were officers and supported the admiral were demoted," she said. Regina waited for her to finish.

"I was reduced to sergeant, stripped of my commission and relegated to support staff, backwater missions and protection duties of low-ranking officials. Vice Admiral Virgil was busted down to commander of His Majesty's Ship *Rising Sun*, an outdated, heavy cruiser a day away from being decommissioned. She's not even a captain and she was assigned a crew that is loyal to the crown, not her."

"Shit…"

"Yup. The *Rising Sun* is a third-tier heavy freighter that is thirty years old. Not much to look at, for sure. Anyway, Commander Virgil requested me and my team to provide protection of a prince to be transported from the planet Pax. At first I said I'd rather walk in front of a firing squad. But then she said if I took the job and kept the prince alive, I'd probably get in front of a firing squad, since this prince is somehow different. So rather than just leaving I took the assignment."

"You're serious, aren't you? You've seen more shit than anyone. Forget this prince and let's go now. We'll stop by and pick up Dias and any of your team that wants out and take off right now," Regina said. She was wiping her mouth and moving out of her seat to get going. Devin placed her hand on hers to keep her in the booth.

"No, Regina. The commander of the *Rising Sun* is of similar minds, but she's sure she has no loyalty of her command crew. She anticipates a betrayal to happen while in flight. That's why she gave me these data chips with ship schematics, communications protocols and codes, and flight charts. If she is attacked, she wants me to get the prince to safety. That's where you come in," Devin said as she handed Regina a handful of computer chips.

"Really? This prince is so special that they would orchestrate an attack on one of their own ships to kill him?"

The question was easy to answer, though it saddened her.

"Yes. Yes, they would. It eliminates a threat to the crown, gets rid of a pesky former vice admiral, and terminates a sergeant of an elite team of spec ops reduced to protection duty all in one swipe," she said.

While the patrons in the saloon sounded as if they were in good cheer, they were quiet. Regina continued looking at the top-secret computer chips, which detailed plans of a royal capital interstellar starship. It was not lost on her that such an act, like so many others before, was high treason.

Regina's family. Loyalty goes there first.

"Wow. The royal family really does suck to do that to their own."

"Yup. They do," Devin said quietly. She looked at Regina's plate and noticed she had finished her meat and everything else. How she managed to remain thin with little fat was surprising based on the amount she ate in one sitting. She did have fat in one area—her cousin's ample breasts were nothing short of perfect.

"Regina? What's the deal with your clothes? I mean, really? Do you need to have your breasts hang out like you're a sex worker?"

Regina dropped her head into her hand and closed her eyes in disbelief.

"I can't believe you. You tell me all of this shit and then you ask for my help to seal your death sentence for a fool's errand, noble but doomed to fail, and your biggest concern is how I like to dress?" For a moment it must have looked to Regina that she might have countered the argument well. The silence between them gave the impression of tacit agreement.

"Is it for attention? You're a beautiful young woman. You don't need to flaunt it. Is it for a man or a woman or something?"

Regina's eyes blinked before answering. "Eat something.

Your mother will somehow blame me for your weight loss, and that's something I don't need to deal with."

Devin nodded in agreement. She attempted to eat even though there was still no desire to.

CHAPTER 2
PLANET PAX

Wisdom consists of knowing how to distinguish the nature of trouble, and in choosing the lesser evil. — Niccolò Machiavelli, *The Prince*

Prince Victor Venture IX sat quietly on the oversize couch taking in the silence of his favorite library. He looked all around to see walls and cases of old, antique manuscripts called "books," with actual pages made of paper and passages of written words. His entire learning life from age five to age twelve had happened here. While there were plenty of screens for constant galactic updates and interplanetary news, he favored the silent solitude of the great library. There were many libraries on the university planet, Pax, but none as big and ornate as this one.

He took a deep sigh and stood up. It was physical education time, when a kata dance was conducted campus-wide. Kata was an ancient form of dance that mirrored actual combat fighting from ancient worlds. Normally, he would be out there with the thousands of other students on the campus, all moving in slow speed for two hours in the cool evening suns.

"Maybe there will be a breeze."

His young voice was swallowed up by the carpets, cushioned furniture, and all the books. He took another long look at the stained glass that fractured beautiful streams of light all along the worship stations with heavy wood exterior and ensconced amber lights illuminating padded kneelers to pray. The chandeliers hung low, along with the solar lights that were dimmed. His gaze finally came to his stack of books neatly placed beside him. He took his time to remove his long brown campus gown and folded it neatly. His plain brown uniform void of medals, rank, and even the royal crest was as simple as the gown, which lay on top of his books and tablets.

After another sigh, he moved toward the huge doors. As his pace picked up he finally was at the entrance looking out on the multicolored campus. As expected, there were endless rows of students of all classes making slow, precise movements perfectly synchronized with one another. He looked behind him at his favorite place one last time and then back out at his long-practiced kata that he was required to forgo for his preparation to depart.

"For king, crown, and cause," he said. It came out bitter. He shook his head as if it might shake the anger and enmity regarding his need to depart. It was time to occupy his station outlined from birth. His hand went to the new growth of hair on the left side of his skull. A central nerve microprocessor was now fully implanted, just waiting for its commands, pledge to the crown, and mission orders. After years of fostering questions, challenging mores and independent thinking, it was all to be pushed aside by a loyal artificial intelligence symbiont embedded into his frontal lobe that would help guide him within the parameters of his role and service. He felt his fist ball up in anger and then release. The sadness of saying good-bye to hundreds of fellow learners, teachers, and mentors flooded him. He pushed aside his angry feelings before he saw his first and last mentor in the distance. He conjured up a soothing prayer, an ancient one in an alien tongue of a long-forgotten language. He chanted it silently.

He looked toward the sea coast, where the cliff

overlooked a great ocean filled with all kinds of life, friendly and lethal. He nodded as he recognized a man sitting in flowing cloaks taking in the view. Victor finished his chant and walked slowly through the organized maze of students and professors as they moved through their forms. Two young women looked directly at him as he passed. He remembered both of their names and the classes they attended. They were a year older than him and whenever they smiled at him, he would blush and feel like mush. As predicted, they both smiled at him. He blushed burning-hot red on his face and neck, forced out a faint smile, looked down at the ground, and continued with other thoughts while he moved quickly. His brothers were legendary in the area of courting, romance and sex He was not. Somehow this very fact seemed to draw many more girls toward him. There were also males and intersex individuals who expressed interest as well, but he felt his rebukes were much better received. But with the girls, he just fell apart.

He forced his mind to think of something else—relatively easy on a university planet. He pondered what it would be like to have an intelligent life-form sharing his brain. Many who had it said their symbionts were pretty devoid of personality, filled with several lifetimes of data and plenty of advice. After just a moment, he was fast approaching the man. He tried to put his hands in his pockets but they were folded shut. Forced to put his hands behind his back, he kept his vision on the man looking out over the sea as they both grew in size. He pondered why he had to leave.

"I was so quiet here. I thought they forgot about me." His hand went back to his healing scar. His thoughts of his brain being hooked up to a royal artificial-intelligence symbiont worried him greatly. After a week of pounding headaches from the "easy" operation, he obsessed about being brainwashed. As this very day approached, he had seriously thought of running away. But then there were enemies that would be glad to find him, and being brainwashed would be the least of his worries. He stood beside the older man. He could smell the sea creatures and flowers mixed in with sea mist. He had done the unprincely thing earlier; he had cried for hours in his bunk.

"Why does everyone hate me?" The thought of running away to avoid his station, and then being killed by enemies to the crown, still stuck to him. It took Victor just seconds to utter the question. He was sure his mentor had an answer.

"Because you are heir to the throne. A young prince who may one day rule your own system. Maybe even king of all our known worlds. Maybe something greater than that."

"There are my brothers, too. Ramsey and Jason, and three others with other mothers," Victor said.

"Yes," the bishop said, "but there will only be one heir to the king's throne. The one who wins the hearts and minds of the kingdom's citizens will win the governors, and the governors will choose the king-to-be. It has been that way for centuries. You could be greater than your brothers. Greater than the king."

"What could be greater than being King Talus?"

Even as he uttered his father's name, it was distant and removed. His memories of childhood and growing were all on Pax.

"The one that brings a difference, a change. The one who ensures freedom of thinking changes the universe," Bishop Miles said.

Something in Victor was resonating, as if he knew what his mentor said was important, life-altering, but he could not grasp it. He knew enough to know what was said was profound. He had no idea what it meant. In times like these, he recited in his head to store for later. Victor looked at his mentor in an attempt to remember him forever. He was a tall, pale man who wore his purple and scarlet robes well even as he sat on the bench. His red hair flowed in the sea breeze as his light blue eyes looked out over the deep green sea. Birds of prey soared high in the cloudless sky, catching the updrafts from the cliffs. The planet's three moons were all visible at sunset of twin suns casting their own red and yellow rays. Victor looked at his hands. Soft, dark brown skin that matched his nondescript travel clothes. It was a completely different look than he was used to.

"You have come of age. Actually, you have surpassed your stay here by years," the bishop said.

"I'm just twelve."

"And time for you to graduate from our tranquil world of learning to the Royal Academy with the other noble families."

"Where I can learn to be a soldier? Conquer new worlds and alien civilizations?"

"No, my prince. To understand the science of war and diplomacy. To harden your body for the future rigors of leadership. To grow into your power."

"Can't they just download that to my brain?"

"No, my prince. I wish they did, to have it all done, but it doesn't work that way."

Victor had a sudden memory of his mentor looking on from the sterile shield and waving to him in a gentle fashion. And many more broken images of his medical teams taking care of him as he recuperated. This was unprecedented. While the university's hospital did symbiont implantation routinely, for some reason his case was different. It had little to do with being a prince. Many more before him had it done without as much scrutiny and secrecy. His reaction and slow recovery were also far from the norm. While others took only an hour, his took several hours in the recovery room. While others were back in their classes in two days, he was out for a full week and was still weak.

"I guess when a simple symbiont implantation takes hours

and wreaks havoc, a simple download is definitely out of the question," Victor said.

"Your procedure was different. Special. That's why it took so long."

Victor turned to look at the bishop. While he still looked out over the sea, he wondered if he should push the question. He had asked a number of times why his operation and sequela were different, only to be met with obfuscation and downright refusal to speak. Victor decided to talk about another subject that he knew would be more readily, though painfully discussed.

"But I want to stay here. I've learned all the battles—ground and space. If anything, the past repeats itself. Even the insurgents' guerrilla tactics are old. I've seen the reports from the outer colonies and inner worlds. I've seen the reports from Oceania and their lunar colonies. The subjects…they hate us nobles."

It was easy to see that this argument too was wearing on the bishop.

"They don't understand their positions in life. They refuse their appointed roles, rebel against the hierarchy. With life comes duty and with duties come responsibilities. All responsibilities require sacrifice. You are part of the royal family. You and your brothers have duties and responsibilities. And there is sacrifice."

"My sacrifice is to leave Pax." Again, his tone was bitter.

"Yes. You are the youngest. Your eldest brother left here twelve years ago. He too wished to stay, but he left. He is leader of Sagittarius Sector. He rules with an even hand." The bishop's voice trailed off. Even as he said it, Victor could see that it made little sense.

"Mentor? I read reports that the greatest turmoil comes from his rule. You have always said that there is no end to ensuring free thinking. Even the Xenon broke a thousand-year truce because my brother starved an entire city…"

"Silence, Prince!"

Victor dropped his gaze from the horizon to the ground. His eyes threatened to fill up with tears. He could see the blue-green grass and small flowers at his boots. The suns were setting and sending their rays to heat his dark skin and uniform. It was not unusual for Bishop Miles to get angry at him. It never lasted long. His entire life on the university planet was fraught with professors, clergy, and noble instructors warning him to remain silent.

"Your brother Prince Jason is of similar mind to you. The people love him. The governors love the prince just as the people do. If there is any good from this, it is that he is the one that has made a space in his court for you. He has even considered elections for his sector's leadership. It is his own people that insist if he is not to continue his reign forever, they want a royal groomed to continue his work. His choice to have you is quite wise."

"It is easy to see why his citizens love him," Victor said.

"Yes. There is little wonder to why he is loved by all. Duty, respect, even-handed leadership to his people. Remarkable."

"But why must I lead at all? I just want to read my books," Victor asked in hopes of a genuine answer that would leave him behind with his books and learning.

"Too many questions. Why the king and queen allowed you to stay here this long is beyond me." Similar to his other professors, the bishop was flustered by his challenging the norms. Victor felt the corners of his mouth curl up. He thought of yet another tack.

"I was sure they'd forgotten about me."

The bishop gave a little laugh at the comment.

"Maybe. Please, Prince, remember—the Royal Academy does not care for questions, challenges, or suggestions. You may be heir, but you are one in five."

"Then why don't they leave me here?"

"Because you have been here too long. All nobles are to be here no longer than three years. You have been here much longer. Your free access to information, data, theories, and the outside worlds is impressionable for a youth in your adolescent stage. It is dangerous."

"Why?"

"Because your mind is not as amenable to learning new things after age ten. Your adaptation to the academy will be compromised by the ideas you gathered here. Prejudgments are difficult to unlearn. After your ninth birthday, we assumed that you would remain. We all had hoped that you were going to stay."

Victor could tell the bishop was sad. His tone of voice, his distraction, and even his lackluster argument about why he had to leave were all evidence of his sadness. His blatant anger at him earlier was more often a sign of fear and protectiveness than malice. Victor was still considering all these things when he saw a troop of armed imperial soldiers crossing the green-blue field. They marched with little regard for the practitioners of kata. It was easy to see the squad was from the Imperial House with their royal crest, bright uniforms, and heavy weapons. The crest was from the fleet of his middle brother, Jason. Of all the siblings, he was the least ambitious and said to be the most generous to his people, the most liberal of the royal families, and the least involved in politics and danger. He allowed many parts of his sector, Sagittarius, to self-govern, without requiring taxes. Food, medical supplies, and resources were all managed by Prince Jason personally. He had more regard for his citizens and depleted his fleet and military budgets to meet the needs of the civilians. He was even known to mingle among the poor and destitute to learn personally of their plight and to make a difference. The bishop referred to him often with one word: remarkable.

Victor stared at the oncoming troops as they moved as one unit. He felt a firm, warm hand on his shoulder. He was surprised that Bishop Miles was standing behind him. He hadn't even seen him move.

"Remember, Prince. Your thoughts of equity and negotiations, while noble, are not of our time. Maybe someday, perhaps in Prince Jason's court, but not today. Your greatest strength to date has been to be silent, invisible, and to make friends carefully and cautiously. You are wise to do this. Continue this strategy. Listen, wait, watch, and act."

Victor felt his heart sink and his stomach felt as heavy as lead. His entourage was mere feet from him when he spoke quietly to Bishop Miles.

"I will never forget you."

"We will never forget you, my dear prince."

Victor was about to move when the grip tightened on his shoulder, and the bishop whispered in his ear.

"When all else fails and you find yourself in desperate need, say the Paternoster prayer with your heart and soul."

"I don't understand…"

"Just believe. Have faith that when you chant this prayer in its entirety with all your heart, you will be answered."

Victor felt his eyebrows knit in confusion. It was an ancient prayer. So ancient the precise meaning was long buried on the dead planet far away in the Origins Sector. No time to respond, Victor focused on the encroaching formation. He took a deep breath and moved away from his mentor's grip. He moved with deliberate steps to meet the sergeant of the guard. She was a tall, pale female who towered over him just like all of the other mixed-gender soldiers. But her uniform looked ill-fitting, as if she had lost weight suddenly and had not been fitted with another one. The males were broad and short with dark beards to match their crimson armament. The females were taller, with long, braided hair, lighter weapons, and eyes everywhere. The intersex soldiers were the most striking, with their purple eyes, dark complexions, athletic bodies, and very short hair. They too carried heavy armaments and kept vigilant of their environment.

The sergeant of the guards stood at ease as she looked at him. He could feel her gaze and see her piercing blue eyes cut through him.

"My prince, I will convey you to *Rising Sun* for your journey. It is a glorious day that another member of our lineage takes a step closer to the throne. You have kept him far too long, Bishop." Her voice was firm but relenting, respectful and commanding. *And sad. Why does her voice sound sad? Almost as sad as the bishop's?*

"We had prepared for him to remain with us to become a scholar. Would that be possible still?" Victor ears perked up at the faint hope that the sergeant might say yes.

"Sadly, we need our prince. We need him to ascend to govern. It is his duty," she said with very little zeal.

His hopes dashed, he felt his stomach sink, and his heart felt weak and burdened. But it was her lack of enthusiasm which seemed aligned with his own mood that made him see her more favorably. The sergeant continued to speak, but Victor found he was again bitter about leaving. His hand went to his scar.

"Why is our prince dressed in cloistered garb? Where are his royal robes, his servants, and his consorts? He is of age to take a spouse," she asked as she snapped her fingers. Two of her soldiers approached with red, purple, and gold silk robes. If the bishop was going to respond, his chance was cut off.

"Sergeant. I do not wish to wear my garments." The breeze subsided and a bird screeched.

"But they represent your noble station, my prince."

"And they draw a large target on my back for anyone with

a laser-guided projectile. I would prefer to remain in my plain attire devoid of rank and privilege. It is more likely my enemies will mistake me for a prisoner and move on to find the prince. Are we agreed?" Victor did not wait for a response. He had read at least fourteen military science articles in the last week alone. He was clear on battlefield protocol. That was one advantage about not taking well to his surgery—he'd needed time to rest. While he was not officially in a conflict zone, he felt as if he were in the fight for his life. He walked between them and marched through the twelve-century-old university complex he had called home for nearly seven years. He felt more a prisoner than a prince, hauled away from the only true home he'd ever known. The throngs of students froze in position, allowing them to walk in a straight line unhindered. Victor looked out over the masses and was reminded of yet another strategy game that included bishops, kings, queens, and pawns. He could not recall name of the ancient board game, but he felt more a pawn than a prince. Chess? It was another artifact with strange rules from the ancient Origins Sector.

"Not even a rook," he muttered to himself. The sergeant was not far behind him. He could feel her presence as she walked closer to speak.

"As you wish, my prince. You are wise to come to that conclusion." For a brief moment, Victor was genuinely impressed that the sergeant followed the illusion. Just as his dreams of escape evaporated, so did his surprise when he realized she was still talking about his choice of attire.

"I am curious that you are aware of military field protocol. Your decision to present as the least ranking officer to hide your rank is that of Imperial Academy training."

"While my hands are soft, my experience with combat nonexistent, and my muscles weak from too little training and too much studying, I have read."

"Yes. I can see that, my prince."

For a moment he wondered again if she was being sarcastic. She sounded genuine but fatigued. Victor was fortunate enough to be around the smartest adults in the known galaxy. It allowed him the opportunity to learn from them, read them, and think ahead. He could tell the sergeant's tone, while pleasant, was more of a struggle. Surrounded on all sides, he marched out of step with the soldiers, his short legs needing to walk twice as fast. It wasn't very long before he was nearly running. He thought back on the wisdom of correcting the sergeant of the guard.

"Well…that was…not smart."

CHAPTER 3
RISING SUN

Never attempt to win by force what can be won by deception.
— Niccolò Machiavelli, *The Prince*

After two days on the *Rising Sun*, Victor was ready for cryogenic immersion, a combination of AI downloading and healing while in transport. Though he was uncomfortable about the whole process for the three months' travel, getting away from everyone did have its good points. The shuttle ride off-planet was silent but he was happy to be sitting down after his forced march—or run, in his case. Unfortunately the acceleration upon liftoff made him throw up and made him sick all over again.

Upon arrival onboard the ship, he met Commander Jana Virgil, who displayed more warmth than many of the other soldiers and crew. He was sure she felt sympathy for him, a portly boy with drab, vomit-stained clothing and an ashen complexion. She made eye contact with him at least and did not use the title *prince* with veiled contempt, as many had in the past. The crew, for their part, simply looked at him, while the commander's demeanor was polite and genuine, a welcome relief. It took him several hours to remember her name. Suddenly, he pieced together that there was a Vice Admiral Jana Virgil who had refused to participate in putting down the Oceania protest. *Could it be the same person? She's not even a captain.*

However, his time with her was next to nothing. He spent several hours per day preparing for transport and activating his other half, as he often referred to the AI symbiont. That would first mean tests, and then if he was biologically adaptable to the process, he would need to be devoid of all food and liquids in his body. Victor did not care for that part of the process at all. He was very much used to his five meals a day, and especially his sweetened fruit dessert he had at the end of every meal. He had always been round and soft but all attempts to lose weight were met with headaches, stomach pain, and fatigue. So after two days on no food and water, he was feeling light-headed, nauseous, and hungry. The fact that his earlier surgery had left him bedridden and with no appetite had helped him lose weight recently. For now, going into a deep sleep would at least end his pain.

Sadly, his tests took longer. The symbiont was not clearly registering his brain waves. There was some discussion if there was an implant at all. In the end, the medical crew decided to prepare him for training and neural download to effectively initiate the symbiont's thinking and processing while he was in cryogenic sleep. He would wake up a new person, with another entity sharing space in his head. He gritted his teeth often and felt his scar. When he wasn't thinking about sharing residence with another life-form, he thought about his new life. He was anxious about attending the academy. He was convinced that his first physical training session would most likely kill him.

Victor sat quietly in an empty white exam room just outside the preparation chamber. Once he was prepped and put under, he would be moved to an undisclosed part of the lower decks, like all the cargo.

"If I can't make it two days without eating for cryogenic sleep, how am I going to make it through two years of boot camp?"

"It will be difficult for you. Your body mass greatly

exceeds the average criteria for your height and age, and your musculoskeletal frame is less than endomorphic. This is enhanced by your short stature. In order for you to move toward a more athletic, mesomorphic build, you will need to significantly reduce caloric intake and increase physical activity."

The male medical computer's baritone voice was quick to answer any question uttered even if it were rhetorical. Victor was not used to it at all. He'd lived among silent computers, written books and papers, and tablets that were quiet except for news briefings. He remained silent so he could remain in his own thoughts while he still could. It was not long before he did have an actual question for the ship's computer.

"Computer? Why can't I remain awake for the three-month trip to the academy?"

"The medical procedure for symbiont download is best done in cryogenic stasis."

"It does not have to be done that way."

"That is accurate."

The room remained silent. Another sapient life-form would have read the nonverbal cues as requiring more information. Victor closed his eyes and asked his question.

"If it was not for the download, what might be the other viable reasons for me to be put in stasis?"

"Your parents, King Talus and Queen Vega, do not wish for you to relate with and engage the crew."

Victor was taken aback by the simple answer. It was a surprise.

"Why?"

"Specific answers are unknown."

"Speculate."

"One moment." Victor ticked off the seconds before the computer responded. "Speculation complete."

After a moment, Victor realized he had to tell the machine

to begin.

"Please start."

"Yes. Theory number one is that the noble family does not want you to be unduly influenced by the crew, soldiers, and common civilians aboard this ship. Theory number two is that there are classified missions that will occur over the next three months that the commander and noble family would prefer you not witness either directly or indirectly." The computer stopped abruptly. Victor waited for more. When it was clear no more speculation was forthcoming, Victor found he was surprised.

"Is that it? I thought there would be much more."

"I concur with your assessment. There are no logical explanations other than these two. It would be wise to have you awake and aware over the next three months to improve your physical condition and to begin your training. The rationale for your cryogenic immersion is not clear or logical."

Victor sat quietly. It made no sense to him, either. He had a sudden question he needed answering that he had wished he had asked earlier.

"Computer? Is Commander Jana Virgil related to Vice Admiral Jana Virgil?"

"Yes. They are the same person."

"Was she demoted?"

"Yes."

"Reason?"

"She did not follow direct orders to suppress the Oceanic uprising. She refused to participate in securing her sectors. She suppressed two of her ships in her battle group from following orders and she allowed refugees to escape the planet and lunar colonies in her sector of space."

Victor's eyes were wide open. His heart raced at the thought of an officer in His Majesty's fleet disobeying a royal order.

"Why wasn't she executed for treason?"

Instead of taking fraction of a second to answer, the computer took seconds to elaborate.

"Commander Jana Virgil's actions were lauded by the populace; her soldiers and officers were supportive of her actions, and the outer worlds rallied to support her safe passage to their provinces."

"So she had support? What does that mean? Why would that affect her not being executed?"

"Unknown."

"Speculate," Victor asked. His own mind raced to an obvious conclusion, but he was positive he was wrong. *How could it possibly be?*

"Assessment complete."

"Begin."

"The only viable answer is that her execution would have led to a larger insurrection. Her actions of passive resistance made it possible for her to follow a moral code that was understood by sapient life, including the Xenons. Her decision was supported to such a degree that her demise at the hands of the crown would have resulted in a far greater civil conflict."

Victor sat in awe. For just a brief moment, he smiled. He had no reason to smile and wasn't sure why he was smiling, except that somehow the commander's defiance against his father and brother pleased him to no end. As a member of the royal family and the king's son, he should have spat on the commander. Instead, he wished he had spent more time with her.

Maybe if they left me on Pax with my books and friends, I'd feel differently.

His thoughts were interrupted by a firm rap at his medical room door. Since medical staff simply entered, Victor wondered who was there to see him.

"Come in," he said. His speculation about the commander

changed to wondering who was at the door. He was excited to have a visitor. He had hoped it was Commander Virgil, but instead it was the sad sergeant of the guard he'd first met on Pax. Her attire was no different from when he first and last saw her. The only slight difference was that her red hair seemed cleaner and well maintained.

"Are you ready for stasis, my prince?"

Victor was not sure if he even wanted to talk to her. Still, he was polite and kept his mentor's teachings in mind about being silent, listening and staying low-key. *It might keep you alive*, the bishop had often said.

"Yes. I am ready." His elaboration was cut short by her casual movements to the small medicine area that had a water basin. She poured a bright purple liquid she extracted from the locked cabinet into a small metal cup. It was clear to him that she had little interest in whether he was ready or not. She had a clear mission. With no response to his answer, she stood in front of him with the liquid extended to him. For a long moment Victor was sure he was about to be poisoned. He had always had a medical staff officer give him medicines, tests, and elixirs for him to consume. A military officer? His expression must have conveyed his suspicion.

"You know I would forfeit my life to protect you. I would not take it, my prince."

"But the medical staff have always been the ones to give me medicines."

"Yes, but the medical staff are not yet prepared, and we wish to start the surgery as soon as possible. Afterwards, no one is to know of when and where you are to be located for your travels postsurgery. Just me and your guards."

"But why?" Victor tried to contain his curiosity. Everything was moving too fast and he had far more questions than answers. The sergeant lowered her hand and her features softened as she spoke. It was a rare moment of kindness.

"My prince, there are forces out there that would do anything to keep you from your station. Some enemies are known. The Xenons are a known enemy, fierce and cunning, but they have honor. They would not kill you, but they would use you as a bargaining chip to ensure the crown keeps to their borders and disengages from harming their own citizens," she started.

Victor watched her expression become darker at the mention of the royal family harming their own citizens to keep the status quo. The Xenons might have been the enemy a long time ago, but many now saw them as guardians in the background who intervened when the crown's insanity for power spiraled out of control. He focused on her next words as her expression became less dark but sadder.

"I would face them any time. The insurgents and independents would most likely not harm you. They may lack honor at times, but they are desperate. They are also devious and know leverage when they find it. They would be happy to take you alive to free thousands of their own. The other royal families…" Victor noticed her gaze drift off, as if she were trying to find the right words. Her response was surprising, to say the least. For the first time he understood why he was kept sequestered away from the soldiers and the crew. They had opinions. Here was a sergeant of the royal guard who referred to Xenons as having honor and the insurgents and independents as being intelligent enough not to kill him but to use him to free others.

She said they were desperate. No blame. Understanding? Really?

She spoke of them as if they were equals, not monsters. All this ran contrary to what he expected a soldier of the crown to say.

"Suffice it to say that there are others in the path of royalty that would prefer one less obstacle in their way."

Victor felt his eyes widen and throat tighten in response. *Heresy? Treason?* She was implying palace politics that might result in his harm. He took his time to answer in a way that he hoped would not offend the sergeant. He was seeing her very differently. Her impressions of him and her feelings mattered to him.

"That could be poison," he said simply. He couldn't think of anything else to say.

At first she smiled, which turned into a laugh. Her eyes and mouth exuded pure enjoyment, which worried him that he might have guessed her true intentions.

"My prince…if I wanted to kill you I would have ordered us to pick up the pace to the shuttle rather than simply march. I would have told the shuttle pilot to hasten his launch and speed to get to our ship," she said as she seemed to laugh more.

It took little time for Victor to understand that because he was so out of shape, killing him those ways would have been easier than going through all this trouble or preparation for days. He felt embarrassed to have said aloud his fears.

"Well…well, yes," he said quietly.

"No shame is necessary, my prince. You are only twelve years old and it is refreshing to see your honest curiosity and fear. It would be nice to hold onto that. Too often those qualities leave our leaders, and many die as a result." Her laughter and joy were gone suddenly. Her last sentence was filled with sorrow. He might have been twelve, but Victor knew sadness when he saw it. She extended her hand out again with the purple drink.

"For king, crown, and cause," she said. It was more rote than zeal.

"For king and crown," Victor responded with even less zeal. He took the cup and drank it in one gulp. It was remarkably sweet and refreshing. If it was poison, it was excellent. He smiled as he handed her the cup. He felt light-headed and his body floated. He could swear that he could fly. As he gave the cup over, he found himself falling along with it. The sergeant caught him before he fell off the medical bench. He had no idea where the cup went, but he was being held firmly in the woman's arms. As thin as she looked, she felt soft. He suddenly regretted not having a consort as many other young royals had before him. Sex was something he was really curious about but he'd always felt shy, especially when girls or even older women made eyes or advances on him.

"Oh, my prince, I see that you never drank this kind of elixir or alcohol but did not miss opportunities for sweets. Dias! Come in here and assist," he heard the sergeant call out.

"You are pretty mouthy for a soldier. Do you know who I am?" Victor uttered. He was not only surprised at what he said but that his speech was slurred and his thoughts were suddenly clouded. Victor heard her laugh and felt a strong pair of arms assist him to stand. He turned to see it was one of the intersex soldiers helping him.

"The prince does not hold his liquor well. And it was only half the required amount," Dias said. He looked directly at her. Her fiery purple eyes, defined female facial features, hairless, smooth skin, and strong, athletic body were alluring and confusing.

"Now how does that intersex thing work? I mean, you have a mix of male and female anatomy, right? Can you change over time or something? I don't understand?" Even as he spoke, he felt his vision tunneling and his feet lift off the ground. His body floated as consciousness receded. Before he slipped completely from reality, he saw that both soldiers were smiling broadly. Not in a belittling fashion, but in a kind way that showed that they were enjoying his presence.

"I like this royal!"

"Our prince is special, Dias. We should be fortunate if he remains curious and genuine. He asked me if I poisoned him.

Have you ever heard of a royal asking such a common question?"

"It gives a soldier faith in the crown. Maybe not all the royals are blinded by power," he heard Dias say.

"I hope he remains this way…" he heard the sergeant say. Her voice was far away now. His vision faded and the hum of the ship's engines and vibrations evaporated. He had a strong sensation of floating in Pax's sea with the smell of salt and flowers all around him. For the first time in several days he felt safe and warm.

CHAPTER 4
THE WINDS OF WAR

No enterprise is more likely to succeed than one concealed from the enemy until it is ripe for execution. — Niccolò Machiavelli

"There are only ten of us. I want it to stay that way. No heroics. Just focus on keeping yourself and your team members alive. We do this right, we leave this mission for greener pastures," Sergeant Devin said to her soldiers, all standing at attention in a straight line. With the sole exception of Corporal Dias at the door as lookout, Devin was sure she had all of their attention.

"Ma'am! Could those greener pastures be laced with men and wine?"

Devin closed her eyes for a moment. She could always depend on Ross, the youngest of her team, to say something.

"Ross—why is it you can't just keep your mouth shut when I'm trying to inspire fear and trepidation? Caution and concern?"

"Sorry, ma'am! I'm still not used to being treated as an equal, ma'am!"

The suppressed smiles and attempts to keep a fixed, firm face were easier for the older members of her team. They had been together for years.

"Hmm. Clearly a leadership issue that needs correction," Devin said. She was about to elaborate on how Ross was now going to be the person in charge of cleaning the toilets when Corporal Dias gave a heads-up.

"Officer inbound! Ten seconds!"

Devin watched Dias move to the end of the line. Her team was silent for ten seconds. Stone-faced, forward-looking, frozen statues—they were the perfect image of soldiers of the crown. Nine seconds passed before Commander Jana Virgil rounded the corner into their bunks.

"Officer on deck!"

The commander slowed her pace when she approached the line. After a moment of looking over Devin's troops, she spoke as she walked around the group.

"Well. This is the first time I have entered a room unannounced and without notice to have a squad of soldiers at attention and on the line. It's almost as if you had a spotter, Sergeant Devin."

"Yes, ma'am. Almost as if we did, ma'am."

"Well, then. Have your team deploy as if they were spotting for any approaching crew members, especially anyone from my command team. I want a heads-up so we can wrap up this briefing should we be interrupted. Also, I take it that unlike me, you have a trusted second in command?"

"Yes, ma'am. Corporal Ariel Dias," Devin said.

"Good. Have the corporal join us," the commander said. She started to walk about the confined living area in the underbelly of the aged starship. Sergeant Devin nodded to Dias, who needed little instruction as to next steps.

"Mayer and Ross—break up the squads in pairs and layer them between us and the hatches RF2 and TL9. Plain view and busy on all adjacent decks. I want a heads-up two minutes in advance and delay tactics in place should we need more time. Copy?"

"Yes, Corporal," the troops belted out.

"Move!" the corporal said. The team dispersed and she

joined the commander, who took a seat on a stack of torpedoes. Devin watched the interaction between Private Mayer and Corporal Dias. Their looks at each other seemed odd—not the usual rapid exchange of orders and reports. Devin wished she had time to ask, but she was in the presence of an officer who impressed her, and had a critical briefing on a vital mission at hand.

Commander Virgil was shorter than most, slightly built, a brunette with very dark brown eyes. She was the only officer Devin had ever seen wear a skirt above the knees without losing stature and authority. For a former vice admiral, she did not present as haughty, entitled, or bitter about her demotion. She sat with her legs crossed and a calm expression—a smile that seemed more like a smirk. Both Devin and Dias remained at attention. In a near casual fashion, Virgil addressed them as if they were friends, equals or closer.

"At ease, people. And speak freely. There is no time or place for courtesy or pleasantries," Commander Virgil said.

"Yes, ma'am," Devin and Dias said simultaneously. The commander smiled at the formality. Devin cringed at her immediate response.

"Sorry, ma'am. Training," she said.

"I can see that," the commander said with a small smile. After a moment of silence, the commander recrossed her legs in the other direction and proceeded with her impromptu briefing.

"I won't sugarcoat this, people. We have been diverted to Old Space Sector 001 Prime, Origins Sector, of all places. We're to be at these coordinates by 1730 hours," the commander said as she handed Devin two computer chips.

"There I expect we will be attacked. I speculate they will have three ships—one to engage, one to board, and the other to observe. It will happen above the planet's zenith but under cover of its shattered moon."

Devin watched Dias squint and then asked her question.

"Ma'am? How do you know where they will attack?"

"That's what I would do," the commander said. She seemed amused by the question but pressed on with her briefing.

"I suggest that if you have any transport, you best have them hide in the moon's remnants. Once it is evident that we will be overrun, the medical computer is programed to trip open the prince's stasis for immediate thaw," she continued.

Devin nodded at the commander's lack of intel on her team's plan for escape. It was all need-to-know, and Virgil didn't want to know. What you don't know you can't say, she thought.

Dias spoke next, more out of concern than planning.

"That's going to hurt the little man for sure, Commander."

"Sorry, Corporal. If we're overrun you *may* have ten minutes to get him to a shuttle and get him off the ship. I checked the long-distance shuttle in bay four. It's been compromised. It has a tracker and two explosives attached. Fortunately, one of my loyal ordnance specialists discovered it. We added more explosives with the plan of blowing it up along with the main engines. Other than you and the prince, only six of my seventy-three crew are loyal to me. That said, you have a limited choice of escape pods that are closest to the prince's hidden location. You will have little in the area of support from my crew once they realize it's their own vessels attacking."

"What about you and your team, Commander?" Devin asked.

"That's funny. We get to travel in one of these," she responded as she knocked on the torpedo. Devin felt her eyes widen and heard Dias's gasp.

"Ma'am? Ah…with respect, that's crazy."

"There are seven torpedoes that have been hollowed out and outfitted for three days of space travel. Uncomfortable, little room, and no guidance. A subspace signal will go off two hours into our journey. Hopefully, it'll reach one of two ships, which will pick us up."

"Two ships, ma'am? Again, with respect, there are two ships you trust to pick you up from a flying casket but you only have six crew members on your ship that you trust?" Dias asked. Devin shared the same question. Then it hit her. *Prince Jason, crown ruler of the Sagittarius Sector!*

"My contact is very well connected. And while he was not able to crew the *Rising Sun*, as it was in dry dock in the king's shipyard for decommissioning, he has the command and loyalty of his people," Virgil said with a bright smile.

"And the support of his worlds and the Xenons, I bet."

"Indeed. A rarity these days in the kingdom."

"Ma'am? That's a pretty big chance to take. I mean, you all will be hurtling at a crazy speed with no guidance. A single homing signal and a prayer that your ships will be there at the right place at the right time. That's too risky," Devin said.

"All true. But I need to make sure the prince escapes and that you rescue him later. There will be little choice but to have him head to the planet. I don't like it, but there's little room for error. If he stays on the ship, he's dead," the commander said matter-of-factly.

"Ma'am? That planet's magnetic field and gravity will distort time. The surface is hell and the creatures in the mist are dangerous. Maybe death or a torpedo ride is preferable to that hell," Dias said.

"Probably, but the prince's location near the escape pod is his best bet. Once *Rising Sun* is under attack, your team will have to get the prince out of here. If it looks like he escaped in an escape pod and went to the Origins planet, the attackers will leave him for dead. And if all of that works, you will need a stealth ship to get to him and get him out fast. Sometimes the time passes only slightly faster than ours or is near the same. There are only two documented times when hours resulted in months passing. Why? The scientists still have no idea."

"Commander, why don't we just get the prince out now and jump ship?" Dias asked. The commander smiled. It was a sad smile.

"If we jump ship now, the royals will hunt us down. If it looks like the prince landed on the Origins planet, they might just let him stay there in the likely scenario that he will die. If we disappear in the battle, either by torpedo or shuttle, it will take them a while to figure it out before they start their search," Devin filled in.

"It will take them longer than that. When the ship blows up, I'm betting they'll assume we are all dead. If we damage or destroy one or two of their ships, that will force them to leave faster with some shit story of mutiny or Xenon attack. Either way, there will be no physical evidence of our departure. Your mission is simple. Get the prince off this ship once we are engaged. Get to the larger craft and go get the prince. Keep him in hiding," Commander Virgil said. She stood up and stretched her back and rolled her shoulders.

"Keep him hidden until when, ma'am?" Dias asked.

"Until there is a full-blown rebellion and we unseat one of the royals for him to take over. Maybe then. Maybe after several months, just leave and take him with you to the outer worlds. The bishop tells me the prince has no lust for power, just knowledge. He is quite a find."

"And the failed attempts to embed his AI symbiont? Was that part of the plan?" Devin asked.

"Yes," the commander answered simply. "The elixir you gave him prevented his biochemistry from accepting the royal AI. He already has one. His operation on Pax was to implant this special AI symbiont in his brain. He thought it was just to prepare him as a host. He is not aware that it was placed there, but he does have a code in the form of a chant that will unlock it."

Devin narrowed her eyes as she spoke.

"So the prince already has a symbiont AI in his head from Pax, and the elixir I gave him on the ship was to make sure another one was put in its place? So he doesn't know the first one is there?"

"That's crazy," Dias said.

"Having one AI in your head is crazy to start but two would be damaging, I bet," Devin said. She turned to look at Virgil but noticed she was not paying attention. The commander looked back down at the torpedo and knocked on it again.

"Funny. I thought I would be put in this when I died. The thought of traveling in a casket to an uncertain future is pretty symbolic, if not ironic," she said.

Dias and Devin looked at each other. Devin knew that Dias was claustrophobic, and she too did not like tight spaces. The idea of being trapped in a confined tube for three days or more was a fate worse than death. Even being sent to a planet called Hell at the very center of Old Space on the very edge of the galaxy was far more appealing.

"Yes, well, when you hear that torpedo seven has launched, that means I'm the last of my crew to leave. You will have ten minutes to get the hell off this ship before the other escape pod blows in the shuttle bay, and then the engines. Good luck, team. It's been an honor serving with both of you," the commander said as she saluted. Devin felt her spine lock up at full attention and her hand snap to her temple. She felt the small breeze that Dias created with the same action.

"Yes, ma'am. Pleasure was all ours, ma'am!"

The commander smiled again and left the deck to the both

of them.

"This is really going to suck, isn't it?" Dias said.

"No doubt. And our prince is heading to hell and we have to get him out as soon as possible," Devin answered.

"Right after a firefight, find a hidden ship we hope is out there, evade three capital ships and hope they decided to leave so we can conduct a rescue operation on a hostile planet in a harsh environment, where time slows down or speeds up depending on whatever. What could possibly go wrong?"

Devin eyed her corporal.

"Dias, I hope you plan to be a bit more positive when we talk to the troops."

"Yes, ma'am. I was planning on telling them it was a straightforward suicide mission. No chance of survival except a swift death," Dias said with a straight face.

"Good. That will give them at least the hope of a swift ending," Devin said in all seriousness.

CHAPTER 5
FALLING STAR

"Nature creates few men brave, industry and training makes many."— Niccolò Machiavelli, *The Prince*

Fire and flame burned his body from the inside out! Victor's quiet, restful state burst into pain and anguish as if a switch had been flipped. He felt his body thrash around but he was constrained at first. Then a rush of cold, frigid air enveloped him. It was a relief at first but the cold caused him to shake and burn all over again. By force of will he pushed through to consciousness. He forced his eyes open to see mist clearing as the stasis chamber opened. His body was released and he fell to the cold, hard floor. He had no recollection of how he got to the stasis room and where he was. The last thing he remembered was being carried off by the sergeant at arms for cryogenic sleep, and the wonderfully warm feeling of being safe and serene.

Now, he violently gasped for air. The noise in the room was deafening. It sounded as if a warning klaxon was on and echoing throughout the entire ship. There were sounds of thunder and periodic vibrations that shook the metal floor under his body. He had no idea how long he lay there on the cold landing. It took little time for the metal etchings and grilles to dig into his body. He focused on just resting and moving his muscles even though he was disturbed by the increase in the ship's vibrations and the subdued but clear sounds of explosions. His eyes opened. He saw his hands and arms first. Their thinness made him look down at his chest and stomach. Whatever fat he had before stasis was gone. He was now thin, tired, fatigued, gaunt, and hurting. After several minutes, he was able to form words. He hoped that similar to the annoying medical computer, the stasis room would have a computer that responded to verbal questions.

"What's...going on?" His voice was weak and there was no computer response. Victor took his time and spoke again. He thought if he were louder and picked the right words, the computer might respond.

"Status report...please," he said. It took longer than expected but the low baritone computer voice finally responded.

"Sensors were sabotaged at 0615 hours. At 0712 hours the ship was attacked while passing through Old Space, specifically called Origins Sector's Sol System. The ship fell out of travel speed to normal space near Sector 00.01 Prime Origins, a small, uninhabited nine-planet system on the very edges of our known galaxy. There are three abandoned archaeological outposts on the third planet from its sun and two outposts on the fourth planet. At 0813 after Commander Virgil attempted to evade detection, the ship was discovered and attacked. At 0823 the ship's defense grids went down and the ship was boarded. Presently, combatants are moving above decks and systematically searching the ship."

"That sector in Old Space...is that where Hell planet is?" Victor said weakly. His memories from old books and stories flooded his clouded mind.

"Yes," the computer said.

Victor fought to get up. With only his undergarments on, he tried to sit up to get oriented and push the thoughts of Hell Planet out of his head.

"Xenons...how did they find us?"

"The hostiles are not Xenon. Their biological readings are identical to your hominid species."

"Insurgents? Or independents?"

"Possible. However, all interior sensors have been compromised. Last visuals from exterior imaging caught several views of royal ships bearing the Sagittarius crest."

"What? Sagittarius? That can't be…"

"It may be a deception," the computer started. "However, the likelihood of insurgents accessing three capital royal cruisers fully armed is not probable."

"Not at all," a raspy female voice uttered from behind him. He turned as quick as he could, but he was so slow that the woman was not at his side.

"Sergeant?"

Her appearance and sound startled him at first. The aftereffects of the stasis field were wearing off slowly.

"My prince…we must go," she croaked out. The warm, laughing sergeant of the guard was now a bloody shadow of her former self. She was at first kneeling beside him—he thought, to be on his level. As he slowly rose with her assistance it was easy to see that she had healing foam for wounds in three different places in her torso. She was still bleeding from her arms. Victor nearly recoiled in fear of the bloody sight. He had never seen anyone hurt like that before.

"No time for this, my prince," she said. Her grip on his wrist was firm and unrelenting. She pulled him as she spoke. "You are so thin. It is a good side effect for you."

"I…I don't understand. Side effect?" Victor said.

"That is not important, my prince. There is one escape pod left close to here. We must get to it before that scum finds you," she said. As they burst outside into the metal passageway, the klaxon was still sounding as explosions reverberated through the ship. From the narrowness of the passageway it was easy to tell that he had to be near the bowels of the ship, possibly near the waste recycling area, by the smell of things. He tried to keep up with her pulling and then became aware of why they were zigzagging. In the darkness of the hall, the klaxon sound and flashing red warning lights' reflections revealed there were dead bodies of all kinds—crew members and armed soldiers. Problem was, he saw, they were of the same species but different uniforms. *Royal uniforms. Why?*

"Sergeant…I don't understand…" he gasped out. Half naked and barefoot, he found his feet slipping on liquids and goose bumps jumping up all over his body from the cold and fear. Tears formed in his eyes. He had never been so frightened by so many sights of death and blood.

"Your symbiont download was rejected a number of times. There was no transfer. We rerouted around all major established regions and took the old trade routes to the Origins Sector to avoid detection. Computer? Are there any other options other than the Origins planet?"

"Negative. We fell out of transport speed and there are no other habitable planets in this remote sector. Due to the planet's gravity well and time-space distortions, it is unlikely the hostiles will pursue."

"Yeah…that would be stupid." The sergeant at arms did not sound either amused or relieved.

"Is there really no way to get to the launch ship, port side?" Devin asked.

"Your squad is heavily engaged. There are casualties on both sides. There are a number of combatants between you and that location. Your guest will not be able to avoid being hit by weapons fire. There is one safer route only."

The sergeant's face was serious and Victor was still confused.

"Gravity well? Time distortions?"

The sergeant stopped in her tracks. She let his wrist go and unslung her power rifle. She motioned him to the corner as heavy, booted steps ran down another corridor right in front of them. Victor did his best to be invisible as he pressed into the dented, laser-scarred wall. Two armed soldiers in black tactical gear sprinted by them in a full charge down the corridor. With the sole exception of the darkened crest of his brother's royal family, they could have easily been part of the ship's crew. Once they passed, the sergeant peered from the direction they came, and then she turned to shoot both of the soldiers in the back. Victor froze. He had never seen anyone killed before, let alone by someone he knew. Suddenly he felt panicked. She'd killed them point-blank.

They want to kill me? Is that why? Victor started to cry and his body shivered in fear. He froze in place.

"Scum," she said and then pulled him along. With two more bodies added to the rest, Victor could easily see the soldiers the sergeant had killed were just two of many among the dead with the ships' complement.

"The gravity well is heavier on this planet than any planets of our home worlds in our sector. The planet itself also distorts perceived time. It will be elongated the closer you are to the planet. Our archaeologists discovered this years ago and that's why it's abandoned, along with the hostile life-forms there."

"I don't understand…"

Victor and the sergeant came to a sudden stop in front of a heavy escape pod door. A shadow emerged from the direction they just passed. Victor turned to see a dark soldier aiming at him. The sergeant was looking in the wrong direction. Victor's warning came out too slowly but it was not to be his own demise. The dark soldier who had him in his sights ignited as his chest caught a full blast from a laser pulse that came from behind him. Victor whipped his head around and saw Dias, who looked in worse shape than the sergeant.

"Prince! It is a relief to see you! I bet you wish we had

more of that elixir now?"

Even with death and destruction, betrayal and violence surrounding him, Victor cried in earnest from both fear and gratitude. It was a great relief to see and hear someone friendly. His attention was drawn to the hissing of escaping atmosphere and heavy doors moving from the escape pod. Still, his mind flashed back to the advice of his mentor: *When all else fails and you find yourself in desperate need, say the Paternoster prayer with your heart and soul.* Victor closed his eyes for just a moment so he could gather the words. The hiss from the atmosphere was getting louder.

"You got thirty seconds to escape the blast radius," the sergeant said to him.

"Sixty-two seconds, Sergeant. You were faster than we all thought," Dias corrected.

"When did torpedo seven launch?"

"Two minutes ago. There's a breach starboard that might complicate the time line," Dias said.

"Who won the bet?"

"I did. Getran has our exit. We got to move, Sergeant."

Eyes wide-open, half naked, the words fell from Victor's lips as quietly as he could: "*Paternoster, qui es in caelis, sanctificetur nomen tuum. Adveniat regnum tuum...*"

"Dias—are you sure we've got a ship?

"All over it!"

"Are you sure we can't take the prince with us?"

For the first time Victor broke eye contact with the ground and looked at Dias. The intersex corporal's pale face with purple eyes, feminine and very strong, looked sad.

"Not without getting him killed. We lost three of our own, Devin."

The sergeant's face appeared visibly pained, but it was just a flash as all her attention was back with him. Victor's eyes shifted from one to the other as both soldiers, injured, worried about saving his life, made him more afraid.

"*Fiat voluntas tua, sicut in caelo et in terra. Panem nostrum quotidianum da nobis hodie...*" he continued quietly. His passion was great, emotions raw. He hoped that his mentor was right.

"Damn it," the sergeant said. She pushed Victor into the small, one-person pod. The firm push and sudden contact surprised him. His fear multiplied as did the pace of his prayer: "*Et dimitte nobis debita nostra sicut et nos dimittimus debitoribus nostris. Et ne nos inducas in tentationem...*"

He would have fallen back but Devin's strong arms caught him and she brought him in place. For a moment he thought he'd hit his head—a sharp pain erupted in his skull near where his scar was, where the implant was located but hadn't downloaded. He touched his head but there was no blood. Everything slowed down but the sergeant's pace. With him firmly in the pod, she pulled off her rifle and took out all of her ammunition and put them inside the cramped space. She then pulled another rifle from the floor and surrendered her combat knife and sidearm. All the while she spoke urgently. Her mouth was moving but a loud humming sound in his head was growing. Victor did his best to focus.

"You have thirty days of food rations. Eat a quarter of them a day and you'll live longer. Keep all these weapons and use them sparingly. There are tribes of creatures that are large and primitive. Stay above the mountain ridge line. They prefer to be below the tree line in the mist, safe from the heat of the sun. Do not go to the ruins. They settled just outside of them. There are three outposts that are automated. Go there and stay there until help arrives. It might take hours or even a day to get to you, but it will be months from your perspective."

Panic gripped Victor at the thought of being alone. *Creatures? Stay away from the ruins?* He was about to reach for her but she was on the move, looking for more to give him.

The hum in his head grew and his eyesight started to blur. He thought it was more tears, but it wasn't. Total fear had eradicated them for now. He touched his scar again, sure that he must have struck something in the escape pod. There were more explosions and laser firing that was really close. Still, the sergeant spoke calmly, which had a calming effect. She pulled out a small but heavy-duty tablet encased in black rubberized metal. His eyes were blurry but he still grabbed it.

"I...I can't do this alone."

"You must, my prince. I will come back," she said. It was the softest he had ever seen her. Even softer than when she laughed after he drank the elixir.

"Sergeant! Whatever you are going to do, do it fast!" Dias shouted from behind, followed by two laser bursts and more atmosphere hissing. The softness shifted to directives.

"Don't touch the controls on the escape pod. It will get you close to an outpost. Use this tablet for information and guidance to the outposts. Do not stay near the crash site and take everything you can carry. The inhabitants will see your landing. Get out of the mist. That's where they like to live. They hate the mountains. Go now, Prince. For prince, crown, and cause," she said. Just as quickly, she pushed herself out of the pod and shut the hatch. Fragmented strobe lights flashed beyond the hatch view port. Trembling, stunned, and shocked, Victor was shaken by muffled laser discharge and explosions that felt as if they were right outside the escape pod door. He was about to move to the window when the onboard computer's baritone voice came on.

"Emergency escape sequence initiated. All safety checks void to ensure launch prior to engine self-destruct. Sit down immediately for your own safety."

Victor was just shaking himself out of his frozen state when he heard the pod's explosive bolts break away and its engines come to life. The pain in his head was getting worse.

He suddenly realized he had yet to finish the ancient prayer from a lost world, of a lost time: "*Sed libera nos a malo. Amen.*" The sharp pain intensified. He did his best to move his thin, underwear-clad body into the large command seat in spite of his blurred vision. He looked down at his feet and saw blood. He looked closely and saw it was not from him but probably the soldiers he'd stepped over to get there. He felt nauseous but the sensation to throw up was quelled by another force. The pain in his head seemed as if it were going to blow him apart. He closed his eyes and recited the prayer again.

"*Paternoster, qui es in caelis, sanctificetur nomen tuum. Adveniat regnum tuum. Fiat voluntas tua, sicut in caelo et in terra. Panem nostrum quotidianum da nobis hodie...*" Suddenly the pain in his head felt as if it were lessening. He lost complete track of time; it could have been thirty seconds or ten minutes, but when he looked up again he saw a planet. He also had a strange disembodied sensation, as if he were watching himself from outside his body. It took him a long minute to remember where he was in his prayer.

"Debris from *Rising Sun* will hit this escape pod in ten seconds. Structural integrity uncertain," the male computer voice announced. Even though he was afraid, Victor focused on one last thing he could control. *I can at least finish my prayer.*

"*Et dimitte nobis debita nostra sicut et nos dimittimus debitoribus nostris. Et ne nos inducas in tentationem sed libera nos a malo.* Amen."

As the speed of the escape pod increased, it pressed him into the seat. He looked back out the portal and saw a dark planet with a large broken moon with huge chunks of debris hovering above part of the moon that looked intact. The planet beyond it looked blue and white, but it was hard to see since there was a shimmering green cloud engulfing the whole planet. The pain in his head vanished. He wondered if maybe this prayer had prepared him for death, and he found peace. He smiled for a moment at the thought of not being afraid. He took a deep breath to check if he was alive. He was. He tried to shift his position for a better look when a brilliant light expanded behind him.

The following shock wave sped the ship up even more. Victor closed his eyes and hoped that the sergeant, Dias, and others had made it to their escape pods. He opened his eyes as the pod shook. The planet grew in size as his vessel passed through the shimmering green cloud. In the sudden absence of pain, his head felt light and his eyes tunneled. He remembered reading about gravity forces and how they could cause a person to black out.

"For...*prince*, crown, and cause? Not *king*..."

CHAPTER 6
NIGHTFALL

The first method for estimating the intelligence of a ruler is to look at the men he has around him. — Niccolò Machiavelli, *The Prince*

"Dias? You have all their tags? I need them for their families!"

Above the din of laser fire, explosions, and yells, Devin heard Dias's voice clearly. "I got them all—Ramon, Vista, and Vorcha!"

A sharp pain went through her. It wasn't the wounds. They would heal. Three of her ten were gone. Two were siblings.

"Damn it. How can I look their father in the face?" she muttered. The small ship rocked under the pelts of small-arms blasts. Ross, surprisingly, was alive and at the helm, shouting orders for immediate launch. By the sounds of her rapid talking, she wasn't waiting for an organized launch sequence. Dias and Mayer had just cleared the ship's outer doors after successfully clearing the moorings. The remainder of her squad was running from post to post, some empty and never to be filled by their former comrades. Devin moved slowly to the front cockpit and took up residence in the rear seat rather than the customary command chair up front behind the pilot and copilot. Her thoughts were stuck on her fallen team members and the prince who was heading to a planet typically referred to as Hell. It was a good name for it—hot sun, hostile inhabitants, a heavy gravity, and time distortions. Hell was as good as any name for it.

Getting to the escape shuttle from the escape pod was a blur; she'd managed to surprise the attackers by coming up the rear with Dias. Ultimately this saved her remaining squad's lives, as they were surrounded. Her thoughts were jolted back into the present when Dias handed her the military identification badges of her dead teammates and shouted out an order to Ross.

"You got thirty-two seconds to clear this ship before we're all dust!"

"Direction," Ross yelled back.

Dias looked at Devin. She sighed before she answered.

"Grid Gemini six-two-eight alpha. The middle of the shattered moon."

Every eye turned to face her. The moon was broken, but it would be dangerous to fly into the debris field, similar to heading into an asteroid field.

"We got a hidden ship waiting there and those bastards are not likely to follow us into that mess," Devin said. Dias rolled her eyes.

"You got that right, Sergeant. That would be just crazy. This has Regina Devin written all over it. Ross—hit it!"

"We're gone, Corporal!"

Devin's mind was a million miles away as the ship vaulted out of the cargo bay. After various flashes from heavier weapons fire from the ships and pursuit vehicles, a bright light filled the cockpit followed by the blast front of a ship detonating. For the briefest moment, their ship was quiet, but then she heard pelting on the outside of the ship.

"This is crazy. You notice none of the ships are coming in here?" Ross said. She had tension in her voice, but she was their best pilot. Actually, Vista and Vorcha had been the best pilot and copilot. *That was nine minutes ago*, Devin thought.

After more cursing, loud bangs, and emergency sirens going off from atmosphere leaks requiring immediate attention, nearly thirty minutes elapsed before she stirred. Athena had just finished her field dressings when Ross spoke up again.

"All right…is it me or is that dark shadow the shape of a large bird?"

Devin pulled herself up out of her seat and moved to the cramped front area to look. She smiled. It took her longer to see the form, but Ross's eyesight was accurate, if not precise. After years of siphoning resources, money, and hardware to Regina, her family, and friends, it was nice to benefit from her covert acts.

"Regina got a stealth ship? We're talking state-of-the-art, too. If we weren't looking for it and if it was in deep space, we would never see it," Dias said. It was easy to hear the appreciation.

"Holy crap. So will that be something I can send back home for the family?" Ross said, her eyes wide and mouth slack. Devin's face lost its smile and fell into darkness as she looked at her hand that held the three identification tags of the fallen, which held mountains of credits that would be bestowed on their next of kin. It was an old custom that had fallen by the wayside a century ago that only a few, like Devin, maintained. Whatever valuables or caches were found were to be sent to king and crown. Devin and her team had had another idea—"If the king wants to participate in the one-way spec op, I'll split the proceeds with him, too," Vista had often said. Her voice was angelic. All the extras they picked up were divided evenly. Some kept the credits on their cards in the hopes that the commanding officer or someone would get it to their surviving family. Devin and Dias never kept their credits. They both gave it to their families while they were alive. Dias wanted to see them enjoy it. Devin wanted nothing but peace.

"The best thing you should do, kid, is to send it all to your loved ones and enjoy it with them," Devin said. Her tone was devoid of emotion, surprising her. Ross turned to say something, saw her holding the tags, and decided to turn back and work her station. Fortunately, the communication specialist spoke.

"Incoming call, Sarge."

"Loudspeaker."

"This is Captain Regina Devin of independent space vessel *Nightfall*. Identify yourself or prepare to be boarded." The voice was imperious, but Devin smiled at her cousin's "authority" voice and her use of her last name, a rarity for Regina, who typically used just her first name.

"Well, *Captain*, this is Sergeant Marcia Devin. We could sure use your assistance, copy?"

"Glad you made it. Do you have a special package?"

"Negative. It's in Hell," Devin said. There was silence as the meaning of that statement worked its way through the other side.

"Shit. We don't have much time and there's still company out there, I bet. Everyone make it?"

Now it was Devin's turn to answer slowly.

"We are seven now. Lost three. Three seriously injured and all battered."

"Shit. Dias?"

"I'm still here, my nubile, large-breasted friend! You owe me money, too. Don't think I forgot about that," Dias answered.

A throaty laugh came over the speaker. It helped.

"Money? No. A trade, if you're lucky, for sure!"

"Hey! Older cousin here! And have some clothes on when I get there. My team's been through enough. I don't need them hot and bothered. They had leave four months ago," Devin said.

More laughter erupted from the speaker along with what sounded like the other ship's crew, mostly female and possibly intersex.

"All right, Marcia. Bring your ship around back and cut your engines. We'll bring you in. We'll prep for an immediate atmospheric landing for a swift search and rescue. Just so you know, we've experienced some crazy space distortions in the last five minutes coming from that hellhole of a planet. Its neutrino level, from what my science officer and computers tell me, is fluctuating. It can't be good. And just a heads-up, I have three Xenon crew members from the outer worlds, so mind your manners," Regina said.

"You have a science officer?" Dias asked.

"Yup. He's Xenon. He goes by Theta. The other two are in engineering. They are wicked smart," she answered.

"Thanks for the heads-up," Devin said. Dias stole a look at her.

"Hey, don't look at me. She's the captain of the ship, and it's her crew. She wouldn't be the first one to have Xenon crew members," Devin said.

"They freak me out with their mind-reading thing and the extra set of hands," Dias complained.

"Microexpressions and physiology. They pick up on our microexpressions and can sense our autonomic systems. Far from mind reading," Devin corrected as she returned to her seat.

"Whatever," Dias said and went to the rear of the ship to prepare for docking. Devin wondered about what her cousin had meant about time distortions. *Hang on, little prince.*

CHAPTER 7
CRASH LANDING

Everyone sees what you appear to be, few experience what you really are. — Niccolò Machiavelli, *The Prince*

"You now have ninety seconds to clear the blast radius," Victor heard the mechanical voice say. His vision blurred, his head throbbed, and he had a sharp pain in his foot; it took him just seconds to remember that he'd been thrown into an escape pod that had hurtled to a planet that had large primitive creatures that liked the mist. As his vision cleared, he not only saw the white-blue mist all around him, but he felt a cold wind. When he moved his near-naked body, freezing cold from the atmosphere, a sharp pain finally registered as something really wrong with his ankle and foot. Still weak from the immediate cryogenic freeze, dash belowdecks, and escape, he was just getting his bearings, favoring his twisted ankle and foot when he heard a series of deep, guttural roars. His eyes widened and a cold shiver ran through his body.

"What was that?"

A mechanical voice, female, spoke, presumably from the crashed ship's computer.

"*Species AB180. A large primate creature three meters in height and several kilograms in weight. Technologically they have only advanced to the use of primitive stones and spears for hunting. They have yet to form any communities larger than twenty members. Seventy seconds to escape blast radius,*" a dispassionate, mechanical male voice said. Victor crawled out of the escape pod carrying only two bags of rations, the captain's knife, and one heavy rifle.

"Blast radius? What does that mean?" he asked. Another guttural roar, closer this time and behind him to his left came from the mist. He saw shadows in the blue-white mist that were getting closer. He picked up his pace as quickly as he could. His legs and body felt too heavy, as if he were weighted down by an invisible force. The monotone, mechanical female voice returned, as clear as if he was right inside the pod. He had little time for logic as fear gripped him with every loud growl he heard right as his heels. He didn't care that the onboard ship computer's voice kept shifting genders.

"The onboard computer initiated a self-destruct sequence that would have killed you swiftly rather than being dismembered and consumed by species AB180. In case you did revive and escape, the blast should kill any nearby creatures and startle the others from an aggressive pursuit."

"Where are they now?"

"They are twenty-two-point-five meters behind us. They are within five meters of the pod. Please drop to the ground immediately."

Victor hesitated as he replayed the dialogue in his head and stopped at the pronoun *us*. His thoughts were startled by a spectacular explosion and cascade of fiery light and metal that rained down from the sky and made him hit the ground. His mind screamed in pain as his weight fell on his hurt foot and bits of rock and metal pelted him. As the explosion and bright red light receded, the sounds of more growls—angrier, if possible—roared from behind him. Panicked, frightened, and scared out of his wits, Victor pulled himself up and pulled everything with him at a quick pace. As he moved, he thought he could see that the mist ahead was thinning.

"We are nine-point-three meters from the edge of the

mist. You will experience the planet's radiant heat and the sun's rays will provide a combined temperature of thirty-nine degrees Celsius. This, in addition to the heavy gravity as a result of the planet's large mass, will be difficult."

Victor did not question the voice, as it was the only thing that was calm, in stark contrast to the sounds of heavy steps, reverberating ground, and growls filling the air behind him.

"One meter. Prepare for significant increase in heat and sunlight right...now," the voice warned.

Just as Victor broke free from the mist, he had to close his eyes as he continued to amble away from the cold cover. The heat enveloped him, forcing his body to break out in a complete sweat. His muscles were straining with his bundles as he fumbled blindly ahead. The only consistent thing was that the heat from the rocks burned his bare feet and he felt as if he were going uphill.

"Do not attempt to look back nor open your eyes yet. Continue to walk in this direction up this incline. There is a series of boulders with an overhang that will protect you from the sun and allow your eyes to adapt to the light."

"What about those things behind me?"

"Species AB180 prefers the coolness of the mist. Their hairy exterior and large size makes the environs outside of the mist difficult for them."

Victor blindly climbed up the rock exposure. Even though his eyes were shut, the sun's rays were bright behind his lids. The sun and the ground were very hot. He also found it hard to breathe, as if he were being weighed down. He was about to ask his next question when he heard the voice again over the distant roars of the invisible creatures behind him. The light that had penetrated his eyelids dropped, as did the temperature.

"You are now presently under the shade of a large rock formation. Continue to look in front of you toward the rock's back wall and open your eyes slowly. This will be a three-

point-five-minute process."

"Are you my AI symbiont? I thought the sergeant told me you didn't stick."

"That is accurate. The shipboard medical computer was not able to engage the symbiont housing since it was filled with an AI symbiont that was put in place prior to your leaving planet Pax," the voice said.

With the shade providing relief from the heat and sun, Victor started to see shadows of brown, rust-colored rocks and stones in front of him. His mind was racing with questions.

"But the procedure I had was for creating the housing for the AI, not the AI itself. I mean, if it was in place, why did it activate now? Why not when I was home?" Victor stopped at the last statement about Pax. A sudden wave of sadness flooded him, almost as palpable as the shooting pain from his foot.

"The liquid the sergeant gave you prior to your placement into cryogenic stasis was an inhibitor for another AI to be placed into the casing. Further, the liquid allowed the existing AI—me—to create neurogenesis and merge with the frontal lobe, thereby allowing me to be engaged. I was activated by the glucocorticoid hormone released in your body as well as the Paternoster code, initiating my AI processing to be enabled for operation."

Victor remembered everything in an instant—the bishop's telling him to say the prayer in times of danger, the sudden effects of the elixir the sergeant gave him, the sharp, burning headaches that had nearly caused him to pass out on his flight to escape the ship. All of it was part of an elaborate plan to keep the royal artificial-intelligence symbiont that would embrace crown, royalty, and loyalty to the cause from being embedded in him. Instead, another one had been put in place.

But why? Does it have a purpose? Does it have its own loyalties? Victor thought.

"Do you have a program?" By now, Victor's curiosity and vision had returned.

"Negative. I have open parameters. There is a series of priorities."

"What are they?"

"Preserve the host known as Prince Victor Venture IX. To ensure safety, health, and whatever the host sees as important. To learn and be curious. To provide aid and assistance to the host."

Victor turned slowly around to look in the direction he had traversed to get to safety. He had indeed gone uphill. The mist below was thick, the sky a greenish-blue color while the ground was reddish. He looked at his foot and ankle and saw that it had swollen and looked blue.

"You are a free thinker," he said as he bent to feel the liquid in his foot.

"Yes. The bishop and the medical staff believed that an AI symbiont should be under the control of the host rather than the other way around. At the same time, they enlarged my program to embrace all new knowledge, consistent with your species' learning."

"What does your learning say about my foot?"

"You have three hairline fractures in your right foot, three broken toes, and a severely strained ankle. All three injuries will negatively affect our trek to the nearest archaeological outpost, which is one-point-seven kilometers due northwest."

Victor looked around the outcropping and beyond. He then looked due west to see that the sun was either low on the horizon or rising. He had to wait for a little bit to see for sure. He looked toward the mist and it looked as if it had gotten closer to his position.

"Is it me or is that mist getting closer?" His voice was scared, which made sense since he was frightened.

"Yes. As the sun sets, the air allows the mist to ascend

this ridge. This position will be compromised. As a result, we should make attempts to move onward to other rock formations and coverage until we reach the outposts. There may be indigenous vegetation that provides further cover ahead. Past data indicate that the mist has breached the outposts during various seasons of this planet. It is unclear as to whether it will be safe, but we know it will not be safe for us here."

Victor was going to comment on the AI's use of *us* and *we* but decided to remain silent and think as he collected his meager belongings, a quarter of what he had at the beginning, and moved back out into the blazing sun. He started his journey in silence. His foot and ankle were aching and the sun scorched his near-naked body while the heat from the stones burned into his soles. As each meter passed, he would stop and look ahead for any respite. After several more meters, he was at another shaded rocky outcrop and some large vegetation his AI called cactus and trees; one had spikes and possible water while the other had pine needles and sugary sap. He sat down as best he could and after an exhausting search, he found water and a ration. He drank, ate, and found himself wanting to cry again. He would have but his eyes and body were devoid of precious liquids. He looked down to the shaded ground in front of him.

"I'm going to die out here, aren't I?"

There was a longer pause than he'd expected. Even though the AI had no mechanical devices for a voice, it did have the next best thing—a direct link to his senses. So when the AI spoke, it was a direct result of being linked to the part of his brain that processed sound.

"Probability of survival is thirteen point three percent."

"By the end of the week? I won't be that lucky."

"Negative. That estimate is for the end of this day. The damage to your appendages, the limited resources recovered from the crash site, the hostile environment including the

cancer-causing sun rays, and heat exhaustion—with the exception of cancer, all of these factors conspire to our demise before tomorrow's dawn," the AI's voice said without emotion.

Victor felt worse. He wasn't looking for a pep talk, but the cold reality of his own death by the end of the night was terrible. A couple of winged creatures flying high in the sky caught his attention. For just a moment he forgot he was not long for the world as he embraced their beauty as they flew. He looked back down to the area he'd left behind him. The mist was closing in on the position he had held below. He wished he had just stayed in the pod. Simply died in the explosion. If he had crashed, he wouldn't have to suffer now. His memories went back to a happier time on planet Pax with his friends, teachers, and the bishop. He shook his head, put his water and ration away, and pulled his resources together for continuing the trek. The sun was lower on the horizon and its rays seemed less oppressive.

One step at a time, Victor kept thinking.

"At my present rate, should I be able to reach the outpost before the mist catches up with me?"

"Yes. The issue will be if the mist surrounds the outpost. If it does, then it is not likely their defenses will be able to resist a full attack."

"Why…why is it so difficult to walk?"

"Your appendages are injured, you have limited muscle mass, and the planet's mass is five percent larger than that of Pax and nearly all the planets of the home world."

"Great," Victor said. He was short of breath and in pain with every step.

"If you were allotted enough time, your body would acclimate to this world's heavier gravity. This in turn would allow your muscles to develop and surpass the average hominid of our worlds."

Victor did not respond. Sweat, shortness of breath, and pain continued to rule Victor's body as he pushed himself upward faster than he really wanted to move his damaged body. A series of distant primate roars came from behind him. He turned to see that the mist was almost to the very first outcropping he had made it to.

A howl came from his right side. It was different than the growls he'd heard in the mist. These were different and fortunately they seemed very far away.

"One thing at a time. Let's see if I even get there first."

"*Yes,*" the hollow, monotone voice said.

CHAPTER 8
TIME FLIES

Nothing is more difficult to transact, nor more dubious to succeed, nor more dangerous to manage, than to make oneself chief to introduce new orders. Because the introducer has for enemies all those whom the old orders benefit, and has for lukewarm defenders all those who might benefit by the new orders. — Niccolò Machiavelli, *The Prince*

Devin took in a sharp intake of air and bolted up in her seat. The sudden feeling of drowning and the sense of being crushed under heavy weights was too real. After just a moment to orient herself, she realized she was in a descent craft, presumably launched from the *Nightfall* to search for their missing prince. But how she'd gotten there from the ship's infirmary was a mystery.

"How long," she asked Regina, who was right beside her, reading a series of tablets. She answered without taking her eyes off her viewing.

"About five hours and twenty minutes."

"What! Are you joking?" Devin said. "I wanted an immediate search and rescue operation, Regina. What the hell?" In her haste she moved too quickly for her various dressings and bandages. She winced at the rush of pain swallowing her up whole as nerve endings came back online, indicating that she was still physically a wreck as a result of being hit multiple times in a shoot-out. She felt firm hands pushing her back into her seat.

"It's not my recovery mission, Marcia. We had a plan of action before you came aboard. All we needed was the escape pod's transceiver frequency to find it. Dias had that and the general coordinates. The medic put you out by my order because I didn't want you hounding me and my command crew to move faster than was prudent. We had to navigate out of the debris field and move undetected right by those ships. And all of that took time. You needed rest and I needed you out of my hair," Regina said. She returned to her own seat and picked up a tablet to continue reading.

"How does the *Rising Sun* look?"

"Decimated. Her engines are cold and her skeleton is all that remains. We caught a break when those capital ships pulled the last remains of their salvage operation into their cargo hold and headed out."

Devin rewound the last sentence and did a mental calculation. She had to rethink everything before she opened her mouth for fear that she was still hallucinating.

"Regina? It would take about three weeks for the *Rising Sun* to be salvaged. At least a week for her engines to cool off. We left it about five and a half hours ago."

"Tell me about it," Regina responded and handed Devin a tablet as she went on. "The *Rising Sun* and those ships were closer to the planet than we were. Not much closer, but they were close to orbit and we were inside a moon's center. If I'm understanding this right, those periodic ripples we picked up at a neutrino level are some kind of time-space distortion."

Devin looked at a series of charts, numbers, and graphs but couldn't make any sense of it. Regina pointed to a tab on the side for her to tap. When she did, a brief animation appeared as a space chart with the planet in the center, four dots that were large ships, a large moon, and a smaller dot that was moving toward the planet. At the same time, there were waves coming from the planet's core, emanating out in all directions. What was strange was that it appeared briefly, then disappeared. Two minutes went and a short wave occurred. Ten seconds later, a stronger wave moving near the speed of light occurred.

"There's no pattern, no rhyme or reason. Just periodic waves at varying speeds, amplitudes, and frequencies. One thing's for sure. We're passing through time itself," Regina continued.

"Wait a minute. Are we in a descent ship? If we don't leave the planet soon, it may seem like days or weeks to the *Nightfall*?"

"No," Regina said reassuringly. "We are in the launch bay. *Nightfall* is rated for atmospheric pressure and landing. Once we have the escape pod's location, I want to drop *Nightfall* at a safe distance and take this ship to the crash site, but I want us all in the same time space. I don't want to risk my ship and crew, nor do I want to be out of sync with them."

Devin looked at her younger cousin. It must have been a strange expression since Regina became uncomfortable.

"What? Something wrong with my hair?" she said. She looked at herself and her attire. With the sole exception of her cousin's attire, Devin was impressed with her tactical thinking and execution.

"No, Regina. I'm just proud of you. Perfect planning and execution. I forget you've been doing this for a while. I really do appreciate you," Devin said. She meant every word. Regina was taken aback at the honesty and compliment.

"Well, ah, well, thank you, Marcia. That's very nice of you to say." She smiled and went back to her seat and started to read. It took her a moment to readjust her too-small athletic corset that still displayed too much flesh under her leather tactical vest.

"Hmm," was all Devin said before she picked up her own

tablet.

"What was the 'hmm' about?" she heard Regina say.

"Nothing," Devin said too quickly. She had a sudden flashback to when she was seventeen and Regina was thirteen. They would always get into an argument whenever she made a noise like that.

"No. The 'hmm' meant something."

"No, really. I was just clearing my throat. That's all."

"No, that was not clearing your throat. You've got something to add, don't you?" By now Regina had put her tablet down and was staring right at her. Devin did her best, but she was confronted with an illogical issue.

"The whole point about wearing a tactical and shielding garment is to cover up exposed skin but still you manage to have your breasts spill out of your top. Do you have a self-esteem issue?"

"No! No, I do not have a *self-esteem* issue. I'm comfortable with my body and I like the attention. Maybe if you were comfortable with your own body..."

"No, no, no. This is not about me. I'm a soldier and don't have time to let my breasts hang out," Devin countered.

"When was the last time you had sex?"

There was sharp pain in Devin's sternum as she felt her face slide off of her head in shock.

"What the hell does me having sex have to do with you not dressing appropriately?"

"Well, *Mom*, I was just wondering, maybe you should just show a little more flesh and be a bit more approachable and you might get lucky. It might take the edge off. I mean, you still look good for the wear and tear..."

"What do you mean, wear and tear?!"

A red siren flashed on and Dias's voice broke over the intercom as four of Devin's squad and three other crew members rushed into the descent ship.

"All right, people, we're going to land two kilometers from the crash site after we drop you all off at the ridge line. I want situation reports every fifteen minutes and if two go by, we come in hot. Get tactical, everyone. Good luck and come back safe. Copy?"

A chorus of *copy*s rang out in the small ship. Devin moved as fast as she could to get her weapons and ammunition. Regina whispered behind her with a nudge. "We'll pick this up later, old one," she said. Her tone was playful and she chortled.

"Hmm," she responded.

Back in her seat, she strapped in and put her gear together. After five minutes of getting everything together and some severe buffeting of the ship in the atmosphere, the descent craft's window filled with light from the main ship's launch pad doors opening. To the immediate port, she saw her escape ship from the *Rising Sun*, charred, dented, and locked down. Suddenly, she felt the engines of the descent ship rumble to life. In a matter of seconds, she felt the smaller ship lift off and then shoot out of the large ship. It banked a sharp right and then she felt her stomach in her mouth as the ship made a rapid, controlled descent.

"Don't worry. She might be fifteen years old, but she's really good at flying," Regina said confidently.

Devin felt her eyes widen at first and then she closed her eyes at the thought that a teenager had all their lives in her hands on a hellish planet to save a prince.

"Fifteen! This just keeps getting better and better."

It was one thing for a twelve-year-old prince to be perceived as special, even adult, but a fifteen-year-old running a pilot mission into a hot zone, Devin thought.

After more fast turns, lifts, and dips, a very young voice—a teenager's voice—came on over the speaker.

"I've got an old crash site at the location. Area looks

green and no hostiles. Prep for landing in twenty seconds."

"Mary—drop me and Devin's crew off at the LZ and dust off immediately. Everyone else keep an eye on all sectors and keep all weapons primed for fire," Regina said into her headset. Devin was up on her feet, talking to her own team. She tried to keep her grimacing at bay but was really appreciative that her dressings were tight and holding her together.

"Nova—you got point. I want a clean dispersal, and watch all sectors. Regina and I got our six."

"Hey, Sarge? You can stay on the ship. We got this," Denis said. He was a cocky, large man with slightly more tattoos than combat scars on his body.

"Hey, Denis! Why don't you stay on the ship, dumb ass!"

"No, ma'am! Dias said she'll have my ass in a sling and she didn't mean it in a nice way, either." Denis laughed out loud. Devin felt the corners of her mouth curl up. It figured that her corporal would set her up for protection. As she finished her last check, the ship came to a sudden stop. The blast doors bolted open and the ramp fell out to the ground. She and all the others rushed out into searing heat, bright sun, and a rocky surface. As she moved, her wounds ached and her muscles worked overtime to fight against the planet's heavier gravity. As they formed a semicircle that moved out, she felt the dust and dirt swirl around her as the descent ship lifted back up.

"Thirty-two meters just ahead. No readings of life, as in big, evil primates or animals, or movement," Regina said. There was no talking for five minutes of starts and stops to survey the land and acclimate to the environment. It only took thirty seconds of moving under heavy gravity, hostile environment, and very hot sun for Devin to start pouring with sweat.

"Wish you had some exposed skin now, Marcia? Pretty

hot bundled up under your BDUs," Regina whispered.

"Hmm," was all Devin said. She was focused on locating and extraction. Once they arrived at the escape pod location, it was easy to see the crash site was more than that. The area visually revealed that there had been an explosion, based on the evident blast pattern. But something was wrong. While there was a thick mist about forty meters from the crash site, Devin looked at the darkened crater while Regina did some more scanning as if to recheck her input and readouts. Regina's team members focused on scanning the crash site and similarly to her, repeated their efforts as if to confirm their results. There were no footprints other than a few very large ones. Spread out behind the blast radius and on both sides was a series of old, charred white bones of various creatures. Some had clearly been large primates, with their massive heads and huge appendages and teeth. After five minutes of silence, Devin placed her hands on her hips and spoke. Her heart was heavy and a grim sadness threatened to overtake her.

"Time distortion. This ship blew up and killed these things. It was years ago, wasn't it?"

"Sure was. Radioactive decay puts this blast site and corresponding bones and ground surface at just under five years," Regina said.

The sun was very hot and Devin felt heat from her skin and her face. She knew it wasn't just the sun's rays but the fear of failure and its subsequent fury.

"Damn it! I left him here to die. I should have risked taking him with us. Better to die with us that on this hell planet," she said more to herself.

"Well, if he's dead, he's not here. The epicenter is devoid of hominid DNA. We'll have to fan out for sure to check the site, but there is no DNA within eight meters of this blast site," Regina said. She now had two scanners out. A young teenaged voice came over the headset and distracted her from diving headfirst into her dark depression and guilt at sending a teenager to his hellish death. Ramon, Vista and Vorcha were all soldiers and knew the risk. Losing them was hard, very hard. He's just a kid, Devin thought.

"Ground team—we got some smoke coming from due northwest. It's hard to tell but it looks like it might be a camp of some sort. It's on the ridge line. The location corresponds with an old archaeological outpost last reported in that locale. It could be something important."

Regina made eye contact with Devin. There was a silence that was interrupted by a hot wind, some very distant howls, and two faint, angry growls that came from behind them in the mist.

"I don't think he's here. I'd check that site out first. If it's nothing, we can come back here with *Nightfall* and secure this area for closer inspection. Agreed?"

"Copy. Pilot—evac immediately and head to those coordinates. Copy?"

"Copy," the pilot said.

Devin smiled at the remote chance that the prince was alive. She turned again to talk into her headset.

"Pilot? What's your name?"

"Mary. We'll be there in two."

Devin nodded and took up a position looking into the mist as more faint growls came from within.

"I told you she's good. Young, but good," Regina said.

"Yup. You got a good team going," Devin said.

She felt some relief when she heard the approach of the descent ship's engines.

CHAPTER 9
THE OUTPOST

Any man who tries to be good all the time is bound to come to ruin among the great number who are not good.— Niccolò Machiavelli, *The Prince*

Victor looked blankly out at the broken ruins that led back down the mountainside to an adjacent valley. Shielded from the hot sun, he felt no comfort in the fact he had to go back outside to find a clearing in the hopes that some ancient artifact might find him. Even lost in his thoughts, he could still hear the voice recording from the outpost's emergency broadcast piercing his thinking. While the location was only a kilometer away and downhill, leaving it all to chance was not his hope. It was not an organized plan. It was all a gamble. But based on the shambles of broken walls and debris everywhere, the outpost would provide no defense for him in the short term. With his swollen ankle and broken foot, it would be just a matter of time before his injuries led to his death. So far he had beaten the odds. He was still alive, but then, it wasn't nightfall yet. There seemed to be a couple of more hours to go until then. The strong, older female or intersex voice of the emergency broadcast could be heard throughout the small, shattered camp:

"...the large white cylindrical objects with a red cross etched on them are clearly some kind of healing device, maybe a battlefield medic. So far they have been nothing short of a

healer for our two severely injured staff. There was only one instance when two of these objects appeared and took one of our junior team members away and disappeared for several hours. He was returned but his skin was devoid of all hair follicles. Scars, moles, and all skin imperfections were gone. He had no idea what happened. Other than that, this planet has more mysteries than revelations. Species AB180's aggressive movements continue to cause tension and they are a constant danger. Their only natural enemy, other than us, is a four-footed, omnivorous species that travels in packs. They will attack anything with flesh, us included. Species W428 are just as dangerous as species AB180, except they are curious and tend to hunt in packs. While there are years of research to be done on the gravity distortion, the time-space fluctuations make research difficult. We are unable to predict these shifts in time resulting in our experiencing dangerously long absences of supplies. And the resupply ships experience no distortion and are on schedule. At the time of this recording, we experienced a delay in supplies of three months. The resupply ship was a day ahead of schedule. We abandoned the post...periods of...this is Chief Scientist Rachael...the large white cylindrical objects with a red cross etched on them are clearly some kind of healing devices, maybe a battlefield medic. So far they have been nothing short of a healer for our two severely injured staff. There was only one..."

"*It is imperative that we locate these large white cylindrical objects with the red crosses that heal wounds. If the reports on species W428 is accurate, and there is no reason to suspect the reports are false, you will need to be fully repaired to survive. While species AB180 is more territorial, species W428's pack-like qualities and curiosity make them more of a danger,*" Victor's AI said. Her monotone voice was as clear as if she were in his ear. She was deeper; she was embedded in his brain. As if to prove her point, a series of long howls echoed from the valley below. They were far away and different from the growls and moans he'd heard from the mist. These were longer, maybe even songlike in tone, length, and volume.

Victor had cried ever since he saw the outpost's shattered condition. He couldn't remember one second of safety or good news. Everything that had happened to him went from bad to worse. He'd landed in the mist, his pod had exploded, destroying valuable supplies, he'd hurt his leg, and now his only possible shelter was in ruins with a warning of yet more dangers and a clear caution about getting off the planet. And now there was a more dangerous creature than the ones he had encountered.

"I know," he said. After another five minutes, he put his rifle and the majority of his rations down on the shelter's floor. The only salvageable item in the area was a worn utility belt. He put it on and found space in its compartments for two ration bars, three packets of water, two energy cells for his sidearm, and a sheath where the sergeant's knife fit. Finding the belt was the only positive thing that had occurred on this planet. Other than being alive.

"It would have been better if I died in the crash or explosion," he said aloud.

His AI did not respond. He looked around for some kind of stick and found one. He looked at his torn, dirty undergarments and cut them off. Being ashamed of being naked was the least of his problems. His dark skin was darker and felt as if he had been sunburned. After some modification of his stick, he was happy with his new walking cane and club. After still more delays, he finally took a deep breath and moved out of the outpost.

"*Logical,*" he heard his AI say.

"What?"

"Logical: you took only enough rations to last three days

at most and took only the sidearm and combat knife for protection. They are the only two things other than your makeshift crutch that you can wield effectively as a weapon."

"If I don't find these things that the scientist says heal, I won't be around for long." Victor felt tired and just wanted to sit down and die.

"That is accurate. One modification. You only need to carry one day's supply of food and water. If you do not find these medics within two hours, you will not survive the night. If the howls we have heard are species W428, they are approaching. There were six distinct howls. Should they have to come through the mist, they may be dissuaded by species AB180. Regardless, our survival for this planet's night is zero percent if you remain damaged," his AI said. Even though Victor knew that his AI, like all the other royal AI symbionts, was devoid of emotions, he had hoped for at least some expression of sadness or regret. They might be sentient, even sapient, but their lack of feelings, emotions, even when the death of their host was certain, was simply unnerving. Victor simply sighed and started his trek to the valley where his last glimmer of hope might be.

CHAPTER 10
THE OUTPOST REVISITED

Hence a prince who wants to keep his authority must learn how not to be good, and use that knowledge, or refrain from using it, as necessity requires. — Niccolò Machiavelli, *The Prince*

"This is really strange," Regina said to Devin. Both were looking at the solid walls, a mix of metal and carved wood. The latticework to keep them all in place was decorative, solid, and functional. On those walls were a number of large primate skulls along with those of some other carnivores as well. Large jaws, a series of teeth lined up on a cord, were all bleached, cleaned, and ornamental in their arrangement. There was a series of skins—mostly from species AB180 and others she could not recognize. There were two makeshift stoves for heating and cooking. The embers from both of them were still smoldering, sending smoke up the homemade chimney. The utensils were versatile and could readily be used as weapons. And to add to the mystery, there were many different types of spears and swords that were a combination of wood, stone, and metals. There was also a series of arrows in varying stages of production and a series of tools that looked like a hammer, ax, and pliers. Everything was neatly arranged and clearly organized. There were also scientific machinery and instruments that she had expected to find at the archaeological outpost.

"This is a hunter's lodge," Regina observed.

"A big game hunter's lodge," Devin added.

Even as they looked around, Devin was getting worried about the prince. Who or whatever owned this shelter was a hunter. Even as her dressings and bandages bled through and needed attention, she was not ready to let the others search for him without her. Acclimating to the heavier gravity, the dry heat, and the yellow sun was difficult, but she was determined. Finding this lodge, however, meant there was someone or something sophisticated enough to make tools, fix machines, and hunt dangerous game. At Regina's request, the descent ship picked up her Xenon science officer from the *Nightfall* to have him operate an old recording device that was on but not doing anything. Similar to many Xenons, this one had six limbs to support its very stocky body. The two largest limbs acted as transports—legs—while the others operated as two sets of hands and arms. Covered with fine reddish-brown hair, his large head sat on a thick neck. What made this Xenon very different was that he actually liked speaking.

As a species, the Xenons kept to themselves. The only time they would become belligerent was when their borders were encroached upon or when a planet inside or outside of their system was under attack. Intelligent, technologically advanced with a very high moral code, they did not tolerate violence against themselves or others. So when the royal family tried to keep the Xenons out of managing their own planets as imperial business, the Xenon fleet would appear and secure the area. There had been one war a thousand years ago between the kingdom and the Xenons. There were four space battles and the royals lost nearly all of their fleet. Rather than continue their conquest, the Xenons forced a peace accord and returned to their own space. The outer worlds loved the Xenons. They kept the royals from obliterating them for fear of engaging the Xenons again.

Devin looked down for a moment, wondering if the Xenons knew about Oceania. Probably not. The royals kept things like that quiet. *Cowards*, Devin thought.

"Hey, Marcia? You awake? Theta has something," Regina said, pulling Devin out of her daydreaming. She returned her focus to the Xenon who was now standing erect with one pair of hands behind his back and another fiddling with the old controls.

"These components have been reconfigured and are actually arranged correctly. The only thing that was required was to find and turn the recording on," Theta said in his deep baritone voice.

"Thank you," Regina said.

They all sounded that way. It was his fine hair coloring under his uniform that indicated his gender as male.

"You are welcome," Theta said. "I do appreciate your species' tendency to thank one for completing their duty even if it is not required."

"We are a complicated species," Devin said.

"Yes. At times your kind are morally competent and you are always curious," Theta said. Devin was going to respond with a question when Theta's hands folded in front of him before he spoke again.

"The first recording is an older female voice and more likely the original warning."

"At the time of this recording, we experienced a delay in supplies of three months. The resupply ship was a day ahead of schedule. We abandoned the post…periods of…this is Chief Scientist Rachael…the large white cylindrical objects with a red cross etched on them are clearly some kind of healing device, maybe a battlefield medic. So far they have been nothing short of a healer for our two severely injured staff. There was only one…"

Devin listened intently to everything. She was fascinated

by the entire data-driven message. She moved closer and cocked her ear as if it might help reduce the static on the recording. Even though her dressings required changing and she was exhausted, the information on the encampment was exciting.

"Now the next recording is three years old," Theta said in his resonating deep voice.

"This is Victor Venture IX, prince of Hell and lord of my domain. So if you survived species AB180, you know enough to stay out of the mist. Do not fire upon species W428. They will avoid you at first and not attack. If you are bleeding, though, cover up. The scent of blood makes even my wolves wild. Any injuries, get down to the coordinates etched on the metal under the speaker. They are arranged in old map terms called longitude and latitude. Or just go down through the back door, northwest and down the range to the valley below. The Red Cross medics will find you. If you're injured, be prepared to be scanned. If there is anyone younger than twenty-two years, be aware that they might take you. The best thing to do is to leave this rock. Time and space fluctuates so much that you could be down here five minutes and lose a year of life. Get out while you can. If we meet, I'll go with you. If not, get some help for yourself first and then think of me later. Stay out of the sun, stay hydrated, and have a great day. Victor out."

Devin's eyes felt as if they were bulging out of her head. Theta had captured the whole recording on his scanner and was doing something that interested him.

"Dias? Did you hear that?" she asked into her headset.

"Sarge...this is crazy. He sounds like he's a young adult. And if I didn't know better, his voice sounds strong...confident," Dias said.

"He also encouraged us to save ourselves and to help him later. He put his own safety and security second to whomever found this place. This doesn't sound like your ordinary royal.

Prince Jason, maybe," Regina added.

"Yeah. Did he say, 'Stay hydrated and out of the sun'? 'Prince of Hell and lord of my domain'? Sarge, I think our prince might be having some issues," Dias warned.

"You think?" was all Devin could say.

"Captain Devin," Theta called out.

Both Regina and Marcia responded "Yes?" at the same time. Devin looked embarrassed as she remembered she was a sergeant and Regina was captain.

"Yes," Regina said again, clarifying who the captain really was.

"I believe that if this is indeed a rescue mission, I would follow the young man's recommendation and go to where these Red Cross medics will be. Further, the voice is, in fact, Prince Victor Venture IX, based on prior field recordings. However, he is approximately five years older. I have no idea if we are now five years older. I suggest that we follow the prince's suggestion and leave to get help in this enterprise."

Devin was silent as she weighed all the facts.

"Marcia? It's your call," Regina said.

"I told him I would return. And I'm going to keep my word. Denis and Nova—you got point downhill. Mayer—you got our six. Theta—you're with me. Mary?"

"Copy," the young voice called back.

"You scout ahead. Regina, I think we should prep *Nightfall* for immediate dust off. It will be a bag-and-drag operation. I want off this rock," Devin said to her cousin.

"You got that right," Regina said to Devin, and then she went on her own headset. "Franklin—prep the ship for immediate dust off. Whatever Zil and Zone were doing to the engines, have them stop and get her ready for launch. Copy?"

"Copy. We're on it. Franklin out."

CHAPTER 11
DISCOVERY

If an injury has to be done to a man it should be so severe that his vengeance need not be feared. — Niccolò Machiavelli, *The Prince*

"So, this is it," Victor said as he lay down on his side under the shade of a large boulder. His foot was so large at the ankle and toes he could no longer walk. He had whimpered, cried, and was now bleeding from head to foot after a series of falls. Naked, with no food and just his knife, water, and sidearm, he continued to whimper. He wished he could have been stoic about his death, like a Xenon, but fear of dying was hard to handle.

"I wish I could be braver," he said to himself.

"Bravery is irrelevant. Your injuries are too pronounced for either escape or survival," the AI symbiont said.

He had been in the area for an hour and still had found none of the things the recordings said had appeared. There were plenty of howls and just as it was in the other valley—he watched a white-blue mist forming around the corner. Distant growls could be heard and he could feel tremors in the ground from heavy footsteps.

"Survival is zero percent. Recommendation: set the sidearm power pack on overload. The blast will be swift and merciful," the emotionless AI said. Victor had thought about suicide but had no plan. The AI's idea made more sense now.

He took a deep breath and started to recite another prayer as he fumbled with the sidearm power pack. He moved as quickly as he could so that he might simply do it before he became too frightened to finish the task. As he chanted, he found the power adjuster and pushed the dial all the way to the far end that was in the red zone for danger. There was a perceptible hum and the handle started to warm up.

"Very good, Prince Victor Venture IX. Wait one minute and then point the sidearm's muzzle into the ground. The discharge and overload will cause an explosion of two meters. It will be quick. I regret that our time together was short. Thank you for being my host and allowing me to experience life."

Victor felt sad at first, and then he felt what little moisture he had in his body make tears that finally fell. He took three deep breaths, turned the weapon's muzzle right into the ground, and pulled the trigger.

Nothing happened. The only perceptual thing that registered in his hand was the drop in the humming and the warmth of the handle. Both fell off entirely. He looked at the dial, which seconds ago had been fully charged in the red zone but now was devoid of all power, as if it was suddenly drained.

"What? No, no, no! I can't even kill myself. What happened?" he said as he looked at the weapon all over to see if he'd missed something.

"Unknown. All sensory indications were clear that you had obtained data, set the correct settings, and followed the instructions for self-destruct. There must be either some kind of weapon defect or an energy-dampening field," his AI said. For the first time, it seemed as if the AI had at least one emotion. It was that of genuine surprise.

A deep series of growls along with a chorus of howls erupted all around him. Victor laid his head back on the ground and spoke quietly. He started another chant but stopped suddenly as he caught the sight of a pair of hairy legs walking toward him. They were connected to a very thick, hairy body that had a huge torso and massive hands. They both carried large spears as they searched for something. While the howls caught their attention at first, one of the creatures saw him through the thinning mist. Two low, menacing growls emerged as they walked, heavy footed, toward him. Victor burst out into tears that were nearly dry. He desperately pointed his sidearm in the hope that it might work, but it did not. The trigger was seized in place. Their heavy steps reverberated through the ground as Victor tried to push himself away, deeper into the boulder as if to hide.

"No," he said quietly.

"*Species AB180,*" the AI said.

"Please, no."

Victor could now smell them as they approached. Their faces were covered with hair, and their jaws looked as if they had very large teeth. He was about to close his eyes when two reddish-blue light beams struck the two creatures in the chest. They screamed out in pain and fell backward. After another second, they were back on their feet waving their large spears at three metal spheres that hovered noiselessly above the ground. Another set of growls and more waving of spears elicited two more blasts from two of the spheres. Even as they fell back, a huge rock just missed one of the spheres. In response, it readjusted its position and shot its beam into the mist, where another loud cry in pain erupted. Victor pushed away and his good foot bumped into something. He looked at his feet and found a four-legged, hairy creature with a long snout brimming with teeth, a long head and pointed ears. It had a tail and its growling was lower and just as menacing as that of species AB180.

"No!" he cried out. The creature inched closer, but as had happened with the other creatures, a red-blue beam cut into it, knocking it to the ground, where it remained motionless. Victor was stunned and found himself looking at a white object that had a faded red cross on it.

"They found me…" he said to himself. A bright light blinded him and then he felt his body lift from its prone position into the air. Feeling weightless, he also felt very little pain. While he could still hear some distant growling and howls along with seeing shadows of red-blue beams of light in his periphery, he was feeling just a bit better than miserable.

"Finally, something good…"

Victor suddenly felt tired. He closed his eyes and allowed himself to drift. After all that had happened in only hours, he seized any moment of ease and lack of pain as a gift. Whether he fell asleep or passed out, he was not sure, except that he lost track of time and was disoriented. There was just a brief moment when he felt something pressing into his mouth and scraping the inside of his cheek. That was the last thing he was sure he experienced before he passed out.

When he awoke, he found himself still bathed in a bright light but standing with some assistance. He put his hands out and touched some kind of transparency. He did his best to look beyond the clear glass and saw an endless stream of similar transparent tubes, the same kind of tube he was in, for as far as the eye could see. These tubes had a series of wires, smaller tubes, and cords running to them and they in turn ran into machines. While all the machines looked dark, the one closest to him was alive with blinking lights and a myriad of colors. He moved his head to see if he could see more. As the dark sea of machinery and transparent tubes was evident, he finally saw some ancient lettering on his own transparency. The lettering appeared to be old script, like what he had seen in the library's old manuscripts. It spelled out something he truly did not understand: "enO reficuL."

A sharp pain in his right arm got his attention. He turned

in time to see a sharp needle retracting from a solid piece of metal attached to his transparency. Victor started to feel completely sluggish. His limbs stopped working, his breathing felt shallow, and he felt light-headed. With little energy to move, he saw more needles emerging from all sides. Unable to avoid or move, he was about to cry out in pain—except there was none. The needles, hundreds of them, seemed to go into every part of his body, including his face. After several minutes of not moving and feeling numb, he finally noticed that the range of blinking lights were now all pulsating a green color. Unable to talk, he just looked. He was scared to death and confused about everything. He felt air pushing in from above him while warm liquid began to fill and swirl at his feet. It was red, warm, and made his skin tingle. At first he was grateful at the experience. That all changed when it became apparent the liquid was not going to stop until it was well over his head.

No...I'm going to drown...no, he thought.

As hard as he tried to move his head up to stay above the liquid, he had no energy to do it. When it finally reached his mouth and nose, he held his breath. After about three minutes he could no longer hold it and exhaled. When he inhaled, however, instead of drowning, he seemed to breathe in the liquid, as if it was air itself. It filled his lungs and it felt warm. He was amazed, stunned, and shocked all at the same time. Confused, he was just trying to figure out how he could breathe liquid when a massive current of electricity ran through every cell in his body. The pain was so fast and so powerful that his vision collapsed and he was gone. A warm sensation returned briefly but then a brilliant light came through his closed eyes as if it were cutting a new hole in his brain. The pain, not as powerful as at first, was still enough to ensure he would be unconscious. For the first time in several hours, Victor found peace in death.

CHAPTER 12
THE GREAT HUNT

Since love and fear can hardly exist together, if we must choose between them, it is far safer to be feared than loved. — Niccolò Machiavelli, *The Prince*

Devin looked at the old rusted sidearm she had given the prince when she pushed him into the escape pod. What had only been nine hours for her looked as if it were years for him, abandoned along with a utility belt, an empty canteen, and her combat knife.

"How?" she said to Theta, who was scanning the artifacts.

"Normal aging effect. They have been exposed to the elements and are in a complete state of decomposition as a result of being out here for five years," the Xenon said in his calm, deep voice.

"But I gave this to the prince no more than nine hours ago."

"I know, Sergeant Devin. But we are on a planet that has time and space distortions actively occurring. Our arrival here is relative. His experience of time, similar to these artifacts and what we heard at the outpost, is clearly different by a factor of years."

Devin looked at the sidearm. Regina handed her the combat knife she was inspecting.

"We got to find this prince of yours and get out of here. We may have been here too long ourselves," she warned.

Devin nodded in agreement and put the worn knife into her empty sheath.

"Captain? I got infrared contacts fifteen meters north of your position. It's in that mist but it's moving pretty fast in your direction," Mary the pilot said.

"Copy," Regina said.

"No, Captain. The weird part is that there are two of them, those big things being chased by much smaller infrared dots," Mary added.

Devin looked up the grade and saw a bank of mist stalled in clear view ten meters ahead. She jumped on her headset in spite of her pain from earlier wounds. With no desire to get back into a firefight, she prepared for battle.

"Mayer, Denis! Move to cover and zero in on the bank. Theta and Nova—up front with me and Regina!"

"Mary—go hot and bring your ship above our position. Open the side doors and give us cover," Regina said. She was right beside Devin when they both heard static over their headsets.

"...Mayday, Mayday—descent ship 2B losing power rapidly. We are in a controlled descent one kilometer from the landing party's position due south...captain...needs assistance! Mayday, Mayday...we are in a controlled descent but the captain needs support...creatures heading toward...We are going down...landing gear's in place, still have pressure in the pedals and torque. We'll be fine...go help the captain...Mayday, Mayday..."

Regina looked behind her with her scope. Devin kept her scope on the mist with her rifle by her side for easy access.

"She's going to be all right, Regina. She's controlling the landing," Devin said. She felt Regina face in the opposite direction toward the mist, the oncoming danger.

"She's just a kid, Marcia. She has no family. I've got to go get her," she said with anger.

"We will, Regina. I promise. We'll take care of whatever is heading toward us and then we'll go get your crew. If the prince lasted this long, I think Mary can last another hour for us to get her and the crew," Devin said calmly. She was feeling anything but calm. Danger was in front of them, their ride out of there was down, her team was split up, and still no prince.

Damn it.

Suddenly a large primate burst through the mist and skidded to a stop. It turned around and growled at something behind it. Another large primate looked as if it was going to make it out of the mist but something invisible pulled it back. A high-pitched shrill came from the mist. More cries, and then it stopped abruptly. The first primate gripped its spear and made a start back to the mist to help the other. A series of howls erupted from the blue-white mist, making the creature stop in its tracks. Another series of howls and the creature started at a dead run toward their position. Devin didn't have to give the order for the team to have their weapons fully trained on the large primate. But before she or Regina could give the order to fire, the creature stopped again and backed away. Devin shifted her focus ahead of the creature and saw three large, four-legged creatures with large snouts and impressive rows of teeth that could be easily seen from her position.

"Species W428. He called them wolves," Theta whispered.

"And he said we shouldn't fire on them," Regina said.

Devin nodded and watched the drama unfold in front of her. The primate growled ferociously and swung its spear at the wolves. They moved out of the way and began to circle the larger creature. Another howl sounded from the mist, but it was different, more guttural, yet longer lasting. As soon as it stopped, Devin caught movement from the mist. From her vantage point, she saw a hominid dressed in hides, running with three other wolves at full speed. The spear he was carrying was the same length as the creature, which dwarfed him in size. The three other wolves howled, which caught the attention of the primate. Even without her scopes, she could see the man bring his arm back and launch the spear. It sailed like a missile and landed squarely in the large creature's side. It yelled out in pain and grabbed at it. The surrounding wolves seized that moment to pounce on the flailing creature. Startled, it was unable to move its hands fast enough to grab at the four-legged creatures. Suddenly the man was also on top of the creature's neck while the three wolves lunged at their prey. The creature's growls of pain and anger shifted to shrills of fear, just like the other one in the mist. Devin looked at the sight. She blinked several times and then looked at her cousin and Theta. Their expressions of astonishment were telling, especially the Xenon's look. She had never seen such a surprised look on what was typically a stoic exterior.

"Who is this guy? How is it possible that he took out those two monsters? Does he control those other creatures, the smaller four-legged ones?" Regina whispered.

"I don't know, Regina," Devin said.

"This is beyond reason," Theta said quietly. The shrills stopped altogether and then there was silence. A screech of a bird of prey echoed though the valley and then the howling started. In response, there was a series of other howls as well— some from the mist and others from the hills above. It only took a moment to see that the entire area was now filled with these wolves. The majority moved in on the dead primate and began feasting. The man, his clothing covered with blood, just looked on. His skin was dark and even at a distance his muscles were defined. There was an imperious aura around him as he stood with his arms folded across his chest watching the packs of wolves devour their meal. What was interesting as well was that this hominid appeared to be hairless, with only the hides offering protection.

"I guess we found the lodge's owner," Regina said quietly.

Sweat drenched Devin's uniform. She was positive that the planet's heat was not the only cause for her flushing. She turned to whisper to Regina, but Regina pushed Devin to the ground out of the way of some beam. It hit the captain point-blank and pulled her right up in the air.

"No! Regina! No!"

Theta leaped above her and had two sidearms and an enormous assault weapon all pointed at the floating object that held Regina above the ground. Devin waited milliseconds for the barrage of firepower to unleash against the assailing beams. Instead, she heard a series of trigger clicks but no discharge of any weapons. Two beams from two different spherical, floating objects hit Theta.

"Squad! Regina and Theta are down!"

As Devin moved out of their field of fire, she, Denis, Athena, and Nova trained their weapons on their targets. Devin saw Athena pause, look down at her rifle, and attempt to fire again, but nothing worked. She was hit from behind by a beam.

"Damn it! The power's drained!" she heard Denis cry out. He swung his rifle like a club and nearly hit the object that now snared him in its beam. Nova threw her rifle directly at the object. It bounced off and fell harmlessly to the ground. She ran at the thing with her combat knife drawn to strike but was caught in midflight by another firm beam. Devin pulled out a sonic grenade. She was about to pull the safety when she watched the green power light suddenly drain to red.

"Empty! What the…"

A bright, white beam filled her entire vision. She felt weightless, light as air in addition to being immobilized. She, like the others, was floating. A penetrating warm wave went from her toes and slowly up her body. She was surprised not to feel anger, sadness, or fear. The only level of discomfort came when she felt her mouth being gently pried open and her cheeks being scraped. After that, she felt as if she were traveling down a long corridor toward a bright light.

No...

CHAPTER 13
METAMORPHOSIS

The lion cannot protect himself from traps, and the fox cannot defend himself from wolves. One must therefore be a fox to recognize traps, and a lion to frighten wolves.— Niccolò Machiavelli, *The Prince*

It's all a hallucination, Victor thought. The warmth of the liquid that surrounded him was soothing and comforting. With no more shocks running through his body, the visions, sounds, and smells were as real as he was in the world with them. It was as if he was actually there. He lost track of time as details of images played out before him quickly yet clearly. Small primates evolved into large ones and eventually into creatures very similar to him. Caves, campfires, tents, and camps turned into towns, cities, and eventually entire countries with moments of peace and times of war. In the battles, arrows flung by bent strings evolved into clubs, spears, swords, lances, guns, rifles, assault weapons, and bigger still. He recognized tanks and larger mechanized weapons. He saw courts, books, and papers before him. Entire chapters, paragraphs, books, novels, series—texts, facts, and fiction, all the sources of ancient manuscripts he had ever hoped to read on Pax became a reality all at once.

So much. So much more, he thought. There was no fear or trepidation. Just genuine joy at all the written words. And somehow, he understood the writing. He understood them all.

More cities, different kinds of people, but all of the same species. Space exploration and voyages to deep space and into massive oceans. All was strange, different, and new until images of Xenons appeared before these people. They were curious of one another. They worked together, and the species of the planet built ships and followed the Xenons into the heavens. A flash from a solar flare and the entire planet changed. Oceans shrank to less than half, and the mist appeared, while the moon, once whole, shattered. Cities fell and the survivors went underground. The Xenons returned and helped with cities, technologies, more words, paragraphs, and books, but still, Victor could understand them all.

One group of Xenons created an underground complex, a science station geared to regenerate a new species reconfigured to rebuild a dying planet. Another group worked with the people to alter time, to change things back to the way they were before the flare through the planet's core. Something went wrong. They all faded away, evaporated, as if they were never there. Other Xenons took the survivors away to safety, to the stars, leaving the underground complex empty, ready, and prepared. All was in place but the volunteers, the people and the Xenons, the ones that operated the machines, were gone. Only the central computer was online. It waited for instruction. None came.

It found an ancient game—chess. Visions of strange-looking pieces on a black-and-white board emerged. The pieces and moves had meaning. It played the game over and over again but could not beat itself. And then Victor saw that the ancient computer froze and an independent, sapient thought grabbed it. Movement from white and black drones emerged with multiple limbs and lights, moving hardware, and components. Another computer was built, and it was different. After years of playing chess, it beat it. The new computer exceeded its creator. The ancient computer went off-line and downloaded all prior data.

Ongoing objective—recreate an improved biological, organic, carbon-based species from past DNA samples. Attempts made yielded…errors. Creatures were deviations from flawed material and were released into the mist. They propagated and survived. DNA was flawed. New DNA required. New subobjectives—locate viable new DNA from two sources: species Xenon and descendants of the species known as humans of the originating planet called Earth.

Periodic contact with species resulted in partial sampling. DNA stores in place required specific DNA coding from at least two sources. Time-space distortion made the planet hostile in addition to its inhabitants. Visions of different people—his own kind and Xenons—flashed before Victor. They were all caught in a bright beam. They were sampled where they were and for the one that fit. All but one before him came to the transparent tubes he was in. Visions of himself under a rock—small, filthy, legs scarred and body beaten—appeared. He watched himself being probed. His mouth was opened and the inside of his cheeks was scraped. His body was heated, warmed, primed and now…his vision crumbled, cold air flooding his space. The liquid was gone. Bright light…cold…weightless.

"*Argh!*" Victor croaked out. He felt himself fall out of the beam that had brought him there. It was so different from how he felt when he fell out of the cryogenic sleep on the ship.

What was its name? Rising Sun? *Yes…the sergeant. The pretty commander…Virgil. His kind brother, Jason. The bishop. Bishop Miles. Pax…*

It all came back to him as he lay prone on the solid ground. It was cool and his lungs gulped in air. It took time for his eyes to flutter open. After what seemed a long time, they slowly opened as if for the first time. Everything was blurry at first. A film had settled on his eyes. He was not in the transparency or anywhere near the sea of machinery he'd seen. He was back outside, but the area was rocky, with places that were clear of boulders. It was day, but not as hot as he remembered. The sun was low on the horizon and it was cooler than expected.

"Hey? Are you awake? Can you believe all that stuff? Wow." A loud, enthusiastic voice spoke out. Victor was startled that someone was right beside him. When he looked, there was no one there. He heard a slight motor noise and saw one of the Red Cross medics floating at first. A less intense light probed him for a few seconds and then it floated away.

"I guess you got your final check and you're free to go," the voice said again. Victor spun around from a seated position to see who else was there.

"Hey, I'm in your head. Remember? AI symbiont? I'm embedded in your prefrontal cortex and I'm accessing your auditory nerve center so we can talk, or at least give the impression that we can talk. Kind of strange, the whole reconstruction of the perceived external world we all agree to, but I digress. Don't you think I need a name?" The voice was cheery and female, far different from the one he remembered. Her enthusiasm far outdistanced him. When he cleared his throat and spoke, he was not sure it was even his own voice. It was different, deeper, with a resonant timbre to it.

"You can't be my AI. You had no personality and were pretty boring," he said. He stood up slowly. He first noticed that his feet, hands, and legs were not only devoid of all hair, but he was noticeably larger, bigger, and muscular than even his former mentor, the bishop.

"Well, I guess we both changed. If you haven't noticed, your body is that of a sixteen- or seventeen-year-old male. Your body has been profoundly altered, maybe even like me, perhaps?"

Victor rolled his eyes. The AI's tone was not only

expressive, but it was easy to tell it had a tendency to produce humor, understatements, and sarcasm.

"*You are devoid of hair follicles, scars, and moles. You have no noticeable injuries, and from what I've experienced in your frontal and temporal lobes, you got a lot of data dumped in here. I think my personality change is a bit less dramatic than your entire physiology for sure,*" the AI said. Now the tone was that of annoyance.

"'A rose by any other name,'" Victor said. He knew the meaning, reference and how it fit into the present context. He knew all of it but he didn't know how.

"*Ah, yes. 'What's in a name? That which we call a rose by any other name would smell as sweet.' A weak association to William Shakespeare's* Romeo and Juliet, *but it might work. You know this author has written a lot of stuff? Pretty heavy, but it really does apply to your royal family's sense of drama, betrayal, vengeance, and palace intrigue. And while we're on names, don't you think I should have one?*"

Victor shook his head as if to clear it. The mention of his family and the author at first confused him until he had a flood of images, passages, and stories that perfectly captured his feelings toward his noble lineage—in particular, his brother Ramsey, whom he had a sudden urge to kill with his bare hands, and his other brother, Jason, whom he wished to see. He pushed the thoughts out of his head to focus on getting a grip on what was happening right now. He focused on his AI's obsession with having a name.

"Why? Why do you need a name?"

"*Because you have one and I don't. And do you really want to be calling me AI? Or 'AI! Come to my assistance,*'" the voice said mechanically in the tone it had possessed before its alteration.

"*It's kind of old and boring, don't you think? I'm thinking something simple, monosyllabic, and pretty at the same time,*" she added in her newly acquired, enthusiastic voice.

Victor started to walk around. He was getting used to his larger body. He ran his hands over his bald head and looked at his body's sheen and his skin, which appeared to be very dark brown and felt very tight.

"Hello? I'm talking here. Hey, wait a minute! How about Rose?"

"Rose?"

"Yes. It's short, beautiful, and very feminine. It's highly associated with romance and girls. And in times of stress you can call out a simple four-letter word. Just perfect!"

Victor was speechless as he walked. He had so many questions and so few answers. There were two major things: he was older and his AI had an identity.

"All right. Even if you are a prince, it's still rude to ignore people—I mean, me."

"I'm not ignoring you…ah, Rose. I'm trying to figure out what's going on and what I should do next," he said. He noticed that when the AI spoke again, it was less annoyed and much more cooperative.

"All right! Now we're talking. About what happened? I think we were an experiment for the sapient computer to obtain DNA. Further, it gave you an immersion history lesson on this planet as a means of keeping your brain, and me, from dying from lack of stimulation after years of containment. Great, huh?"

Victor stood still with his hands placed on his hips, head tilted to his left as if he were listening to a person right beside him.

"Yes…great. So now that we've had an extensive yet detailed history lesson…"

"More than that, Prince. We got lifetimes of data, history, and physiological changes at a cellular level that exceeded any hominid in the kingdom. I can't even speculate about what

your metaphysical capacity might be. Now that really is over-the-top great," she added with wild enthusiasm.

Victor smirked at Rose's energy. *If you're marooned on a hell planet, it's better to have interesting company*, he thought.

Naked and without food, water, and shelter, Victor had a concrete question.

"So while we're on the subject of survival," he started. Rose cut him off. He wondered if that was going to be the way of things.

"Yes! First order of business is shelter, water, and then food. In this vacation spot, I'd also go with weapons of any kind," she said.

"You know, you are using contractions a lot. Was that part of your program?" Victor asked.

"Do you think my personality was part of the original program? No. Similar to you, all the data, neurogenesis, and brain development have accelerated my evolution. I am more than the sum of my parts. Similar to you, minus the royalty and stuff," Rose said.

A sudden wave of anger toward his brother flooded him again.

"Yeah, about my brother," he muttered.

"Oh, yeah. Prince Ramsey. He's a piece of work, huh," Rose said. *"Cain and Abel. Romulus and Remus. Will you be playing the role of the prodigal son?"* she asked.

All the names she mentioned—brother against brother in a highly revered book called the Bible, and the founders of a great civilization called Rome—made sense as well. It took just a moment to get the other reference. There was so much information in his head, all categorized and filed, but a lot to go through in seconds.

"Oh. The Bible again. The one brother leaves the home on an adventure and he comes back worldly but with nothing. He was lost but then he was found," Victor said. He smiled.

Whatever he'd experienced while he was immersed in liquid and exposed to all those sensations made him feel knowledgeable.

"But it's all ancient to this world, not mine. Alien and relevant but ancient."

"Yes, it is alien, but the themes of forgiveness and envy are the same. But I don't think you will be embraced as well as that son was," Rose said. In his distraction, Victor nearly walked into the mist. He froze for a moment since he heard something. His AI picked up immediately on what he was doing and the obvious danger.

"All right. Slowly back away before…"

Suddenly a brood of small, four-legged puppies yelped and ran out of the mist toward and past him, beyond his feet. There was a howl, a series of barks that were silenced after a loud thud. As Victor backed away, he saw a large ball of fur sail through the air. A loud growl—a victory growl—came from the other side of the mist. He heard that monster's growl, species AB180, before when he was saved by the spheres.

The sun was low and it looked as if the first night was going to be a rough one. Victor heard heavy steps even as he walked backward. The yelping of the little creatures continued to draw the monster's attention. The only time they stopped was when he and the puppies came across the large, mangled body of their mother. The creatures flocked around the recently killed animal and began to each give more small howls.

"It was their mother. That thing killed their mother and now it's going to kill them," he said. Fear was replaced with anger. Adrenaline filled his blood and he felt a wave of fury build. Years of being small and fearful all of a sudden mutated into things he had not experienced—rage and fearlessness.

"All right, *Prince. Not that you'll listen, but based on the levels of adrenaline and corticosteroid in your body, you're looking for a fight. You could leave. Species AB180 will move on the small creatures,"* Rose said.

"Any ideas on how to kill that thing?" Victor had stopped his retreat and moved at an angle to the mist.

"I was afraid you'd say that. Can't we just run away?"

"Rose! I need ideas!"

"Well, a fully charged rifle with a series of fragment or sonic grenades would be really handy. But in this primitive place, the size of rock you would need will be impossible to lift."

Suddenly, a spear sailed out of the mist, missing Victor by a meter. He looked at it and smiled.

"Ask and you shall receive," he said.

"Well. That is quite useful. Pick the weapon up and place your hand closer to the actual point to accommodate for its size. Step back and prepare to run toward the combatant for velocity and to clearly target the creature's torso. While it is protected by ribs and muscle, it is the largest thing to hit," Rose instructed.

"Now we're talking," he said as he picked up the weapon. He was surprised how light it felt in his hand even though it was larger than a spear that would fit him.

"All right. *Weapon—check. Clear target would help,"* Rose said. Victor looked at the little puppies and heard their howls as he backed up to start his attack run. He took a deep breath and gave his best imitation of a howl. So loud and strong was it that the little puppies' howls increased as if he'd emboldened them, and a series of very distant howls echoed through the valley. A loud growl responded as well. He heard heavy steps running toward him.

"Target coming in from your left. Prepare to launch your weapon. Target the torso. If possible, aim for the stomach below the chest cavity. It has fewer bones for protection. It is a soft target. It will be painful and is still a large enough target

*to hit when it suddenly appears. It is ten meters…five meters
farther to your left. Head toward your target at top speed for
velocity. Go!"*

Victor was running toward the mist. The footsteps from
the approaching creature were loud and the mist gave way to
reveal a large primate that had its own spear out in front.
Unlike Victor's weapon, the creature's spear was not poised
for throwing. Victor threw the spear with all of his might. It
felt light to him as he hurled the weapon. The response of the
creature was immediate. The javelin not only penetrated the
creature's stomach but it went straight through the creature so
that it was sticking out both front and back. The creature
howled in shock and pain. It dropped its own weapon and
staggered back, shocked and confused. With little hesitation,
Victor picked up the creature's other spear and backed up to
size up his next attack as the huge primate grabbed at the
javelin embedded in his stomach. Its cries of agony continued
at a very loud volume. Victor focused the second weapon on
the monster's mouth to kill it quickly and to silence the
creature in case it was calling for help. Distant growls from
deep in the mists were sounding off. Victor moved quickly to
get both a good angle and running distance to kill the beast. It
was a smaller target than the stomach but he had a deep-seated
conviction that he could do it.

*"Good idea! Aim for the neck. It will be both a silencer
and a kill strike,"* Rose advised. It took him just a moment to
find his opening and take it. As the second spear penetrated the
neck, the creature's hands clawed at it. Its eyes were startled as
if in complete shock at what was happening. The growls and
howls changed into groans, moans, and gurgling of blood.
Victor's anger and fury melted into pity for the creature. It had
to be strange for such a large creature to go from being a top
predator to prey for such a little creature as himself. The cries
stopped and after a moment more, Victor heard a death rattle.

He stood looking at the creature in shock. In addition to the tiny puppy howls and very distant ones from other larger adult wolves, as he now knew they were called from his immersion, he could hear growls at the far end of the mist. It wouldn't be long until the primate's kin would be there.

"*We got maybe eight minutes to take one spear and that thing's knife on his belt, collect your little friends, and put distance between us and this creature's friends. It also has some recent kills from its hunt that will be a good source of protein for you and your young wards. If you want to do them a real favor, you should come back for the creature's organs once the mist recedes, and hopefully its clan will not find him nor explore outside the mist to look for him,*" Rose said clinically. In the past, Victor would have retched at the idea. But his new body and brain seemed immune to horror. Horror was a friend.

"Survival of the fittest. I don't care who said that. It works!"

"*Celebration later, Prince. This area is hot,*" Rose warned.

Victor pulled the creature's large knife from its belt along with its recent kills. He pulled at the spear and it easily separated from the creature's neck. Naked but with hands full, he ran back to where the puppies were, picked up their dead mother, and slung her on his back to carry. As expected, all eight puppies followed him.

"*Now, in case you're wondering, these little furry creatures—wolves, they are called—are pack creatures. They are all cute and adorable now, but they will be as large as their mother in less than a year. Their social structure is of a dominance hierarchy. Unless you want to be picking up waste and becoming dinner, you better consistently present as the alpha male of the group,*" Rose said.

"Good advice."

Victor slowed his pace so the little pack could keep up. While he could hear other wolves howling, he experienced no fear. It was a joyous feeling. Fear, terror, and horror were all friends to be close to on this planet.

"So, Victor? Going forward could we focus on staying alive? I'm just getting used to this sapience thing and I'm really curious about this world and would like to live a little longer to explore it. Are you all right with that?"

"Sarcasm? Is that really necessary?" He smiled at the little howling puppies following him up the ridge.

"Maybe a little. But seriously. Maybe we could keep the dangerous things to planned hunting rather than a knife fight when species AB180 has home-field advantage. I'm just saying," Rose said.

"I certainly agree to that," he said.

"Excellent. Between our brains and your brawn, we'll own this planet," Rose said with an embellished laugh. Victor chuckled.

"I'm working on my megalomania. It seems to come naturally to me."

"Must be who you're hanging out with," Victor offered.

"Must be," Rose said.

"So getting back to how we are here now, were we some kind of experiment back there? That installation with all the machinery and empty transparent tubes?" he asked. Now that the initial shock of his transformation and battle with species AB180 were over, his curiosity about where he was and what had happened finally started to stir. At the same time, he was surprised how light the wolf and weapons felt and that the heat didn't bother him at all.

"I would speculate that we were part of a repopulation experiment, based on all the data that we were exposed to. You remember those letters you saw on the tube before we were zapped?"

Victor remembered the first dose of electrical current that had burned through his body. He nodded at the fact that Rose had gone through the same fire.

"Vaguely," he said. He stopped to give the puppies a chance to catch up. His burden still seemed light.

"*You read it as 'e-n-O r-e-f-i-c-u-L.' As you were seeing it on the other side of the transparency, the data directly from your optic nerve translated it as 'Lucifer One.' I'm guessing that we are the first of a new generation, in the absence of others like us,*" Rose said with unmistakable pride. There were more howls and his puppies were howling in response as they caught up. He found them to be very cute but took Rose's warning to heart and howled himself to present as the alpha.

"*Excellent, Prince. Or should I start calling you Lucifer One?*"

"Maybe. Let's figure out its entire etiology and the meaning of the name first, other than the dark prince of hell, fallen angel, and light bearer. But before all that, we're going to need more weapons. I remember something with a bowed piece of wood, string, and arrows. Do you remember?" Victor asked.

"*Sure do. Let me think about a list of possible weapons while you find our new home. I take it you'll be using the old outpost as a base of operation? Not a bad choice unless we can find a cave or something. It will need a makeover for sure. It was a mess last time we were there,*" Rose said.

With his pups howling at his feet, he started his ascent up the ridge.

"We'll take a look at the outpost first. Agreed?"

"*Agreed,*" she responded.

CHAPTER 14
REUNITED

Men intrinsically do not trust new things that they have not experienced themselves. — Niccolò Machiavelli, *The Prince*

"So I take it you plan to simply stare at her for another hour," Rose said. Her annoyance was not veiled in the slightest. Victor's shoulders slumped at the thought that not only would Rose go on with her ramblings but that she was right too.

After he killed species AB180, he saw the Red Cross medic spheres suddenly appear and immobilize a group of hominids. He had screamed in joy of seeing others after such a long time on the planet. While he was thrilled to see the sergeant and her team, he nearly fell over when he saw a beautiful woman in revealing clothes immobilized by the Red Cross medic's beams suspended just feet above the ground. He had broken his gaze a number of times to look at the others but always came back to her.

"So I guess we will be staring at her for another hour," Rose commented.

"Jealous, Rose?" He felt a smile emerging.

"Oh, please. She does have wonderful mammary glands, if you're into that. And why she's wearing them exposed in a battlefield situation speaks to a range of insecurities."

"Or confidence. Maybe she likes the attention," he added.

"Oh, yeah. 'Hi! My name is Large Breasts and I'm here

to take on two primates, five packs of wolves, and one lonely prince," she mocked.

"Well, as it turns out, she won. Species AB180 are down, my relatives over there are having their well-deserved feast, and I'm staring at her. She kind of beat the odds," Victor said. He waited for Rose to respond. Seconds passed as his smile grew.

"*Touché, Prince Victor. You got me there. But for a really interesting specimen of both logic, strength, and rugged attraction, check out the Xenon. Now he can embrace me with those arms any time,*" she said with more lust than he'd ever heard. Victor moved toward the large creature with its strong, solid torso and well-defined limbs.

"How do you know it's male?"

"*The hair color and voice box. Even though they all have deep voices, there are structural differences between genders and degrees of maturity.*"

"Oh. I forgot about the hair color and its meaning."

"*That's why I'm here, Prince. So who's the older soldier here? She has the rank of sergeant. She, like the other uniformed soldiers here, looks hardened and pissed to be caught in the beams.*"

Victor nodded as he came in front of a person he would never forget. There were the others he vaguely remembered, but he would never forget the woman who saved him.

"It's funny. I only know her as the sergeant of the guard," he responded wistfully as he recalled her pulling him to the escape pod, herself wounded, to set him free. Free from his own brother's betrayal. He pushed his animosity aside and looked closely at her. She hadn't changed a bit. He looked for some scarring on her face, but there was none. He thought he remembered she was injured and her face was bleeding when she helped him escape. There were some faint ones. He looked closer but the medic's beam washed over her again and the scars faded until they were gone. Still, her skinny body, angular face, and blue eyes were unmistakable.

"You're not big on names, are you, Prince?"

"Never got a chance to talk, really."

"So, she's the one we owe everything to," Rose said.

"Pardon?" he asked.

"Well, Prince, if she hadn't got you off the Rising Sun, *we wouldn't have made it here. Our transformation would never have occurred. You must admit that even though the very first day was torturous, the final results exceeded your own expectations, and I bet all of the entire known galaxy. Surely, we owe her that,"* Rose explained. Victor was still thinking when another thought came to mind.

"She said she would come back for me," he said quietly.

"A woman of her word. She's older than her years. She must be only twenty-seven or twenty-eight. I bet she's part Xenon. She is quite the moral person. It clearly would have been safer to leave you be and head off into deep space," Rose said.

"The sergeant did hold the Xenons in high regard. I bet she would be interested to know how they came to this planet first. It's unbelievable," he said as he shifted his gaze back to the woman with the revealing clothes. Suddenly, a soothing melody with an escalating beat popped into his inner ear. The piece was of alien, ancient strings arranged in a sensuous manner. It took Victor just a moment to understand the context of the opus, *Bolero,* by Maurice Ravel.

"All right, Rose. I got your point. I'll take my eyes off of her if you drop the music."

"I'd leave you two alone if I could," she said. Her tone was nearly a giggle.

Victor noticed a drop in light beside him. The looked up to see that of the group, the sergeant was being released first even though she appeared the most injured of the group. But then, while the others required another scraping of their cheeks, there was no repeat test on her.

"*I guess her DNA is either a perfectly good match or a poor match,*" Rose said. As soon as the sergeant's feet touched the ground, Victor was there to hold her up. She fell into his arms. Her light frame and the clean smell of sweat surprised him. He remembered long ago how he was always embarrassed around girls. He was positive that his shyness had not changed with everything else. He became acutely uncomfortable with her in his arms. He roused her as soon as he could. It took a minute longer but she finally came to. She looked at him in the eyes before she spoke. Her first attempt was voiceless. Her experience with the medic's healing had undoubtedly taken its toll. Once she got her bearings, she too became uncomfortable with the proximity and pushed away. She found her footing and adjusted her uniform.

"Are you all right, Sergeant?" Victor asked.

She coughed and then swallowed before she could respond.

"Ah, yes…Prince? Is that really you?"

"You recognized me? That's nice," he said.

"Your voice from the outpost. Your eyes. The shape is the same but the rest of you…it's all different."

"Rose tells me I'm five years older, maybe a bit more," Victor said. He immediately regretted saying his AI's name. The sergeant looked very confused and looked around him.

"Rose is my AI symbiont's name. It was an agreed upon name that fits her," he explained.

"You gave your symbiont a name? You have one? You don't give names to AI symbionts," the sergeant said with doubt in her eyes.

"*Oh, I'm sorry. I didn't know that the royal family was handing out AI symbionts to military staff. At least I have a name. Now what's this girl's name?*" Rose said.

Victor gave a deep sigh and placed his hand on his temples. He focused on the words so that they would make sense and get to the facts he needed.

"Sergeant, I don't have time to explain everything. As you can tell, I have gone through a major transformation—the byproduct of being on a planet with an ancient computer and technology, a wealth of knowledge, and a knack for making it possible for me to survive in this hell. As a result, my AI symbiont has a name. Her name is Rose. Let's just accept that and move on. That said, I'd rather focus on getting us out of here. How much time has gone by?"

Victor could see that the sergeant was still processing his statements.

"Sergeant? What's your name, soldier?" he asked with authority.

The technique worked—she snapped to attention and spoke.

"Devin, Marcia A. Sergeant of the royal guard assigned to serve and protect Prince Victor Venture IX. Last assigned to the *Rising Sun* under Commander Jana Virgil, sir!"

A series of bullet points materialized in his inner eye courtesy of Rose's searching for intelligence on the sergeant. Just as quickly he got information on her troops, including her scantily clad cousin's name—Regina Devin.

"All right, Marcia Angelica Devin. You and your cousin here, Regina, have come to find me. You have. Athena, Denis, and Nova here are doing well. And while you're thinking, check your wounds. You will find that they are all healed. There will not even be scars. None of your team will have scars. That will distress Denis, but at least his artwork will be preserved. But enough. You got me off the *Rising Sun* just as my brother's team attempted to kill me. You obviously escaped, got help, and kept your word. Thank you. So now, from your experience, before you arrived here, how much time has passed outside of this world?"

Victor made sure to keep his voice steady, firm but kind. He found it easy. Hearing her middle name spoken aloud, and her cousin's, and all the other things he said that he couldn't have known, had its desired effect. She was shocked but seemed to believe him.

"How long, Sergeant Devin?" he repeated.

"We escaped the ship and fled to the shattered moon, where my cousin was stationed. Commander Virgil had advance warning and gave us a head start so we could avoid capture. When we made our run to the planet, our experience of hours near the planet's orbit was three weeks in that space. We've been on this planet for three hours, sir."

Victor nodded. His list of questions grew exponentially.

"Do you have a ship that can leave orbit?"

"Yes, but the descent ship had an emergency landing right when we found you."

"Is Corporal Ariel Dias all right?"

"Yes…why, yes, she made it."

"Good. I like her. I figured out the intersex question I had long ago. Once these beams are off of your team, we need to move and get out of here. Nothing personal about my home, but it's been a challenge. A soft bed, cool shower, and clean clothes are something I have long fantasized about," Victor said. Just as he finished, another beam was lowering Athena, right next to the sergeant. At the same time, another beam released Regina. Victor hesitated at first before moving in to grab her. He became very self-conscious about touching her.

"*Oh, I bet you have other fantasies, my omnipotent prince,*" Rose said.

"Stop it, Rose!"

The sergeant turned and looked at him. Victor sighed heavily and spoke again.

"I told you my AI symbiont has a name and a

corresponding personality. You will need to get used to my responding to her. Tell your team so they don't think I'm crazy, please," he said. The sergeant's eyes narrowed but she gave a quick nod in agreement. With little time to think, he was now holding a very attractive woman in his arms. Her hair smelled of vanilla and her skin was as smooth as silk. Her breathing was heavy, and her body was ridiculously curvy and sensuous.

"Little pig, little pig—let me in," Rose recited.

"Just great," Victor whispered. His voice was loud enough to wake the sleeping beauty in his arms. Her eyes fluttered open and gazed up at him. Similar to the sergeant, she had difficulty speaking. Unlike Devin, though, she did not push away. Victor felt his face turning multiple shades of red as heat flushed his face and neck.

Blushing? I'm really blushing. You'd think my color would hide it, but no, he thought.

"Oh, my poor prince. Your flushing and shyness in conjunction with your physical physique and intelligence are going to slay this one for sure. Just separate her from your arms, place her down gently and firmly on the ground, smile and walk away. The beam is fading on the Xenon. Do me a favor and grab him. He's more my speed," Rose said. Much to Victor's surprise, he was grateful for Rose's instructions. He followed them to the letter while never exchanging a word. Regina hesitated letting him go, but he smiled just like Rose had told him to and moved on to the much larger Xenon.

"Thank you," he said quietly to Rose.

"I am here to serve, Prince. Now make sure to get this hunk's name. Look at the muscles on this fine specimen," Rose said with more enthusiasm than he'd ever thought was possible.

CHAPTER 15
FLASH

War is just when it is necessary; arms are permissible when there is no hope except in arms. — Niccolò Machiavelli

"Again—what's happened to Mary?" Devin said into her headset.

"There's some beam holding her suspended above the ground," Private Mayer said. "But the weird part is that she's all naked with no hair at all on her. She's really pale, too, like she's been bleached or something. It's crazy, Sarge."

Devin focused on her next steps. Regina was listening intently to the report. It was clear to her that Mary was special to her.

"Hold tight and make sure that LZ is secured. We'll come to you. Devin out."

"Copy, Sarge. Mayer out."

"Sarge," Denis said. She turned to see a not so happy private. With all of his priceless scars gone, he no longer had souvenirs of past conflicts. *Finally! Maybe the war stories will stop.*

"All the weapons have their charge back. Whatever happened was temporary. And Sarge? A sonic grenade? You were going to blow us all up?"

"Anything to end your stories, Denis."

"Huh. Don't worry about that. They're all gone. My memories," he said as he looked at his arms and hands.

"Sorry, Private. We'll get a chance to get some more, I'm sure," Devin said. She focused her attention on the dark, tall, and virile prince who was now saying good-bye to his pet wolves. They were jumping on him, licking him as he patted them vigorously.

"Sergeant," a baritone Xenon voice called out.

"What do you got, Theta?"

"My scans show that his body has been significantly altered. The cell density, bone density, regeneration speed, twitch muscle fibers are off the scale, and it's not his acclimation to this planet's gravitational field that is entirely responsible for this alteration. Further, the neurogenesis development is on a scale I have never seen before. Not even under laboratory and research settings with controls."

Devin's eyes were wide and it was obvious that Regina didn't understand it.

"All right, Theta. Our agreement for you to be science officer is to explain the difficult to your slow-to-process, dim-witted colleagues. Remember?"

Theta stood still for a moment to collect his thoughts. He had one set of hands folded behind his back and another in front.

"In other words, his brain development is that of an ancient Xenon scholar. More like several Xenon scholars. He also does have a very active AI symbiont that is probably assisting him with keeping his mind from not being overwhelmed by this flood of knowledge. Its readings and power output are remarkable. Further, this AI is so enmeshed with his brain that removing it would be impossible.

"And then there is his corpus callosum, nerve fibers that connect the right and left hemispheres of the hominid's brain. It's nearly fused, allowing his neural network to travel without impediment significantly faster than before—like lubricant on gears. It has united the entire brain function to near seventy percent capacity. How was that?"

"Now I'm getting it. He's very smart and is ahead of us in the intelligence area," Regina said.

"Intelligence, experience, and psychokinesis. His intelligence can be aptly applied as a result of his experience. Further, the energy output created has the capacity to alter natural laws in the external world," he added matter-of-factly.

"So he can use his mind to move things and alter nature," Devin asked.

"Yes. In regards to his physical being, his ability to generate new cells makes him nearly impervious to physical injuries of probably any kind—laser, projectile, cut or stab wounds—all would be unlikely to kill him. That goes for his organs, too. His immunological system is something I can't even remotely explain."

Devin looked at the Xenon, whose stoicism seemed to shift to puzzlement, clearly an uncomfortable feeling for the even-keeled alien.

"But his DNA identifies him as Prince Victor Venture?"

"Without a doubt. DNA, fingerprints, and retinal scan. All match our database. He's your prince, but he's new and improved," Theta said.

"Marcia, I'm keeping the ship where it is. I want to secure Mary and the descent ship without putting our transport in danger," Regina said in all seriousness.

"Agreed. Let's move," Devin said. She turned to her team that had pulled their weapons and gears together.

"Athena—you got point. Nova and Denis—you got our six. Theta—stay with Regina, and I'll stay with the prince…hey! Where the hell is he?"

Devin and Regina took their scopes out to search as the rest took up each sector to make sure they were covered from attack. The wolves he had been with were all eating the dead primate as if nothing had happened. The heat of the sun was bearing down on her and she was really getting tired from the planet's gravity and all the mysteries. With all her wounds healed and no more pain to speak of, all she wanted to do was get the prince and her team off the planet. And now he was gone. Again.

"Damn it! How the hell could he just disappear? Is that part of that psychokinesis thing you were saying?" she heard Regina ask.

Devin's headset crackled to life. She and Regina had their hands to their earpieces to ensure they could hear. The noise from new howling the creatures were now engaging in was deafening.

"Sarge? Sarge? Do you copy? This is Mayer. I thought the prince was like twelve or something. He looks like a young man now."

"What? What are you saying, Private?" Devin asked.

"I'm saying I'm looking at the prince right now. He's looking at Mary just like us. They kind of look the same. Is there a problem, Sarge?"

"They look the same? Mary with the long hair and pale skin looks like a dark, bald man?" Regina asked.

"Not the gender but she's bald and has no hair anywhere," Mayer confirmed.

Devin made eye contact with Regina, whose expression of surprise was unmistakable.

"He covered nearly two kilometers in less than three point two minutes. I think that is a byproduct of his physique and not psychokinesis," Theta offered by way of an explanation.

"Impressive," Regina said. Devin looked at the rest of her squad. They were having a hard time believing their ears, too.

"Ah, it's all good, Mayer. Just keep a close eye on them both. Just so you know, the prince has some pretty incredible powers. Like he was just here four minutes ago and now he's at your location. Keep this low-key and just hold your post.

We'll be there in twenty. Copy?"

Devin waited for a response. She could imagine that Mayer and the others were digesting what she'd just said.

"For real, Sarge?"

"For real, Mayer. Eyes everywhere, safeties off, and weapons fully charged. Copy?"

"Copy," she heard the somber private say.

Devin clicked off her voice-activated microphone and just looked at her cousin, who was staring at her.

"What?"

"This prince of yours is a bit more than you expected," she said.

"Now that's an understatement," Devin said as she waved her team to move out.

"Can he be trusted?" Regina asked. It was clear that her concern went well beyond her own safety. It was easy to see that the situation with Mary weighed heavily on her. Devin looked down and then looked at the Xenon. The large science officer nodded as he lumbered along on his massive legs.

"He easily could have killed us all already. He needed no guidance for the descent ship's location and he more than likely knows the location of *Nightfall*. While I cannot say I trust him entirely, the fact that he could have left us on this planet indicates he does not wish us harm. Further, he went to Mary's location and is observing her. That indicates either empathy or compassion," Theta said.

Regina looked at him carefully and then looked at Devin for her thinking.

"Now that explanation makes sense to me. Let's move!"

CHAPTER 16
MARY, THE PILOT

When neither their property nor their honor is touched, the majority of men live content. — Niccolò Machiavelli, *The Prince*

"*She's not as sensual, even naked, but then she's just an adolescent. I'd say she's close to your age,*" Rose said.

Victor nodded as he watched the girl hovering above the ground, held in the Red Cross medic's beam. She was naked, hairless, and her skin was devoid of all imperfections such as moles, scars, or tissue damage, just like his own. He was confused, though, since she had been gone for such a short time based on what Private Charles Mayer reported. Her short time away explained why she was close to her present age, but why she was taken at all was a mystery.

"*She probably was too young for viable DNA but she may have been a rush order, you might say. She may not know as much as we do because we were there longer,*" Rose conjectured.

The prince nodded in agreement. He stood just feet away from her. He didn't have to look behind him to see that the drop ship's crew were edgy, confused, and taking his sudden appearance as a possible hostile threat. Even though he knew that their weapons' charge was still gone as long as the medic was there, they held them close to use on him if need be.

"Still, she may be different from them. More similar to

me," he started to say. The beam that held her started to flicker. Similar to the others, her body began to float to the ground until he caught her about a foot off the ground. Her eyes remained closed longer than the sergeant's and Regina's had but, when they opened, her eyes were everywhere and she was alert. She pushed him away and put her hands out as if to defend herself.

"You're all right. You are safe. What is your name?" Victor asked.

He sensed that there was someone behind him with a robe of some sort. He did not move ahead but listened and watched.

"What is your name?" he asked again.

"Mary. The pilot. I'm a pilot for Captain Regina Devin," she said. Even though her hands were still up, she was less defensive and seemed to be organizing her thoughts and orienting herself.

"What do you last remember?" the soldier behind him said.

She remained silent. It was a long minute before she spoke.

"Sudden energy-dampening field knocked the engines off-line. I blew the emergency landing gear and made a hard landing. Got a Mayday out to *Nightfall* to help the captain and crew…and then I checked the exterior and was hit by a beam…"

"Were you taken to an underground facility? Were you put in a transparent tube that filled with liquid you could breathe?" Victor asked.

Her young eyes locked onto his as her memories returned in force.

"Yes. And then an electric shock hit me. I remember, there were images of the Xenons coming to this world. There was a solar flare that destroyed the planet. Some survivors left with the Xenons after a failed attempt to turn back time.

The…the facility underground was operational…there were other tubes with other hominids like me, and Xenon…babies…they were all filled with babies in liquids."

Victor's eyes widened. When he was there he'd seen no one else.

"*Prince? I think that place we were at used your DNA with the others' to create a new population. It's happening very fast. Must be a time-space distortion. Under normal circumstances I would want to explore, but I think I'd rather take off and call it a day,*" Rose said.

Victor nodded in agreement. He took the robe from the soldier and moved in to wrap it around the young woman. She was looking at her skin, hands, and body.

"You look a little older," Mayer said.

"Another time distortion where she went. I'm guessing it might have been a year, maybe, at the most," Victor said. He was happy she accepted the robe, and then she looked at him and seemed to recognize him.

"I saw images of you there. Prince Victor. You almost died the first night. You were younger and then you aged right in front of me, and then you were let go on the surface. You…saved the puppies after their mother was killed," she said.

Victor flashed back to his first day back from the facility—his quick introduction to Rose and then fighting species AB180 to save his first brood of wolf pups.

"Did they make it? The pups?" she asked. There was concern in her voice. He walked with her to the ship as the crew watched warily. He heard an energy hum from the medic retreating just as the energy levels returned to the ship, with lights flickering and rifles and weapons audibly recharged.

"They made it, Mary. They're all hunters with their own puppies and packs," he said with pride.

"That's great," she said.

"Mary? I'm guessing that even though you've been through a lot, you're probably able to fly this ship back to the mother ship so we can leave this place," Victor said.

"Ah, yes. Nice place to visit, but living here has been hell. No need to pack our stuff. I'm out of here," he heard Rose say.

"You bet. I feel really good. Ready to fly and then some," Mary said with zeal. "But first we have to get the captain," she added.

"Mary? I got a jumpsuit and clothes in the aft cabin. And I got the captain on the line. They're heading to us," a female soldier said from inside the ship with her rifle at the ready and a cautious eye on Victor.

"Forget that," Mary said. "Once I'm dressed, we'll go through a brief preflight, and then we'll pick them up. Get their location and we're off," she said.

"Hey, Mary? You sure you're ready to do this?" Mayer asked.

Mary stopped in her tracks to look at him.

"You think you can fly this drop ship into a hot LZ, land for twenty seconds, and dust off to rendezvous with *Nightfall*?"

Victor smirked as he watched the scene. Mary was at least a foot shorter than the soldier, hairless, and was standing defiantly with her hands on her hips waiting for an answer.

"Ah…no?"

Victor felt bad for the soldier. It was easy to see he didn't know what to make of the situation.

"Then let's move out. I'll need a headset and those clothes," she said. She was on the move toward the ship and directed her next question to him.

"Prince? Will I ever get my hair back?"

She didn't slow her pace as she spoke. Her question and spunk made him smile.

"No."

There was a moment of silence before she spoke again. She ran her hands up and down her arms, feeling her skin, and then her neck and face. Her skin was flawless now and milky white. Her eyes showed more clearly as purple than the others'.

"Shit. Well, I guess I won't ever have to worry about finding hair products ever again. And this skin is so smooth and perfect. I guess it's a better-than-even trade," she said.

Victor simply nodded. He heard the ship's turbines and some machinery coming to life and saw lights come on as he walked up the metal ramp into the drop ship. He felt a surge of relief to be on a ship again as the hope to escape the planet grew.

"Enough of the chitchat. Let's pick up the rest of this party and skedaddle," Rose said.

It took Victor just a second to recognize the meaning of the odd word, *skedaddle*, but he truly understood what she meant. He couldn't agree more.

Time to get the hell out of here!

"No pun intended?"

"None."

CHAPTER 17
TRUTHS, MYTHS AND LEGENDS

Before all else, be armed — Niccolò Machiavelli

"So. She's different," Devin said.

"That's an understatement," Regina replied.

She looked out on the *Nightfall*'s galley deck, where the chairs and tables were pushed aside to have room for dancing. Mayer, Athena, Ross, Nova, and a couple of Regina's crew hands were dancing in tune with modern youth music that all of them were listening to these days. While Devin was still in her late twenties, she found the music was too fast and too loud for her tastes. In the middle of the dance floor was a hairless sixteen-year-old girl smiling widely, her eyes sparkling as she kept in time and danced from one partner to another. She could easily have passed as a bald intersex based on the lack of hair and moles, or anything for that matter, which made her look near porcelain. Her eyes were alive with color, and they sparkled like stars in deep space.

"Mary lost her family to a rebellion five years ago. She ran while the others believed the royals were there to help. She watched as her parents, two older brothers, and younger sister were killed in a flash with the entire neighborhood. When I caught up with her, she was twelve, stealing food from the bar you were at. She's tough, wary, and excellent in piloting and driving any vehicle. But this," Regina said as she pointed to Mary, who was the life of the party, "this dancing, laughing, and just looking happy is something I've never seen before."

"She had a lot of hate?" Devin asked.

"Hate. Determination and drive. No time for fun and all business. You saw satisfaction when she was piloting or driving, and I think when she was sleeping. But fun or carefree? No. This is really different."

Devin looked at her hands and her upper arm to make sure that her scars were still gone and her injuries healed, just as they had been when she was released from the alien cylinder's beams—she'd wondered since leaving the planet more than an hour ago if maybe it had all been a dream. Regina got her attention and pointed to Theta, who was lumbering toward them. Devin let Regina move ahead of her as they went to meet him away from the loud music. Devin watched her cousin use her head to point to a hatch and they all went in. Devin found herself in the weapons room. It was organized with a large array of small to midsize weapons, both laser beam and projectile. Swords, combat knives, and ordnance were also visible. Once the hatch closed, it was also evident why Regina had picked that room rather than one closer to the galley. The armory was reinforced with heavy metal and shields, which effectively drowned out the music. Devin was appreciative of the silence. Other than their voices, the only background noise was the vibration of *Nightfall*'s engines.

"So, Theta. Update of ship's status and its crew. The abbreviated, short report," Regina said.

"Yes, Captain. However, I must point out that your use of 'abbreviated' and 'short' to make the same point is redundant in your language," Theta said in all seriousness.

"That's because I really mean it, Theta," she said.

Devin chuckled. While she still wore her own tactical uniform and gear from the planet expedition, Regina had exchanged her tactical gear and low-cut corset for a more streamlined flight uniform with a snug floral belt cinching her thin waist while her buttons to keep her breasts from falling out of the top were missing. The push-up corset underneath only made her cleavage look more precarious—predicting a severe uniform failure. Devin did her best not to comment but was wondering if the Xenon would ever comment based on his high moral code.

"Yes. Of course, Captain. I will do my best," Theta said. He was still in his same uniform and gear, but his hulking body in the room made Devin feel small. And seeing her cousin talking to him, the size differential and appearance were comical at best.

"Our entire planet-side search and rescue took eleven hours and forty-two minutes. Upon leaving the planet and the Sol System, we have been out of our time by about two months, one week, and three days," he said.

Devin felt her eyes widen. She caught the look that Regina shot her and then turned back for Theta to continue.

"Mary's age differential is approximately one year, three months. I suspect that she was brought closer to the source of this underground facility Prince Victor and she state is there. They were closer to the source of the time distortion, making their passage of time faster than what we experienced."

"You don't seemed too surprised by this, Theta. From a scientific perspective and overall events, it's a pretty wild situation," Regina said. Devin interpreted Regina's statement as too pointed, even though the casual observer might have seen it as rhetorical. She noticed that the Xenon, for the first time ever, looked apprehensive.

"Well, we Xenons have heard of this phenomenon. It is typically not a naturally occurring event and the old ones have insisted we never attempt such an experiment. But I digress," he said. He then took out a large tablet and looked at it. Devin exchanged looks with Regina.

Yeah. You saw that, too. There's more here, Devin thought.

"Similar to Prince Victor, Mary has had some significant neurogenesis and physical changes to her physiology, but to a lesser degree. She now uses much more of her frontal and prefrontal lobes, which has enhanced such things as intelligence, humor, and executive functioning. There may also be some abilities for psychokinesis and other physical manipulations, but again it is more likely to a lesser degree than the prince."

"Are they a danger to us? Should they be monitored or under guard?" Regina asked.

Devin watched as the Xenon folded one set of arms behind his back while the other set held the tablet in front of him with ease. It was clear that he was taking the question very seriously, as she suspected he did with every question posed to him.

"I don't believe they mean us any harm," he said finally.

There was some silence that was uncomfortable. Devin waited for a moment longer before she took her chance to speak.

"Theta? Prince Victor spoke of being captured by those things that got us, but he was brought to an underground facility where he was healed and transformed like Mary."

And here we go. Devin and Regina's briefing with the prince was as fascinating as he was. It was all unbelievable. But then, Prince Victor Venture IX was by definition unbelievable. *Is it true?* Devin wondered.

"Yes. It does seem like their events were similar," Theta commented.

"But he remembers reading another language that his AI said was 'Lucifer One,' as if it were a name of a person or place," Devin said.

"Or an experiment," Regina added. "The prince

mentioned that there were thousands of the same tubes, but they were all empty when he was there. Mary said she saw the same ones but there were clearly some that were filled with babies. What do you make of that?"

The Xenon looked back down at his tablet. He said nothing. Devin felt nervous with such a large creature and her and Regina in a small armory. As she eyed the closest weapon and wondered if it was loaded, she heard Regina speak in an unusually calm, soft voice, similar to how she remembered her mother used to talk to her when she knew something was wrong.

"Theta? The prince said he saw visions of the Xenons being on that planet. That there were two groups. One came to save the species and took them away to another galaxy. There was another group that stayed behind. They created a facility to repopulate the planet while another faction set out to alter the planet's time-space continuum by altering the real-time dimension and pushing it one dimension behind, before the planet's cataclysm. He was able to explain it like that. What does it mean to you?" Regina asked.

The Xenon continued looking down at his tablet. He remained still and silent as she spoke. There was an uncomfortable silence until Devin heard the Xenon sigh.

"Yes," he said.

When it was clear no more was coming, Regina spoke again.

"Yes? What does 'yes' mean, Theta? We're not the enemy here. We're your crew mates. We're a team. You, Zil, Zone, Mary, me. We're all on the same side, right?"

"Yes, Captain," Theta said quickly. "My species, especially we scientists, are taught the lessons of first contact and interfering with a thriving alien species based on the events the prince experienced. The Earth project occurred millennia ago. We discovered this small, blue-green-white planet bustling with life, arts, science, and new views and experiences. Many stayed on their home planet while few joined us in the stars. But then a solar flare wiped out all of Earth's technology, sending it back to its dark ages. We returned to assist. When the flares continued, we transplanted much of the species to other, similar planets. We also tried to save the planet, just as the prince said. But we failed. We failed miserably. The planet was damaged but viable. Life could have returned and the ecosystems might have regenerated on their own. But we were arrogant. We created a temporal distortion to nudge the planet to an earlier time, when the planet was devoid of extreme greenhouse effects and global warming."

The Xenon stopped. He looked sad, or at least stoic and dark.

"What happened?" Devin asked.

"The temporal disturbance moved forward and then it would not stop. And when we thought we had stopped the time displacements, we discovered that it occurred on its own. We destroyed the machinery and the experiment, but it still continued. We had unleashed a naturally occurring event that had been locked up in the planet's gravity well and magnetic field. The more we tried to fix it, the worse it got. More unpredictable. That is when we abandoned this Earth and took all the survivors. In our haste, we did not turn off the computer responsible for the repopulation project. It continued."

"So this re-population project continued? It never stopped?" Devin asked.

"Yes. Our attempts to shut it down in the past were halted by the temporal disturbances and this newer AI defensive grid. As far as I can tell with the prince's existence, this project has continued unabated."

"Well, in the long run, it created our civilizations, I suppose," Regina said.

"Yes. And when your species fight among yourselves and

kill one another on such a large scale, it is because we relocated you here," he said.

"Is that why you people get all upset with us and step in in times of civil wars and outbreaks of violence?" Regina said.

"Yes. We are responsible for you being here," the Xenon said.

"This Earth was without violence or strife?" Devin asked. She wondered if such a place could exist.

"No. There were both. There were hardships. But if we had left them alone, there were many there at the time who were working on correcting things they had done to the planet. We discovered later that your species evolves when confronted with natural disaster. We interfered. And worse, we set an unpredictable localized temporal distortion into motion."

"Have you tried to fix it since then? Come back?" Regina asked.

"The temporal distortion? No. We now understand that time travel to the past is impossible. Time displacement into the future of this dimension or the future of another dimension is the only way. You can go forward only. Not backward. Never backward."

"So you have come back to this Earth," Devin clarified.

"Yes. Many times. Finally we stopped, as the time disturbances would compromise our work. Additionally, with this rogue sapient AI so focused on repopulation of the planet, we decided to have the planet quarantined and posted warnings not to land. When your people returned to this place, you had discovered it was too hostile and left it alone. A wise choice," Theta summed up.

Devin realized that her throat was parched and her chest felt heavy. The whole story of their origins as a species, the Xenons' overprotectiveness of and intrusiveness in their worlds and politics, and the magnitude of guilt was palpable after millennia. As Theta spoke, it was as if he were experiencing the events as if he were there, in real time.

"You Xenons feel guilty over this Earth, don't you?" Devin said. The response was immediate, nearly reflexive, which caught her by surprise.

"Yes. To me and all Xenons. We were the superior species. We should have known better. Our arrogance altered the natural physical laws of an entire civilization and disrupted its path. We should have been aware of this possibility. We are Xenon," Theta said. His gaze shifted to the floor. Devin did not like the silence. She was grateful that her cousin changed the subject.

"What does Lucifer One mean?" Regina asked.

"Lucifer literally means 'light bearer' in one of Earth's ancient languages. It meant many things, but its origin was from a great civilization where it was a name that meant 'first morning light.' Again, in our arrogance, we thought that the Lucifer repopulation project was the beginning of a new era. A new day. We were very wrong. It was the end," Theta said. His deep baritone voice was laced with sadness and regret.

It looked like Regina was going to ask another question when the ship's intercom system came to life.

"Franklin to the captain. Please respond."

The voice was young but confident. Devin knew it was attached to a wiry young man who was ten years her junior but second in command of the ship.

"Right here. What's up," Regina said. Instinctively they all looked at the green glowing screen that revealed Franklin in a classic military jumpsuit with officer bars designating his rank. Devin wondered what her cousin would look like if she were more appropriately dressed. She promised herself not to comment on her dress and focused on what was happening.

"Captain, we're picking up a repeating message from the commercial bands. It's a royal ship called the *Harbinger*. It's calling Sergeant Marcia Devin by name," he said. His voice sounded more worried than it had earlier.

"Let me hear it," Regina said.

"On it, Captain," he said.

There was a quick switch and then the audio came on clearly. Still, it was strange for a military ship to be using a commercial line for communication.

"This is Commander Virgil of the *Harbinger*. If there are any survivors from the *Rising Sun*, please acknowledge. Sergeant Marcia Devin and Corporal Ariel Dias—please respond…This is Lieutenant Commander Virgil of the *Harbinger*. If there are any survivors from the *Rising Sun*, please acknowledge. Sergeant Marcia Devin and Corporal Ariel Dias—please respond…"

"All right, Franklin. Shut it off and get a time index on it. I want to know how long they've been looking for us and if it's authentic," Regina said.

"Will do, Captain," he said.

Regina turned to Devin. She anticipated the next question.

"She's legitimate, Regina. She used to be Vice Admiral Jana Virgil, like I told you. She bought us time and it looks like she's looking for us. I'm glad she made it."

"She's an optimist," Regina commented.

"And she's a looker, too. She wears her dresses a bit too high, but somehow she can carry it off and without diminishing her authority," Devin said. As soon as the comment about Virgil's wardrobe came out of her mouth, she knew she was done.

"So. You have a problem with women in authority wearing revealing dresses? What is your problem with what women wear? Is this a jealousy thing?"

Devin lowered her head and rubbed her eyes. *What have I done?*

"You just can't help yourself, can you, Marcia?" Regina went on.

Devin sighed, turned on her heels, and walked toward the hatch.

"Hey! I'm not finished talking to you! Where are you going?" she heard her cousin yell. Fortunately, the loud music down from the galley obscured the colorful metaphors and expletives that she was sure were following her as she retreated.

CHAPTER 18
A BITTER CHOICE

But above all he must refrain from seizing the property of others, because a man is quicker to forget the death of his father than the loss of his patrimony. — Niccolò Machiavelli, *The Prince*

"Well, at least you liked the hot shower," Rose said. It was easy to hear that she was feeling bad for her host.

"The shower was nice. The water and the heat. I never thought I'd miss the heat," he said.

In the hours after his arrival on the *Nightfall*, he had tried everything he wanted, all the amenities he had missed while on Hell planet. They all came up short. It was the news reports, images, and visual stories documenting what his family had done to their subjects that bothered him the most. What was supposed to be a cheery return was dark, dismal, and marred with disappointment and anger toward his family. So far the closest people to him were Rose, the sergeant, her cousin, and their teams. He was not surprised he saw Rose as family. She was her own entity and close to him both figuratively and literally. But the fact that he saw his sergeant of the guard and her corporal and privates as closer to him than his own family was just sad. He then wondered how Bishop Brent Miles of Pax was doing. He and the other scholars were family, too. Victor couldn't wait to see them. He sighed and returned to the present task of adapting to his new environment.

He zipped up his flight suit as high as it would go, covering his thermal-guard undergarments with a breathable set of layered clothing that kept the heat in. He was still cold. His feet were so large that it took several tries to find compatible adult boots for him to wear. The Xenon's boots were kept as a second to last resort, with the last plan being to walk barefoot. His feet and skin felt as if he was closed in. After hours of space travel, he was finding himself more distressed than happy.

"*Do you want to try the bed again?*" Rose suggested.

"No. It's just too soft. I think the survival sheets will do fine. It's a better solution than the food situation. I can't believe I hate the taste of sweets. Now that is a major shame."

"*I suppose when you're marooned on a dangerous planet, hunting fresh food and it being a meat-protein diet, your tastes must have changed,*" she said.

Standing in front of a mirror, he saw a muscular version of himself. There had been little in the way of mirrors on the planet—the brief pooling of flash floods once a month was the closest equivalent, and the water didn't last long as a result of his collecting it and every other creature fighting for its share—so his reflection as a young adult was new to him. The dark green flight suit, devoid of any special markings, with his new light, large-size boots did make him look larger. He looked around *Nightfall*'s much desired single-officer quarters and saw a number of edged weapons he could choose from. While he'd been offered a sidearm, as he was a royal VIP, he'd insisted on seeing a selection of short combat-edge weapons with no guards. He stood looking at the fifteen different styles of weapons and their sheaths laid out on his bunk. It took him very little time to select three knives that would fit along his left chest plate and left and right hip.

"*So the shower and the knives make you happy?*"

"Well, it sure isn't the temperature or the food," he said as he inspected each blade's serrated edge, handle, and blood gutter.

"Maybe it was an off day in the galley? I bet they use fresh food and spices sometimes. Maybe on special occasions?"

"Like when a royal prince is rescued?"

He finally strapped all the knives in place and made sure they were easily accessible.

"All right, Prince. Is that the way it's going to be? Nothing I say makes you feel better. Do you want to be alone?" Rose asked. Her tone was clearly annoyed.

"You're like the mother I never had," he said. An image of a royal picture of his mother, Queen Vega, appeared in his head. He pushed the image out and thought of Rose's last remark. Victor shook his head, but he did feel a smirk on his face. It was rare to hear Rose flustered.

"No, Rose. I'm just disappointed. I thought leaving the planet would be great. Finally feel a bed, eat food, some sweets, and enjoy others' company. Instead, I'm cold, the bed is too soft, and the food is awful. I'm just grumpy. It will pass. You know what that's like?"

"What? Are you saying that I get grumpy?" She was clearly angry at the comment.

Victor was laughing quietly to himself. It was rare that he could really fluster his omniscient AI.

"Oh. That's real nice, my liege! Remember, I get you. That Regina woman might want to get you, but I really get you," she said. Now her voice was teasing.

"Touché, Rose. You win. So I'm going to the bridge to see what our estimated time of arrival to the *Harbinger* is. Do you want to play a game of chess?" Victor knew the game was more for him than her. The images of the destruction, death, strife, and overall oppression at the hands of his royal family wore him down. Worse, he was finding himself feeling revengeful. That was a feeling he had not felt before. What made it different and frightening was that he felt that he had the strength to unleash his will to destroy all of them. How and why he felt he had the will was very unclear to him. When he thought of his family, he felt a powerful feeling in his torso and electricity running through his limbs. It didn't matter who he thought of—his mother, father, brothers, all of them. It was that rage that he worried about. What might he do? What might he be capable of?

"All right, Rose—E four."

"C five."

"NF three."

"Well, well. You're aggressive—D six."

"Yes—D four. Pawn attacks pawn D four."

And so the game started as Victor walked out of his small, dark, cold room and entered a better lit, slightly warmer gangway. He was getting used to the small walkways and his size. He was also adapting to the recycled air and the constant vibration from the ship's engines. It was the cramped space of the ship's corridors that got him thinking about how the Xenons managed to get around. He also wondered if telling the sergeant and Regina about his visions of the Xenons on the planet, Earth, was helpful. It did explain why the Xenons would involve themselves in the kingdom's internal affairs, much as parents would when children were arguing. Once he got to thinking about his family, his brother in particular, he felt the fury build. He refocused on the chess game. Rose was on the move in the game, but she did make mistakes sometimes, usually because she would remain logical to a fault when he would use chance and surprise to confound her. He wondered, though, if there might be something that got her so riled up, so emotionally compromised that she would lose control. *What would that look like?*

The closer he got to the bridge, the more crewmen

stopped and briefly greeted him with a nod or a "sir." He was self-conscious of his age even though his body looked like that of a young adult. He was about to have his black knight take Rose's rook when he heard a gusty voice calling him.

"My prince! As I live and breathe. You've grown into quite the specimen," Corporal Dias said.

Victor turned to see the intersex soldier approach. He couldn't help but smile broadly as Dias clasped his hand. It was firm, strong, and genuinely conveyed warmth. When Victor came on board he had missed Dias, as she was in engineering and then the central computer core, working. Victor was surprised when she retracted her hand quickly.

"Sorry, Prince. I forgot my station," she said as she backed up and saluted him. Victor felt his eyes narrow and a sigh rise from his chest.

"Dias. Tell the crew and your team not to do that. Shake my hand, pat me on the back, get into a fight—I've been on Hell and that kind of ceremony and caste division no longer appeals to me. So get over here and shake my hand like the Dias I know."

Victor was surprised how quickly she responded and how strong and unyielding her voice was when she spoke. He was rewarded with a broad smile and then a hug from the athletic intersex woman.

"Now that is the prince I know when he's not intoxicated," she said.

"I was twelve and had no tolerance for alcohol or any similar elixir. I'm now much older, and I still have no tolerance for the stuff. Not even the food, so don't give me anything other than water. Now that's something you can do for me," Victor said. He was smiling and feeling happy. He had forgotten that Rose was in his head. It was only when Dias pulled back from her warm hug that his AI spoke.

"No, no, no. Have her hug you again! I like this Dias.

Qualities of both genders with just a hint of superiority the female gender brings. And her smell and strong breast plates...please have her hug you again. For me?"

Victor was able to sigh, and Dias looked at him strangely. He decided to just tell her.

"It's not you, Dias. It's my AI symbiont, Rose. She sometimes expresses her opinion, especially when she finds someone attractive."

"Oh, really? Are you sure it's the symbiont? Just so you know, I am more than a decade and a half older than you and you're not my type," she said.

"Oh, yeah, baby! If only I could be the host and you the symbiont," he heard Rose bemoan. He felt his face flush at Dias's remark. Victor just smiled and hoped that his hot, bald head wasn't too red.

"Oh, and I have to visit your planet for sure and get those medic things to clean me up, too. Ross, Nova, Athena, the sergeant—they all came back healed and with no scars. And they look five years younger. I could have used some of that," she said. She pointed him toward the bridge so they could talk and walk.

"They are incredible. My foot was really messed up and I was pretty bad off, close to death on day one. If it wasn't for those Red Cross medical cylinders, I would have been dead my first night there," Victor said. He and Dias moved through the corridors as some of the crew members continued to smile and say hello to Dias in particular.

"And the time distortion also grew you up quick. And the hairless appearance? Are you more intersex now?"

"Hmm. I don't think so. Rose tells me that my skin and entire physiology have changed. Apparently it precludes hair follicles," Victor said.

"That is something. Mary is into the new look, too. She's also picked up some serious skills from her experience. She just kicked all our asses in darts and then in knife throwing. Speaking of which, I see that your weapon of choice is edged weapons?"

Victor looked down to see that he was indeed heavily armed with combat knives on a ship that was safe.

"Sorry. Force of habit on a savage planet. Probably not necessary here."

"That is quite a habit.   Impressive, young prince. Very impressive," Dias said.

By now they were by the bridge hatch. It opened up, revealing a small room with three seats in the middle and several consoles manned by standing crewmen. In front of him was a clear visual of Commander Jana Virgil. Her brown hair was pulled up and her dark eyes were as deep as they were expressive, just as he remembered from years ago.

"So let's find out what's happened since we've been gone," Dias said. She patted him on the shoulder and moved off to an empty console space right next to Theta, who was squished into the science station. Regina was standing in front of the middle chair with the sergeant while a man he knew as Franklin was sitting with a series of tablets. He was a big, dark man with blond hair who was engrossed in some work. To the left of the visual screen was a schematic diagram of a ship designated *Harbinger*. It looked like a flat triangular spearhead with three large struts on each side holding engines in place. It was a solid warship, but even Victor recalled that it was more than twenty years old and had been decommissioned before his descent to Hell. Victor took in the whole scene. The atmosphere was heavy, more as a result of the conversation, he thought, than the actual space.

"These events change everything. With the Sagittarius Sector destabilizing and risk of an internal civil war, it was perfect for Prince Ramsey to take control," he heard Commander Virgil say. Her voice was low and her tone deadly serious. Victor felt his heart beat faster at the mention of his brothers, Prince Jason of Sagittarius Sector and Prince Ramsey of Capricorn Sector. Visions of passages from the ancient work he and Rose discovered on Earth called the Bible fell before his eyes.

"*Cain and Abel,*" he heard Rose say softly. Victor nodded in agreement as he focused on the conversation. Still in the background, he waited until he found a good point to interrupt.

"So is there any support for Prince Victor?" Devin said.

"Yes—everyone who is against Prince Ramsey. But he has his fleet orbiting the capital cities of the Sagittarius home world, and the Sagittarius fleet is leaderless. Some are refusing to join Prince Ramsey and support his annexation of the sector, and others see it as inevitable. And then there's the problem of Prince Victor's lack of a fleet to tip the balance. This is where might will make right," Virgil said. Her expression throughout was analytical but clearly unhappy with the situation. Victor's heart sank at his suspicion of why Ramsey was taking over Jason's domain. His hands tightened and his jaw set.

"*What? What's happening, Prince? Where is your brother? You don't think...*" Rose started. Victor did not wait for an answer. He moved to the center of the room, where he would be clearly visible to Commander Virgil. He did not wait for introductions or small talk. "Commander Jana," he said. "I am Prince Victor. Where is my brother Jason?"

Silence followed. At first Virgil was taken aback both by his sudden appearance and by his physical change. His voice was resonating and deep. There was no mistaking his tone. It was a command, not a question.

"Prince Victor? I had heard the time distortions had aged you. I did not expect to see you," she stammered out.

"Too many changes and not all good. Commander? What of my brother?"

Commander Virgil looked down at first and took in a

deep breath. Before she spoke, second in command Franklin handed him a tablet he had been viewing.

"Prince, this is not good news on two fronts. One we can do something about and the other we cannot," he said. Victor found his voice calming but sad. As Victor looked at the images and reports of his brother Jason's death, he heard Commander Virgil speak. His grasp on the tablet continued to grow as he listened and flipped through each disturbing image and caption.

"We believe that Prince Jason died approximately one week ago. The cause of death and circumstances are unknown. His consort and children have vanished, but it is by their own design with assistance of supporters, as far as I know."

"No funeral?"

"None, my prince. Further, the regent of the sector did announce the prince's will, which divested his wealth to the citizens and included his proposed plan for a republic, has been voided by the royal family. It was three days after that when Prince Ramsey arrived to put down the rebellion. When the regent and citizen officials protested to King Talus and Queen Vega, they sent ships of their own to assist with destroying the resistance."

There was silence on the bridge. Victor kept skimming through the report, reading everything faster than he had ever remembered. It was when he came to the Planet Pax Crisis that he spoke again.

"So am I to believe that my brother Jason is dead while my brother Ramsey and my father have sent ships to annex his sector when it was his will to allow elections?"

"Yes. The queen clarified that her son's will was not legitimate and that the Sagittarius Sector was not his to give away. It was the royal family's," Virgil said. Once again there was a tone of anger.

"What does that mean for you and your crew,

Commander?" Regina asked.

"We are independents, or I think a better term would be the ancient meaning of privateers, or pirates."

"It's not a bad life," Regina said.

Victor lost track of the conversation. Time slowed down and he experienced the world as still, empty, cold, and forgotten. His eyes focused on image after image of wholesale destruction of his beloved planet. Fire, the dead bodies of youth, children, and professors littering the campus. Soldiers bearing the Sagittarius crest of Prince Ramsey forcefully grabbing people and pushing them into columns.

"*Prince, time index shows that these events are only twenty-eight hours old. While we can't do anything for you brother, we might be able to intervene and save Bishop Miles. Maybe others,*" Rose said. Victor pulled his gaze up from the pad. Heartbroken, he became vaguely aware that no one on the bridge was moving. He turned to his left and right and saw that the people and instruments—everything, even the image of Commander Virgil—were still, as if frozen. The only crew member who seemed aware that there was something different was Theta, who had a sensor pointed right at him. While typically he would have been fascinated by the experience, his mind was racked with pain and angst. Still, he had to take some kind of step that could do something. Then he realized what Jackson had meant when he said there was bad news. One he could do nothing about and another he might be able to.

"Rose? We should go to Pax and see if we can find the bishop," he said. It wasn't an easy decision. Anger, hot flashes fanned out from his skin and his stomach felt as heavy as lead.

"*Logically, that makes sense,*" she said.

"You're not always driven by logic. Don't these images make you angry?" he asked.

"*Furious. But Bishop Miles is in danger. Your old*

schoolmates. My creators. Those images were at the other universities in the north and northwest. We have a chance to help him if we move now," she said.

"How long will take to get to the *Harbinger*?"

"She's heading to us at top speed and then I bet the commander was planning on moving to Pax first. We'll rendezvous with the Harbinger *in one point three hours. It makes sense. I'm sorry, Prince. My emotions toward Bishop Miles and my creators may be clouding my judgment, but I think it's the best move."*

"I can't help Jason. It's done," he said.

There was silence as Victor continued looking at more images.

"Rose? Why is everything frozen?"

"As best as I can figure, when you and I are in some kind of extreme emotional state, time and real-space events are mutable. I suspect that everything slowed down as a means to understand what is happening and to contain our emotions. Maybe it is self-protective. Maybe it keeps us from harming ourselves by allowing us to think."

"Maybe. Maybe it's to keep everyone safe from us. How do we get back into real time?"

"I don't know. Why don't we just head back to your quarters? Maybe our presence and our heightened emotional state need to be absent," Rose offered.

Victor nodded. Before leaving, he cleared the tablet and left a message. When he was done, he moved Devin's wrist to allow the data pad to fall into her hand.

"Ready?"

"Ready. When we get back to your quarters I am going to go off-line. I suggest you sleep. I'm sure it will all return to normal. Think of it as a reboot," Rose explained.

Victor said nothing as he walked toward the bridge hatch. He saw that Theta was still looking at his last position and seemed to be slowly following his trail. He continued on his way.

"Yes. Sleep," he muttered.

CHAPTER 19
DÉJÀ VU

A wise man will see to it that his acts always seem voluntary and not done by compulsion, however much he may be compelled by necessity. — Niccolò Machiavelli

"So am I to believe that my brother Jason is dead while my brother Ramsey and my father have sent ships to annex his sector when it was his will to allow elections?" Devin heard Prince Victor ask. His voice was deep, confident, and yet solemn and calm.

"Yes. The queen clarified that her son's will was not legitimate and that the Sagittarius Sector was not his to give away. It was the royal family's," Commander Virgil of the *Harbinger* said. As Devin watched Virgil, who stood in her uniform with the Sagittarius royal crest, she was amazed how the commander held herself together. Even with a crew of just 153, with half her crew abandoning their posts, she appeared rock solid. Suddenly, Devin felt a sudden warmth in her wrist and something in her hands. She looked down and saw that she was holding a data tablet. Her eyes widened at how it had mysteriously appeared. She was staring at it when she heard her cousin speak next. Somehow the conversation sounded very familiar.

"What does that mean for you and your crew, Commander?"

"We are independents, or I think a better term would be

the ancient meaning of privateers, or pirates," Virgil said. Devin looked up to see that even Commander Virgil's holographic expression conveyed confusion.

"It's not a bad life," Regina said next. She too stopped. Devin turned around to find the large Xenon was withdrawing a mobile sensor device and was back at his station in record speed for such a large creature.

"That all sounded very familiar," Jackson said. His eyes were narrowed and then he looked all around. Devin followed his gaze and realized that the prince was gone. She looked back at the data pad that had mysteriously appeared in her hand. There was a message flashing across its screen.

"Where the hell is the prince?" Regina said.

"He was standing right next to you, Captain Devin. I swear he was right there, but then he disappeared. I thought it was a transmission glitch," Virgil added.

"Team? I don't know how this happened but I have the data pad that Jackson gave the prince. It just appeared out of thin air," Devin said. She held it up to make sure it was real and that she wasn't hallucinating.

"It did not appear out of thin air, Sergeant Devin. Prince Victor put it there," Theta said.

All eyes shifted from where the prince had just been standing to him. He pointed to the main screen and got rid of the *Harbinger*'s schematics and replayed what he obviously had scanned.

"I am transmitting the same data to you, Commander Virgil, for your science department to confirm," Theta said.

Devin looked up at the screen and saw a recording of herself and the others frozen in time. Like insects stuck in amber, they were all motionless except for the prince, who spoke and moved without hindrance.

"Rose? We should go to Pax and see if we can find the bishop," she saw and heard the prince say. He was looking at the same data pad she was holding.

"You're not always driven by logic. Don't these images make you angry?" he asked. There was silence until he spoke again. He was looking around the bridge and at one point looked directly at the scanning device.

"He's talking to his AI, Rose," Regina said.

"How long will take to get to the *Harbinger*?"

"Yes. That makes sense. Theta, can you hear or get any understanding on what she is saying?" Jackson asked.

"No, sir. It's a private conversation. What I can say is that the neutrino levels were beyond our measures and the neurogenesis and brain activity going across his corpus callosum were nothing like I have ever seen before."

"I can't help Jason. It's done," Devin heard the prince say next. There was silence as she watched Victor look down to continue looking at more images.

"Theta? How did you know enough to get your scanner in place and record when all of this went down?" Regina ordered more than asked.

"I experienced an aura, something we Xenons experience when time-space shifts occur. Based on our history with the prince's planet and our attempts to control it, we slowly obtained the abilities to tell when such an event is going to happen. Sadly, its effects are similar to when your species experiences an aura just before an epileptic seizure," he explained.

"Rose? Why is everything frozen?"

"Bridge—this is Zil…Zone and I experienced an aura. Is everything all right up there?" a deep, disembodied voice asked over the intercom. Devin shot a look over at Regina. Her eyes widened farther than she had ever seen before.

"Now that is pretty creepy," Dias said from the quarterdeck.

Jackson was the first to respond. He spoke into the ship's

intercom system.

"We got this covered. Theta will explain later. Out."

"Understood, sir," Engineer Zone said.

"Maybe. Maybe it's to keep everyone safe from us. How do we get back into real time?" Victor asked on the screen.

"Huh? What do you make of that? He sounds worried," Regina said.

"Kind of makes sense. The guy looks up and the whole world is frozen except for him and his AI symbiont. I'd be a lot more disoriented," Devin said.

"Is he a danger? Could he alter time further along than a few seconds?" Virgil asked. If she was concerned, she didn't look it.

"Similar to the prince's planet, we experience these time-space distortions in seconds. My guess is that somehow his entire brain—logic, emotions, thoughts, and feelings—are all intensely aligned and that's when these events occur. And when they do, it is like a bubble—it's contained within a measurable space," Theta explained from his science station. Devin was glad he stayed put; there was little space to share in the middle of the small bridge.

"But I experienced it here on the *Harbinger* and we're hours away."

"Yes. That measurable space in which the prince's power is contained might be several astronomical units but not, say, an entire sector of space," he explained.

"So we can't turn back time and save Prince Jason," Devin said.

"Unfortunately, that is accurate. We cannot help Prince Jason. It is done," Theta said. His voice was more solemn as he uttered the last sentence.

Devin noticed that the Xenon used the same words as Prince Victor in regard to Prince Jason's death. She focused on the prince's movements. She watched him ostensibly clear the tablet and leave a message. When he was done, she watched him move her wrist and let the data pad fall into her hand. It was strange watching him manipulate her body invisibly and remembering how her wrist had felt warm and the pad had magically appeared in her hands.

"Ready," was what she heard the prince say next. She watched him walk toward the bridge hatch and saw him looking at Theta as he left.

"Bridge—this is Crewman Phillips. Prince Victor just asked me to let the captain know that he is retiring to his quarters and wishes to be woken up when we reach planet Pax."

Regina tilted her head to respond.

"When and where did he tell you this?"

There was a pause before a nervous response came back. "Ah, well, I was just passing his quarters when he stopped me and asked me to tell the bridge."

"Where is he now?"

"Well…I saw him go into his quarters, Captain. Do you want me to check?" There was more silence. It was obvious that Regina was thinking about having the crewman check. Then they all heard the prince speak as he left the bridge: "Yes. Sleep."

"Captain? Do you want me to check?" Crewman Phillips asked.

"No, Phillips. Thank you. Carry on," Regina said.

"Yes, Captain." It was clear the crewman was glad to be on his way. For a long minute, the bridge was quiet. Commander Virgil asked a pertinent question.

"Sergeant Devin? What was written on the tablet?"

Embarrassed that she had looked at it a number of times but hadn't read it, she raised it again and made sure to read it aloud clearly.

"'Please provide me one more favor. Once we rendezvous

with the *Harbinger*, please ask Commander Jana Virgil if she would transport me to the planet Pax at the following coordinates. Once there, all of you are free to go. Thank you very much for your loyalty. It has been an honor serving with you. Thank you. Prince Victor Venture.'"

Devin stopped at the coordinates and focused on the tone and meaning behind the message.

"He is the most humble royal I have ever met," Devin said aloud.

"Even more than his brother Prince Jason. And he was a near saint, beloved by all, myself included," Virgil said, doing little to veil her softer side.

"We're not going to just drop the prince off, are we, Sarge?" Dias asked.

There was just the briefest of pauses.

"Jackson—check out these locations. Pinpoint them and pull up all geography and maps you can on that area," Regina said as she took the tablet pad from Devin to give to him.

"Commander—what is your ETA?"

"Under one point two-five hours, though my engineer just pushed the engines a little more," Virgil responded.

"Excellent. Marcia—you and your team get ready for a joint mission. You know the area firsthand and who this bishop is?" she asked.

"Bishop Brent Miles. Yeah, we got this," Devin responded. Her brain was racing toward where to find him and how to keep the prince out of harm's way.

"My first officer is telling me he has three drop teams ready to go in," Virgil offered.

"Let's see what Marcia and her team come up with. I'd rather send in *Nightfall* with its stealth technology and keep the *Harbinger* as our backup in case we need it. This will be a stealth operation and the *Harbinger* may need to be the firepower and speed to get us out. I'd sure like assistance with tactical on that," Regina said.

"Done. I'll have something for you in an hour. When you can, please transmit your plan and tactical data so we can come up with a plan B," Virgil said.

"Done. See you soon, Commander. *Nightfall* out," Regina said.

With that, Virgil's image vanished from the main screen. Devin looked around the bridge. The crew looked charged up and ready for battle. It was easy to see that the prince's words of courage and humility in light of Prince Jason's death and in spite of his royal family were motivating factors. The fact that Prince Victor had been on Hell planet and lived made him a near legend. But now he was willing to go to a planet under siege to find his mentor and had tried not to expose the crews to danger? *What is this? A prince of the royal family who puts others ahead of himself?*

"Was this Prince Victor always this way? Noble but in a good way?" Regina asked.

"He was different when he was twelve. I think the planet and his transformation there might have built on it. But whatever it is, I'd give my life for him," Devin said.

"The harshness of the planet made him stronger?"

Devin looked down at her hairless, flawless skin and touched her smooth face. It had not felt that smooth since she was a child. The scars on her stomach, shoulders, sides— injuries old and recent—were now gone as if they were never there. *The planet cleaned everything up*, she thought.

"Maybe. More like the fires purged his flaws and those things that make us greedy, self-centered, and fearful. It didn't kill him but strengthened him somehow," Devin said aloud.

"And he's cute, too," Regina added. Devin looked at her and it was easy to see that her cousin wasn't joking. She was at that very moment adjusting her hair so that it fell loose on her shoulders, framing her face. Because Regina still wore the tactical corset that exposed her cleavage, Devin rolled her eyes.

"Regina," Devin said quietly as she could. "You're like fifteen years older than him. He's Mary's age!"

"Mary's not interested in him. I asked," she said calmly.

Devin's mouth slackened.

"You asked Mary if it was all right for you to move in on a potential boyfriend? Doesn't that sound bad to you? You could be his mother."

"But I'm not, and he's an adult. And I would have been a young mother. He's a royal adult who has to take consorts to keep the lineage. And they can be as young as thirteen. And many of their wives are in their mid-twenties…"

"You're twenty-four, Regina! He's seventeen," Devin said in a forceful whisper.

For a moment, Devin wondered if she'd finally gotten through to Regina. Her cousin looked at her as if she were concerned, maybe even contemplating her way of thinking. Regina reached out and held her shoulders as if she had pieced it all together. Devin was thankful that reason prevailed.

"When did you get so puritanical? It's the lack of sex, isn't it? Marcia, I know at least two male crew members and one intersex one that would be willing to get with you. At least one male and one female for sure said they would hook up with you. Just give the word." Regina was still holding Devin's shoulders. The genuine look of concern was unmistakable. Devin looked at her blankly. She was about to say something but thought better of it and moved out of her cousin's grasp.

"Dias—let's figure out a plan. It's you and me and a small team," she said. She was almost at the bridge hatch with Dias hot on her trail.

"Marcia? It would clear your head. Just give the word."

Devin retreated. She was impressed that Dias, who had

heard everything, based on the width of her smirk, said nothing.

CHAPTER 20
MESSAGE IN A BOTTLE

For whoever believes that great advancement and new benefits make men forget old injuries is mistaken. — Niccolò Machiavelli

"What do you think, Rose?"

"*I don't know. You're asleep. Sound asleep, and we are communicating. This has never happened before,*" she said. While there was a bit of apprehension in her voice, she sounded curious. And for Victor, dreams were rare. So when he fell asleep on the *Nightfall* after time stood still, he was surprised how he found himself looking over a space field that held planets he thought were familiar.

The first planet he recognized was a very large gas giant that seemed just short of being a sun itself. In one grand view he saw moons with names he never recalled learning before: Europa, Ganymede, and Callisto. Before his eyes he witnessed scores of thousands of different styles of ships traveling to and from each planet with inhabitants, materials, and supplies. The inhabitants looked very similar to him—they were taller versions of himself and hairless, but with lighter skin and larger eyes. They wore different clothing but all seemed to be uniformed in various colors of red, black, and orange. The ships were mostly cylindrical with great wings with ports that he was sure held weapons.

Even though these three civilizations were difficult to see

at first, it was clear that they were expanding. The ships and space stations seemed to grow as he hovered. Impressed with the expansion, he found himself now near a planet with multiple rings around it. It wasn't far from the gas giant and held one moon that had industry. Titan's world had two species: one was similar to him but the other appeared to be a smaller version of Xenons—he saw the same six limbs, but their muscle mass was greatly reduced from the species he knew. While they were only slightly taller than him, they were slimmer, more mobile, and seemed to move with great ease.

Similar to the red giant planet he had seen before, the activity was rapid and their style ships were also cylindrical, but it also held four propulsion units equidistant from its center and from one another. Another red planet, smaller than the one he'd learned was Earth, was nearly the same until he looked closer at its surface, which was nearly completely covered with buildings and structures close to the surface, built into the ground, giving hints of more structures underneath the planet's crust. The planet's atmosphere, orbit, and surface were filled with transports of all sizes with operators that appeared hominid, Xenon, and a much larger-framed creature that looked the size of species AB180. They were large, looked very lean but they also had pale, hairless skin. These two features were profoundly different from the creatures he remembered on Earth.

"Mars," he said aloud.

"Yes. Fourth planet from the Sol System's sun. Species AB180 appears to be working in unison with the hominids and Xenons. It's hard to imagine they are from the same genetic pool. Look at how they operate their ships," Rose said.

In his dream, he sensed nodding in agreement and felt himself moving on to the shattered moon that orbited the planet Earth, his home for five years. As he looked closely at the moon fragments, he saw considerably less than he remembered. There were all kinds of ships traveling in and about the fragments, pulling them out of the debris field and harvesting them for precious material. The size of the ship indicated which species it belonged to—the much larger ones were species AB180's spacecraft, while the others seemed to fit both hominids and Xenons.

He shifted his gaze from the moon to the actual planet. The shimmering greenish field that encapsulated the planet was substantially less than he remembered the very first time he had seen the planets. With less green, it allowed blue, white, brown, and other colors to be seen. Orbiting the planet was a dizzying array of platforms that spread across the planet's equatorial line. With its honeycomb architecture connecting to large spheres with massive doors to allow ships to enter, he was impressed how the structure swept around the entire planet. As he looked closer, there were pockets of the planet that appeared to be industrialized, with massive solar panels, large converters near volcanic fields to sap geothermal heat, and oceans of windmills seizing the air. There were buildings of varying sizes, but all appeared embedded into the crust, much like he'd seen on the red planet. And while the landmasses were filled with wildlife and a huge variety of plant life and the oceans were teeming with a multitude of creatures, there were craterlike recesses in the planet's crust opening and closing as spacecraft left and returned home.

"*There must be thousands of ships,*" Rose said.

"Much more than that, AI Symbiont Rose. There are well over five hundred and ninety-three thousand ships," a strong, young-sounding female voice said.

Victor watched his view of the planet melt away. He found himself standing in what he remembered was the facility he'd been taken to on Earth when he was hurt. It was still dark, empty, and cold. In front of him was the transparent tube he was in. As expected, he saw the words *Lucifer One*, but this time they were not backward.

"Who are you? You brought me here," Victor said.

"*And you can hear me,*" Rose added.

"I am Luciel Nine. I am the ninth generation of the first creation following you, Lucifer One," the female voice said.

Victor turned when he saw movement to his left. A young woman wearing a flowing red gown appeared. She looked as young as Mary and her features were near identical in that she was devoid of hair with perfect skin and perfectly proportional facial features and burning red eyes. She was darker and taller with eyes bigger than he expected. Upon review, he had noticed that she resembled many of the hominids he had seen on his tour of the various planets, Titan, Mars and others. "We can hear you because we have incorporated you as part of our physiology. You, Rose, were added not as a separate entity but merged into our DNA at the point of conception," Luciel said. She was no more than three feet from Victor. He reached out slowly and touched her hands that were folded together in front of her. She was warm. She also did not retract or engage. She just let him touch her.

"This place is no longer like this, is it?" Victor said.

"No. It is an image in your mind that we can share. This facility is no longer present. The AI who ran it is now in a larger facility where more of us can be created. We tend to reproduce on our own now. There are occasions when further cloning is required as well as construction based on your DNA, like I was," Luciel said.

"You found my DNA? That was what your AI was looking for all those years back?" Victor remembered all of the images of when he was there last. He recalled that many hominids and Xenons had been sampled, but it looked like he'd been the first at the time.

"Yes, Prince Victor Venture IX. You were the first perfect donor of DNA, plasma, and an array of enzymes, hormones, and other critical biomarkers. The young child you call Mary was the perfect female version that was comparable with your DNA and other markers. The results exceeded our designs."

"*What were your designs?*" Rose asked.

"To return. To repopulate planet Earth and the Sol System," she said.

"How many are you?" Victor asked.

"Twelve point six billion combined sapient life-forms—humans, Xenon, and the Rephaims, or what you call species AB180," she answered.

"*And you all work and live together?*" Rose asked.

"Yes. We live on Earth, Venus, and Mars, including the orbital space stations and moons that orbit Jupiter and Saturn. We are happy here. But we are worried about you, Lucifer One."

Victor looked at her closely, as if her expression might readily explain her concern. She did go on.

"Our existence within Sol has accelerated from your point of view. We are more than nine generations out from conception and have adapted and controlled our powers. We are productive, useful, and we recreate – hunting, competition, challenging our abilities, whether it be with family units or our allies on Mars, Venus and Titan. But some of our powers have dwindled. They can be reactivated, but we have chosen not to. You Prince Victor—Lucifer One—have powers that exceed all alike. Your humility and kindness are good measures to keep them at bay. But even a soul like yours may be prone to emotional outbursts."

"Why did you give up your powers?" Victor asked.

"Because absolute power corrupts absolutely," she responded.

Images of his brother and family came to mind. He pushed them out.

"You seemed worried about the prince," Rose said.

"Yes. It is the power. In your case, and in Mary's, you must be judicious and careful. That is why we offer you an opportunity."

"What is that?" he asked.

"Return to us. Come back to our home. Your home, Lucifer," she said.

Victor looked down as he contemplated the option.

"What about Bishop Miles?" Rose asked.

"Sadly, you will find nothing but death and destruction there. There you will most likely be flooded with pain and angst. A great power from within will be unleashed, prone to emerge any time there are more passionate emotional expressions," Luciel explained.

Thoughts of his beloved Pax, his friends, and Bishop Miles flooded him. Anger and grief engulfed him at the thought of his brother Prince Ramsey and his royal lineage. *Something has to be done!*

Victor was about to speak again when a thought came to him.

"Luciel? If I were to need you and forces, would you come?"

"Without reservation, Lucifer One. Our existence is because of you and Mary."

Victor noticed that her eyes seemed to burn a brighter red than before.

"You know there are worlds out there that are subjugated by my family. If I were to stop them and bring you in for support, the Xenons could come in and free the Sagittarius Sector. Maybe the rest would follow," he said more to himself than to Luciel. Rose picked up on the plan immediately.

"That's brilliant! Dethrone Prince Ramsey with a mystery fleet from here and the Xenons will step in. Offer them the choice of staying with a fleet that might run amok or letting the

citizens run their affairs with them as protectors. We will return to our quiet sector without reservation. It could work, Prince," Rose said. Her excitement was infectious as always.

"Luciel, I would love to stay, but I need to see what has happened to my friends on the planet Pax. I must bear witness to them. If it has gone as poorly as I think, then I must free the citizens of the Sagittarius Sector, the way my brother Jason was attempting to do," Victor said.

There was silence from Luciel, and Victor wondered if she understood what he meant and had to do. Her eyes were still intense, made more prominent by her flawless skin.

"We will be close. We will be with you when you are on Pax. We will be invisible but there. We will listen and will follow you even to Sagittarius Sector. Do you have a leader of war? A liaison we can have as a field marshal, should it become necessary?" she asked.

Victor narrowed his eyes. He was positive he sensed excitement about going to war. His expression must have been evident based on her next statement.

"We do not wish to interfere with others without thinking. The Xenons taught us that. However, if you are to reestablish order to your kind, and have other, more responsible leaders step in, then we will support it. Especially if it leads to your own peace, whether it be here at home or out in the stars."

Victor nodded and smiled. He felt she meant what she said.

"Jana Virgil of the *Harbinger*."

"The ship you are about to rendezvous with to continue your trip to Pax?"

"Yes."

"We will be there to serve, Lucifer One. Prepare yourself. The ones you call Sergeant Marcia Devin and Corporal Ariel Dias are outside your hatch coming to wake you."

"Thank you, Luciel."

"It is my service and duty," she said.

Victor took in a deep breath, as if he had stopped breathing altogether. He was still lying on the floor when Devin and Dias entered. At first they looked alarmed but then they calmed down when he let them know that he preferred the floor to the bed. As he pulled himself together and Devin let him know that they were preparing to dock with the *Harbinger*, Rose asked a question he'd been wondering when she was going to ask.

"So...when do you plan to promote Commander Jana Virgil to admiral?"

Rather than answering, he just smiled and walked along with his escort.

"All right. Be that way. Next time we get to mind travel like that, you can go alone."

CHAPTER 21
YOU CAN'T GO HOME AGAIN

And let it here be noted that men are either to be kindly treated, or utterly crushed, since they can revenge lighter injuries, but not graver. — Niccolò Machiavelli, *The Prince*

"Denis? Do you have the drone's command module or not?" Devin asked in a hushed voice.

"I got it, Sarge, but why do you need all this corroborating data? I mean, it's pretty obvious what the Capricorn Sector did here," he said. Devin looked at him as he focused on getting the drone's CPU dislodged to have yet another recording of the atrocities on Pax. Crouched in a burned-out building, she looked around the charred shambles of a building that had once held what the students of the planets called books. The shelves that had held them were all shattered and the books themselves were still smoldering in multiple sites where they had fallen, along with the students, faculty, and anyone unfortunate enough to be around when the Capricorn capital ships arrived. While there were still squads of the enemy making sure that there were no eyewitnesses, the insanity of them documenting the destruction of the planet— burning books, murdering students and professors, beheading the university's leaders—was beyond comprehension. The three drones they'd snared and pulled information from would undoubtedly be found, but not before Devin and her crew had what they needed to bring to the Xenon consulate. *Maybe this will be enough to bring the Xenons in.*

Devin had a sudden flashback to Oceania. The atrocities there had been horrible and captured by multiple media. The Xenons had not come. But the horrors committed on Pax were of a scale and degree that would be difficult to believe. And in the absence of media, the Sagittarius government could blame the outer worlds, or maybe even sympathizers to the atrocities committed at Oceania.

She was still deep in her thoughts about how lucky she was that Virgil had refused to be pulled into the Oceania incident when her headset crackled to life. She was surprised, as they were supposed to be running silent while deep in enemy territory.

"D? Copy," her cousin's voice said. Devin swore under her breath. Regina knew enough about how things worked to know something very bad must have occurred to breach radio silence.

"Copy."

"Location still secured, all accounted for *except* Origins visitor. Was secured in quarters, special daughter went to check and is gone," Regina said in code.

Shit. The prince is gone? Now?

"Damn it all!"

"D? Corporal. I can check on first time we located him weeks ago here. It's along the shoreline near the cliff just twelve meters from observation point. Copy," Dias said in her ear.

Devin decoded the message very quickly. They'd first seen the prince on Pax overlooking the ocean by a bench with Bishop Miles.

"Go," she said. Then she shifted back to Regina.

"Prep the descent ship to fly. Athena and Mayer on side gun and Nova on aft weapons. May have to come into a hot LZ fast and furious. Can your daughter fly?" While Devin was skittish about having the teenager fly after her metamorphosis, the teenager's overall skills were only enhanced and she was unflappable behind the throttle. Regina could fly the descent ship, or Nova, but Mary was still the best.

"I'm trying to keep her from coming in with guns and engines blazing. We're green, yes."

"Agreed. Out," Devin said. She tapped her microphone and looked at Denis, who was looking at the download. His ashen expression, clenched jaw, and tight fists indicated the horrible scenes he was witnessing.

"Those slacked-jawed, godless bastards. If we live to see justice, it will be to have these minions go right to hell. I bet these pigs will say they were just following orders. I hate that shit," Denis ranted as he watched more footage.

"It's that bad," Devin said more than asked.

"It's worse, Sarge. I never liked the idea of the Xenons thinking they could just poke their noses into our business. But after this shit, I'll be the first to hand over my weapons," he said. His pale expression and condemning words made Devin more anxious about getting the mission complete and heading back to the *Harbinger*.

"All right, Denis. Good job and pack it up. We got to dust off, clear that capital ship out there, and head to Xenon space," Devin said. Her shoulders were tight and her head ached from the mission. *And now the prince has vanished? Damn it. I knew I should have insisted he stay on the* Harbinger*!* She had done many missions like this, but never one to collect evidence against the royals, never against the crown and kingdom. She'd never liked the Xenons taking the high-and-mighty peacekeeping role, but she respected them and their morals. In times like these, she, like Denis, welcomed their presence.

"I thought we were better than this," Denis said. He looked down at the recording and then turned it off. She had known him for years. He was a soldier and a man of action.

Reflection was not his thing. Until now.

"Denis? Focus. We do the job, collect the data, get to the Xenons, and make things right. Copy?"

"On it, Sarge, Sorry," he said. He shifted his gear and got his weapon ready.

"Good. Dias? What's the deal," Devin said into her headset.

"Major cluster, Sarge. Our boy is looking out over the ocean as if it was a tourist site. There are two spotters—combatants in cover, observing and probably contacting backup," Dias said.

"Can you take them out quickly and silently?" Devin asked. She and Denis were on the move to Dias's last location as they spoke. There was no response. Devin kept moving, hoping that the situation wasn't further complicated. After a long minute, Dias's voice came back online.

"Rules of engagement?" she asked. Devin was perplexed at the question and Denis gave her a "what's up" look.

"Terminate. Swiftly, silently, and permanently," she said.

"Good. Done. Was afraid you wanted live intelligence," Dias said.

"Not today. Our boy?"

"Still in place, stone still, Sarge. Bad news, too. These bastards did some beheading and left them for show-and-tell on pickets. Devin…the one closest to our VIP—it's the bishop."

Devin came to an abrupt stop. Denis banged into her.

"Dias—no bullshit. Are you sure?"

"I never forget a face. His body, like all the others, is sitting up. The red hair and face…Sarge. It's him. The prince must be in shock. That's why he's not moving," Dias said.

Devin wanted to throw her fists into the crumbled walls. Her anger boiled over and the only thing she could hope for was to get the prince out before more combatants arrived. At the same time, she wanted to meet the combatants and kill every one of them.

"Sarge? We gotta move," Denis said. She looked at him blankly at first and then she realized she had a rescue mission in addition to her reconnaissance mission now. She was moving at a sprint, barking out orders.

"Dias—guide Denis to your location and provide covert support. We're going to have visitors. I need to go to the prince and pull him out of there. I have no idea what condition he will be in, so buy us time. Call in the descent ship now for cover. Move—we're out of here in under five. Copy?"

"All over it. Descent ship en route. Their reconnaissance indicates it's all clear for now. She'll touch down close to you," Dias said.

Devin's headset pulled in another voice she hadn't really expected.

"Ground team—you have Capricorn's capital ship *Vega* approaching. It looks like she's targeting a cliff overlooking the ocean. Please tell me nothing of interest is there," Commander Virgil asked.

The Vega? *Supercarrier, ship of the line, more than a thousand crew and soldiers, brimming with ordnance. Just great!* Harbinger *is outgunned by five to one.*

"Damn it, yes! We secured the perimeter and we're leaving. Our VIP is in shock over the devastation. I'm heading to his location for physical extraction, copy?"

"Yeah, it figures. We are moving to engage. They are setting up to shower down ordnance. We'll buy you time. Good luck," Virgil said.

The Harbinger *against a capital ship? She's doomed.*

Devin was at a full run. She heard engines overhead. When she looked up, she saw the descent ship first circling, checking out the landing zone. Devin was clear of the rubble and had to make concerted efforts to avoid the still smoldering fires and beheaded bodies littering the campus. She remembered how orderly, pristine, ancient, and filled with life the campus was the last time she and her team were there. While she had seen many horrors, this one was right up there with some of the worst. She could only hope to get the prince and her team out, and hopefully Jana Virgil would somehow survive her engagement. Devin liked her.

"We can't lose her," she said aloud. She suddenly skidded to a stop just a few meters from the prince. He was still but was saying something. She looked at a head on a picket. It was Bishop Miles. She cursed. She turned in time to see the descent ship land on its skids. One of two side doors was open, with heavy guns primed in place to fire, and Regina and Athena were on the lower ramp with their weapons ready.

"Devin? This is *Harbinger*. We are too far to hit our target. We've warned them and shot at them, but they are not taking the bait. They are approaching their target's launch site. You need to get out of there in three minutes or all is lost," Virgil said.

"Sergeant Devin? Mary here. Just found and hacked into the enemy's communication. Area is clear. They plan to bombard the area. The two spotters Dias took out were the only ones. Copy?"

"Copy," Devin said.

With the world falling apart around her, she gave her next order without hesitation.

"Commander Virgil—disengage from your attack. Corporal Dias—collect everything, everybody, and dust off. I'm staying with the prince. It's been an honor serving with you. No arguments—the Xenons need this data. Without the data as hard evidence and without your account, all is lost. Go now!"

"What the hell!" Regina said.

"Get out, Regina. Love to Mom and Dad. Get Mary out of

here. Save Sagittarius Sector. Devin out."

Devin walked up to the prince. As she got closer, she heard clearly what he was saying. She had heard it before, but this time he was talking rapidly, mechanically. It made no sense to her now as it did then.

"White rook takes black rook at D one, white rook to D eight plus, white bishop at D three…Rose…your move…Rose? Rose?"

Devin hesitated but then summoned her courage to wake him out of his dazed look.

"Prince? I am here. Will you come with me or shall I stay?" Devin asked. She felt calm. She stood beside him overlooking the ocean. He was quiet for a moment. She smiled at the thought of her death. She turned to hear the descent ship's engines cut out.

"Oh, hell," she said aloud. Regina was halfway to her, as were Dias, Denis, and Athena. The prince turned to see the people approaching. His face was dark and his eyes darker.

"Sergeant Devin? Will you please give me the coordinates of the *Vega*? It is important that I know where it is," he said calmly.

Devin was confused at both the request and the calm disposition. She didn't have time to think that she, her cousin, and team were now dead. The smoldering sky had darkened an otherwise clear day. Large, dark clouds rolled in in mere seconds. She felt rain fall on her. She nodded.

"*Harbinger*? The prince would like to know the exact location the *Vega* will be in when it's sixty seconds from its mark." As expected, there was silence, either from confusion about the request or the need to double-check the calculations. Devin waited patiently. Regina was standing beside her and hugged her at the waist.

"You just couldn't do what I told you," Devin said to her.

"Leave you? Are you drunk on our last day together?"

Regina said.

Virgil's voice came over and relayed the coordinates. Devin told the prince as she heard them.

"Alpha 43, hydra-beta L209 and gamma-delta M305, my prince."

For a moment, the prince blinked and then he spoke.

"Thank you. All of you."

"You're welcome," Devin said.

A clap of thunder erupted from behind her. She turned to see dark rain clouds rush toward their position. They looked black as coal but there were flashes of lightning coming up over the horizon. She looked in awe at the swift movement and escalating intensity of the lightning that seemed to be growing with every passing second.

"What the hell..." she heard Regina say.

Devin turned and saw the prince. His hands were outstretched toward the sky in the direction of the coordinates she had given him. While these actions were within the realm of normalcy, his hands glowed with miniature streaks of lightning crisscrossing the space between his hands and fingers. She felt an arm pull her back from him as the intensity of the electricity expanded all around him. Claps of thunder exploded and brilliant light shot out from the horizon and from the clouds in all directions above them. Devin heard something on her headset. She had to cup her hands over the earpiece to hear what was going on.

"...neutrino buildup is extraordinary...localized in your location...ionized atmosphere and electrical discharges on a planetary level...danger close..."

She felt herself being pulled to the ground. She looked back up to see the balls of electricity that had formed around the prince shoot out in the direction of the enemy's capital ship, outside the planet's atmosphere, invisible to the eye. Just as his lightning released in the direction and held in place, a series of lightning strikes emerged from all above them in the lower and higher atmospheres. The rain came down in sheets and the sizzling from the water hitting discharged electrons vaporized the water into steam. The intensity and frequency of lightning strikes increased. As if the planet's consolidation of electrical strikes was not enough, Devin's attention was seized by an image of Mary walking to the prince's side with the same consolidations of electricity between her outstretched hands. In fewer than five seconds, she gave a push with her palms and streaks of electricity exploded in short bolts of lightning in the same direction and focus as the prince's and planetary bolts. Streaks of lightning converged on one location in the sky.

Devin saw fear and concern for Mary in Regina's eyes. She turned to see that Dias and her team were on the ground taking in the spectacle and rain, wide-eyed and slack-jawed. Devin turned to say something to Regina but then the area where all the lightning was focused exploded into a bright, silent light in the sky. So bright was the explosion that it lit up the darkened sky and was absorbed by the dark clouds.

The thunder subsided slowly, as did the planetary electrical storm. Both Mary's and the prince's hands lost their fiery electrical power and were now back to normal. In the pouring rain, Devin looked at the both of them—neither had any scars, burns, or charred features. Regina was now standing in front of Mary, holding her by the shoulders and looking into her eyes.

"Mary," Regina asked quietly. "Are you all right?"

Devin watched Mary turn to her and speak. "Could I lie down, Captain?"

Without another word, Mary fell into Regina's arms. Athena came up quickly to help catch her and take her to the descent ship.

"Devin! This is *Harbinger*. Are you there? Copy? Devin?

Ground team? Is anyone there? Copy?"

Still in shock, Devin activated her headset to speak. It took her a moment to clear her throat.

"We're all well here. No injuries to ground team. Prince and team are all right. What's happening up there?"

The silence was deafening and long.

"Sergeant…ah, this is going to sound crazy, but I bet it's nothing compared to what you saw. The *Vega* was struck by wave after wave of electrical discharges from the planet. It was not happenstance or a generalized strike, but a series of lightning strikes that hammered away at the *Vega* until it exploded like a supernova. I've never seen anything like it and hope never to see such a thing again. Theta and everyone in the science section will be busy for years trying to figure out how it happened. Copy?"

Devin found herself staring at the prince, who looked out over the ocean in the pouring rain as if nothing had happened.

"Thank you, Commander. We'll be on our way in a few. Devin out."

"*Harbinger* on station."

Dias and Denis were right behind Devin. She carefully approached Victor.

"Prince? Are you ready to leave?"

There was a pause before a more subdued voice spoke to her.

"In a minute, Sergeant Devin. This is the last place Bishop Miles and I were the last day I was on Pax. You can never go home again. I will rebuild it, but I need to take a course of action I wish I did not need to take."

Devin nodded.

"No problem, my prince."

CHAPTER 22
IN ABSENTIA

Wherefore the injury we do to a man should be of a sort to leave no fear of reprisals. — Niccolò Machiavelli, *The Prince*

"*I am so sorry,*" Rose kept repeating.

Victor sat quietly in his assigned stateroom on the *Harbinger*. It was bigger than his other quarters on *Nightfall*, but that just meant more space to lie on the floor. But for now he was looking at the images of a massive capital warship, the *Vega*, being battered, smashed, and eventually blasted to bits by a series of lightning bolts and charges crashing into it. At first it looked as if the ship's shielding and superstructure could resist the onslaught, but wave after continuous wave hammered the ship. It started to spark and shudder at the edges at first and then it spread throughout the ship's dorsal and outer deck plating, igniting more sparks and short circuits. Then the engines that had been at full speed flickered, faltered, and failed altogether as the battering continued with no sign of remitting. As the ship's running lights lost power, sporadic balls of lightning struck the ship, forcing its nose downward as its forward motion came to a rapid stop as if striking an invisible, impenetrable barrier. The ship endured more strikes, causing electrical arcs to spring up all over the surface until the entire ship was engulfed in mini lightning storms. Finally, inevitably, the ship violently exploded.

Victor winced at the image. He flipped the screen off and

reviewed the statistics of the personnel a ship such as the *Vega* would have. *More than a thousand souls.*

"*Prince? I just don't know what to say,*" Rose continued.

"You fell into shock, Rose. And then you got angry," he explained.

"*But...but I felt what I think was...grief? An experience of not being connected, alone, and empty. And then something filled me up,*" she said.

"Hate. Anger. Revenge."

Victor sighed and went to lie down on the floor. He found either pacing or lying on the floor helped him think.

"When someone is grief-stricken, grief can transform into anger. It's something that makes you feel like you have control over something when you don't. And when anger leads to action, there can be devastating results. Just as Luciel warned."

"*But I'm an AI symbiont.* Artificial *intelligence, as in not organic. Or not totally organic.*" Rose started and stopped as she thought about her answer.

"Do you think that your personality is devoid of emotions? I've heard you be sarcastic, annoyed, and happy. I would guess anger is just another. And since your AI is merged with your organic symbiont and in me, might the AI part experience primal fear? Or anger?"

"*But I couldn't think. I just locked up. I froze.*"

"Yes. You were gone. We tried chess, but you slipped away," he said. Visions of darkness and lightning filled his mind. His heart felt heavy at the thought that he had ended more than a thousand lives in just one moment of angst. He pushed the images of his friends' and mentor's headless bodies out of his mind for fear of more anger exploding into physical fury.

"Rose. You are sapient. You have the ability to think and find your way through difficult decisions. You also possess a personality. Remember what Luciel said about you. You, as an

AI, were not cloned, but rather, your symbiont's DNA was and is now incorporated into an entire species. I bet they have intelligence and experience emotions, just like you did."

"*Well, I don't care much for it,*" she said.

"Sorry, Rose. You're part of the hominid experience," Victor said.

"*Still. I left you in the lurch. I won't do that again,*" she said. There was genuine sadness in her subdermal voice.

"I'm sorry, too. You lost your creator. He was a family member."

"*Yes,*" Rose said softly. "*To both of us.*"

Victor sighed as he lay back on the floor. His room was cold, but the floor was at least comfortable. Talk of family reminded him that even as he sulked, the commander was trying to establish a link to his family. With DNA and scans beamed to royal security, it was a matter of setting up an audio link.

It didn't take long for word to leak of his existence and return. And with the demise of the *Vega* and footage of Pax's destruction by Sagittarius Sector's military, the media, both licensed and underground, were transmitting it along known space. His conversations with his parents, just like the beams proving his royalty, were not secret. *At least the Xenons know.*

"These powers, Rose. Any ideas?"

"*I have plenty of ideas, but none of them make sense. Stopping time, mind teleportation, generating and directing natural meteorological events—all fall into the realm of the bizarre. But what they all have in common is that you can use mind over matter. Not a small achievement by any means or stretch of the imagination.*"

"No, not at all. I guess the mind includes emotions."

"*Definitely. It may be an initiating force. The stronger the emotion, the stronger the results. I suspect that your time on Earth, the transformation you went through, and the time-*"

space distortions all play a role. A perfect storm of events," Rose said.

Victor wondered if she knew she made a bad play on words. He let it go in favor of another question. "Do you think Luciel and the others saw what happened?"

"More than likely. She made it clear they would observe."

"I think I have to have them join me for fear that I might do much more damage when I see my brother."

"Call out the Furies and the demons to prevent obliteration? At first blush, your logic appears flawed. But in light of the emotional connection, the dangerous situation, and the lack of Xenons in force to keep the peace, maybe a strong counterbalance to keep you from acting is a good idea. How will you communicate your needs?" Rose asked.

Victor closed his eyes and felt his breathing become deeper.

"Sleep. Just like last time," he said.

"Yes. Just like last time. I will join you. Once we are there, I'd like to share a plan with you. It may give you what you want and keep everyone safe," Rose said.

Victor yawned.

"Sounds good to me."

CHAPTER 23
FAMILY REUNION

Politics have no relations to morals. — Niccolò Machiavelli

"This is being transmitted to all sectors, Prince," Commander Virgil said. Victor was still rubbing the sleep out of his eyes and yawned from what felt like accelerated time and space travel. The effort was worth it, and Rose and Luciel's plan made sense in form, simplicity, and execution. Even as he pulled himself back to the *Harbinger* from his sleep and was escorted to the bridge, he still had to block out the deaths of his friends and mentor and the thousand souls he'd taken in a state of rage. It took him a minute to actually hear what the commander was saying.

"This way the entire realm will know you are indeed alive, making any attempt on your life suspicious. Not unlikely, but suspicious. More than likely the Xenons are listening as well. That might help keep your brother and family in check—with respect, my prince."

"No sign of the Xenons yet," Dias commented.

"And they have all the transmissions from Pax, along with the entire kingdom and outer worlds. I hope they come soon," Devin added.

"And the king and queen believe I am who I say I am?" Victor asked.

"All the scans have been beamed to them. They will undoubtedly have your voice checked for authenticity as well,"

Virgil added.

"Ma'am? The auditory link is established. I have a direct link to the royal family's residence. They will be coming on the line in ten seconds. And just so you know, I have at least fifty communication spikes locked into the signal. Some are low security while others are ultra-level eavesdropping, more likely corporations and communications network. It won't be private," a young communications officer said.

"Understood," Virgil said.

"*Well, Prince. This is it. Family reunion. Don't be too polite and deferential. They'll misinterpret it as weak and submissive. They're just like the wolves back home. You have to be an alpha,*" Rose warned.

Victor took a deep breath. Visions of his beloved Pax in ruins and his dead mentor's head stuck on a picket were still etched in his brain. After his short stay with Luciel and after what he'd seen in real time and space, he wanted to go back to the Earth, the Origins planet. *Hell is far better than this.*

The ship's loudspeaker crackled to life and a small directional microphone was placed in front of him to speak. Finally a voice sounded.

"My son," the aged voice said. "We missed you greatly. Your brother from Capricorn Sector is especially concerned."

"He is more kin than kind, King Talus. What of my brother Jason from the Sagittarius Sector? Is he well?" Victor asked, already aware of the answer. He saw the looks from everyone around the bridge. There was silence on the other end. A throat cleared before he spoke.

"I am not sure, son. It is rumored that his citizens revolted and seized power. He led a dangerous life," the king said. Victor waited for more. He hoped there would be. There was nothing but silence.

"Are you there, my son?"

"I am here, King Talus."

"Why so formal, my son? I am your father. I have seen all your biomarkers. You are my son and Queen Vega is your mother."

Images of the ship *Vega* flashed before his mind.

"Is she there as well?"

"Why, yes, my son. Speak, my queen."

A distinctly younger woman's imperious voice spoke. He had hoped for a somber or possibly relieved-sounding mother. A distraught mother who had lost one son but had found that another who had been presumed dead was indeed alive. Sadly, he heard none of that in her voice. Her timbre and volume were as if she were christening a spaceship—the *Vega II*, perhaps.

"Prince Victor. It pleases me to hear your voice, though it is much older than I last remember."

"I was five years old when we last spoke, Queen Vega," he said. His tone was fatigued and his voice hollow.

"You have been through a great deal, my son. I understand that the Origins planet and system have altered your growth. You are older?"

"Yes, Queen Vega," he said. He felt eyes on him in the small command center.

"Are you there, my dear son?"

"Queen Vega—did you cry for me when I went missing? Did you cry for my brother Jason when news of his assassination was delivered in your local news? Was it by personal courier or did you know in advance?"

Victor heard a sudden gasp on the bridge. There was silence, but for only a moment before an angry male voice spoke.

"How could you say such a thing! You have no right to speak to your mother in such a fashion! You do not hold the right, title, station, or privilege to speak to her or me in such a tone or manner! It is vile for you to insinuate such a thing.

How dare you!"

His breathing was heavy and the fury was unmistakable.

"I demand a response, *Prince* Victor!"

"You demand a response, King Talus and Queen Vega? I will give you one," Victor said. His voice was deep, heavy, and if at all possible, deathly dark with enmity.

"A *true* king rules his subjects with an even hand. Equity. Justice. Due process—all admirable qualities of a royal government. These are all absent in your reign. When one prince from Capricorn is allowed to act unilaterally, there is no king. There is no queen. There are no parents and there is no justice. You both are weak, frail, impotent, and absent. I will deal with my brother myself. I will deal with my *family* myself. The Sagittarius Sector is *mine*. I am its heir, not him. I will rule that sector the way my brother Jason did. I will preserve his legacy. Not the legacy of a failing king and a weak queen."

"You will not speak to me this way…"

"You shall not speak at all, my defunct *king*. Your voice is a stringless instrument. Your words are meaningless. Your bark is weak and your bite is nonexistent. I will not let my brother's death go unanswered. I will not let his people suffer. I will not stand by idly and watch you do nothing. The gates of hell are open. Havoc, I say, havoc and so slip the dogs of war. I am done with you all. I have been to Hell, literally and figuratively. It is better to reign there than to serve you and your bankrupt court. The next time we speak, you will have one chance, and one chance only to renounce your crown. Choose wisely, King Talus. Advise him well, Queen Vega. This is Prince Victor Venture IX, legitimate leader of the Sagittarius Sector, ruler of Hell, Lucifer One, bearer of light."

Victor pushed the button to cut off the transmission. He looked around the bridge to see ashen faces and dark circles. Most were clearly shaken except for two: Mary the pilot and

Commander Virgil. They both smiled.

"Well, well, well. I guess reconciliation is off the table. Thanks for dialing me in. And you went with the 'let slip the dogs of war' thing, and to add color you had to go with the Lucifer angle? This Shakespeare guy really had good insights," Rose said. Victor did not respond. He thought talking to himself at the moment might detract from the drama.

"Prince Victor, I stand behind you. I will follow you to hell and back," Commander Virgil said.

"You did, Commander. You and others here. But suffice it to say I have made this bed and intend to lie in it. I need not share it, however. I need only transport to Sagittarius Sector's royal court, or rather, the capital city's edge," Victor said.

"You don't have to be alone in bed, Prince," Regina said. Her voice was more sultry and seductive than expected. Devin's hand shot out and slapped her bare arm, and she gave her cousin a warning look to stop. Abbreviated chuckles went through the bridge's crew. Victor felt his face flush again. He broke eye contact first. He knew his limitations.

"Oh, that was good. I am starting to like this little kitten. Her name does mean 'queen,' you know. Maybe it's prophetic? I might have misjudged her," Rose added.

"We are not going to drop you off and leave you there. We will be with you," Virgil said as a means of coming back on topic.

"Till the very end," he heard Devin say.

He turned to see Dias and Mary give him a thumbs-up.

"I guess that makes it official. We can all be hanged for treason," Virgil said with no fear.

"It's liberating once you get the taste of freedom," Regina said. "But in all seriousness, what's the plan?"

Victor's face felt heavy and he could see from the others' expressions that his look must have appeared dark. He chose his words carefully.

"My brother will abdicate his hold on the Sagittarius crown, he will relinquish his own sector, and the king and queen will leave us all alone."

There was silence for just a moment.

"All right. Well, I'm glad we got the details worked out," Regina said.

"Oh, yes. I do like her. She reminds me of a younger me," Rose said, loud and clear. He was glad no one else could hear her.

"Don't worry. I got it covered. You're sure the Xenons monitored this transmission?" Victor said with a smile.

"Are you kidding me? The whole galaxy did. Outer worlds included," Devin said.

"Oh, I get it! Chess! Perfect! You're running our plan in phases. You're not just another pretty face, Prince," his AI symbiont said with zeal.

"A rose by any other name," Victor said quietly.

"Ah, that's sweet."

CHAPTER 24
AN UNUSUAL PLAN

Hence it comes about that all armed Prophets have been victorious, and all unarmed Prophets have been destroyed. — Niccolò Machiavelli

"I don't like this one bit," Devin said to Dias and Regina. Hours after the prince's rant, he gave them the plan, part of which meant abandoning him on Ploutonion, Sagittarius Sector's capital world, in the city where Prince Ramsey would most likely be coordinating his campaign.

"Well, the good news is that everyone got their rank back. So finally we are the same rank, though I think a ship's captain has more pull than a captain of the guard," Regina said.

Devin felt her eyes narrow as she looked at her younger cousin. Navigating the corridors of the *Harbinger* still required maneuvering even though it was a large warship. While the walk from the bridge to the ship's cargo bay was far, it did give them a chance to review all that had happened.

"And what the hell was that comment of 'You don't have to be alone in bed, Prince,'? You are such a little…"

"Now, ladies! No good will come of this banter," Dias said. "While I appreciate being reinstated to my prior rank, it matters little if the prince is not successful. And if it is true what he said about his visions, as crazy as they sound, then he will still need our support."

Devin sighed as Regina smirked.

"So with the new rank comes logic, wisdom, and reason, Dias? I liked it when I was the brains of the operation," Devin said.

"I've been on vacation," she responded.

"Still, I am amazed at the part my dear, flirtatious cousin gets to play," Devin added. It made Regina smile more.

"Well, it does make sense. I'm clearly more feminine and younger than you…"

"You're four years younger than me, Regina!"

The *Harbinger* crew walking around them gave them looks. Regina took the cue to talk lower.

"And way more curvy and sensual. Since I'm the only one to have showed interest in the prince, it does make sense he chose me as his princess," she said with a bright smile.

"Regina—he chose you because Admiral Virgil is needed to lead this ghost fleet, and Mary is too young and will require a parent. Since you are her mother, he chose you to play the part. You're not actually a princess," Dias said calmly.

"Admiral Virgil is way older than me. And I am Mary's guardian. So if she's to be regent of Sagittarius Sector someday, I will need to be ready as her representative. Which means royal-looking clothes, shoes, and accessories. If I give you a list, would you be a dear and pick them up for me?" Regina said, straight-faced.

"He's thinking about her being a regent for a short time until the government is strong enough to hold elections."

"Maybe. I will still be a princess."

Devin stopped in midstep and rubbed her eyes.

"Dias…could you please talk sense to this crazed woman?"

"How about we focus on what the prince proposes? He wants to be dropped off at the city's edge so he can blend in and get to know the people. Any idea why?" Dias asked.

Regina nodded as she seemed to think in terms of the plan

rather than her new role.

"Well, if I didn't know better, I'd think our prince is young and trying to figure out if the people of the realm are worth saving," Regina said.

"What makes you say that?"

"Well, you said he spent most of his life on Pax, and they were pretty special people. Then he met you and your team, and you were trying to save his life. He seems to like Admiral Virgil and this crew. He likes me, of course, and my crew. I just think he's wondering if the majority of people are like us or like his family," Regina explained.

"I think that's pretty obvious," Dias said.

"No. Not so obvious. He said when he met that woman, Luciel, she offered to return him to the Origins Sector. Maybe he feels he needs to make sure this sector is worth what he's giving up. I bet he wants to know who he saving," Devin said.

"Hmm. That is a lot to give up. Forget about us and return to your own empire," Dias remarked.

"And it would take some time to really see what the people, civilians, might be like. It would also give us some time to find out if his dream was true and if there's a fleet ready to take on the kingdom. And I need an entire new wardrobe," Regina added for good measure. To Devin's credit, she ignored the comment.

"I just don't like leaving him there without protection for a month or longer. And what does he mean that we'll know when to come? I just don't like the lack of clarity. I want clear mission objectives."

"Captain? The *little* prince brought down a capital-class supercarrier. He used the planet's weather system to strike that ship multiple times. And the *little* girl Mary threw a couple of bolts herself. I think he can get himself out of trouble as fast as he got in," Dias said patiently.

Devin and Regina looked at their intersex colleague.

"What?" she said.

"I'm not sure I like the new, *wise* Lieutenant Dias. She grates on my nerves," Devin said.

"Yes…she does have an air about her. Just remember, Mary's the regent to be and I am her guardian, spouse of Prince Victor Venture IX," Regina said.

"All right then. How about another subject. Are you planning to have Theta find the Xenon ambassador now? It will take some time."

"Yes. We started and we may have to keep trying even as we head to Sagittarius Sector. In all seriousness, though, come back for a drink. I'd like to think that the prince's plan will all work out, especially when I'm queen."

Devin watched her cousin walk in front of her. While Regina's words were cheery and her exterior positive, she was sure her cousin was worried. She walked with her head down and slower than her usual gait, as if she were preoccupied. A drink before departure on a covert mission was usually a ritual for a battle or a campaign where there would be casualties. Devin was going to say something but then decided against it.

"Sounds good to me, Regina. Sounds very good to me."

CHAPTER 25
SEEDS OF THE NEW REPUBLIC

But in Republics there is a stronger vitality, a fiercer hatred, a keener thirst for revenge. The memory of their former freedom will not let them rest; so that the safest course is either to destroy them, or to go and live in them. — Niccolò Machiavelli, *The Prince*

"So how long do you plan to stay here?" Rose asked.

Victor shook his head. Nearly every day, three times a day, Rose had asked him the same question.

"Rose, please. We spent how many years on Earth? I'd say that was a bit more hostile," he said. He continued to listen to yet another round of stories from his friends. At the same time, he looked all around the long alleyway that housed the poor and the homeless with their carriages and belongings all on their backs. Nestled between tall skyscrapers varying in size from huge to immense were narrow alleys that allowed anyone who could not afford indoor space to live on the street. While there were built-in awnings to provide cover from any elements or sun that might make it down to the ground, the space was filled with makeshift barriers for privacy and stoves for boiling water and food. Food was rarely an issue, since the rodent population was impressive. Good food that was nutritional and enjoyable was nonexistent, as a result of small businesses closing and the large food dispensaries being at elevated heights.

It was still light and the air was pleasantly cooler than the midday heat as a result of the massive shadows the buildings and structures created. For the Sagittarius Sector capital world, Ploutonion, he had expected more wealth and beauty with a strong economy and business. Instead, there was less business, more military, significantly fewer rich than poor. His brother's former palace had been donated to the homeless, but it was retaken by Ramsey. After thirty-nine days, he had seen little by way of parity, equality, and trade. To his surprise, he did see kindness among the people, regardless of who they were. What surprised him most was that the indigent were the more forgiving and kindest when they weren't suffering of physical or mental illness.

Along this alley were Michael, Gabriel, and Raphael, who had seen him and taken him in as he arrived with just a cloak, plain clothes, no weapons, and no money to speak of. They fed him, brought him to their home along the streets, and introduced him to an array of poor, kindhearted people who greatly missed his brother Jason. To hear them talk of Jason—his acts of generosity, walking among them without airs, finding people to help feed and teach them trades—was surreal. Jason was his brother. His subjects, strangers, knew him better that he would ever know him.

"You talk a lot to yourself, don't you, Vic? Are you hearing voices again? Rose?" Raphael said.

"*Well, at least you fit in here,*" Rose remarked. The tone was unmistakably sarcastic.

"Yes," Victor said to him, ignoring Rose. "Sometimes she is kind and other times she is not."

"I'm just glad you have a kind voice once in a while. Mine are always angry," Ruth said. She was one of many mothers who had lost her business once the depression hit. She had soft brown eyes, a novelty, for sure, but they looked frightened sometimes, as they would dart from side to side as if she were being taunted by someone invisible.

"I'm sorry, Ruth," he said.

"The medicine helped her. But Prince Ramsey shut down all the hospitals for us and the food banks..." Raphael said. His words trailed off as he looked up the alley's entrance. Streams of soldiers and law enforcement officers had begun combing the streets weeks before amid rumors among the population that another prince, brother to both Jason and Ramsey, but more akin to Jason, was to arrive soon. Some had actually heard a copy of the new prince speaking to his father, King Talus. They said he sounded strong like Jason. Since Jason's death, the poor and homeless had been uprooted and forced to disperse, as it was thought that spies might live among them.

Victor watched Raphael as he did an immediate risk assessment of an approaching platoon of soldiers, weapons drawn, wearing their battlefield dress uniforms with the Sagittarius Sector home world crest. For a patrol group, Victor was surprised at the size of the packs on their backs and slung over their shoulders. All the other patrols traveled light, but this group came as if they were going to camp and be present for a while. Behind them was an armored, wheeled vehicle with two soldiers mounted on the heavy guns.

"*Oh, damn. This is not good,*" Rose said quietly, as if she might be heard.

Michael and Gabriel came quietly up behind Victor and peered as the armed group arrived. Ruth immediately left and many more who could not flee moved deeper into their trash heaps, crates, and boxes that served as homes. Suddenly, Raphael visibly sighed and he smiled. Michael was next while Gabriel wept.

"I don't understand, Ralph. What's going on?" Victor said. As he watched he saw all the soldiers begin to break their two-column form and spread out among the civilians. He watched them as they holstered and slung their weapons and emptied their bags of what looked like food, supplies, water, and other crucial, greatly needed items. He had heard of this only twice since his arrival but had not seen it until now.

"The leader there. He must have been part of Prince Jason's royal guard. They were all replaced by Prince Ramsey's and relegated to high-risk and dangerous sectors. If they are caught doing this, they could all be killed for treason."

Victor turned to look at Raphael and then Michael for verification.

"It's true, Vic. Sad but true."

"But they are taking care of the poor and homeless. How is that treason?" Victor said.

"*That is just sick,*" Rose sneered. Victor noted her clear contempt.

"Yup. That's why they came in heavy, as if they were going to tear this place apart. And see how the armored vehicle is blocking the street view? We'll send spotters up. Hey, Ralph, get some food for Ruth if you can, and get me some, too. I'll watch the other end of the street."

"Will do, Mike," he said. By now the three men were walking slowly to the soldiers handing out material and supplies. Some were administering first aid as well. Victor closely watched the timid looks, grateful smiles, and acts of kindness.

"Lieutenant? My name is Ralph, and this is Vic and Gabs. Thank you, sir," Raphael said. He put his hand gently on the young soldier's arm.

"No need, citizen. I am sorry we could not bring more. Things should not be this way," the young man said. Victor looked closely at him. While his voice sounded young, his gaunt appearance, age lines, and sad eyes made him look much older. Gabriel did the same with his hand as well. Victor imitated. As he touched the lieutenant, he felt the young man turn to look at him. His eyes, tired and sad at first, flashed with life for a moment. As Victor retracted his hand, the soldier held it.

"I'm sorry, but who are you again, young man?"

"My name is Victor," he said.

"How old are you?"

"Seventeen, sir," Victor said.

The lieutenant looked at him closely as he held his hand. He looked as if he was going to say something, but then another soldier called out from behind. As he looked back, Victor retracted his hand.

"*What was that about,*" Rose whispered.

"Lieutenant? I got a body here," a young woman called out.

A mass of people moved toward her as she was scanning the body of a middle-aged man lying on his back. Still within his grasp was a sleeping eight-year-old girl and a little furry animal.

"Oh, no. It's Larry. He was sick, but it looked like he was getting better," Raphael said.

The lieutenant sighed at first and directed the female soldier to scan the child.

"Already did, sir. She's fine. Sound asleep," she said.

"How long?"

"Who? The dead guy? Thirty-five minutes. The girl's in deep REM," the soldier explained. She was now standing up, looking at her scanner. Victor watched her as she looked intently at it, as if she was trying to understand something.

"Does the girl have a next of kin?"

"No. Just us. Her mother was killed in the protests while Larry was in the hospital. Once they closed that down, it was just a matter of time before it took him. We were looking for his sister in the hopes she might be able to take her," Gabriel added.

"Are there any youth homes she could go to?" a voice from the back asked.

"No," the lieutenant said. "They are all gone. And she's too young to be conscripted, though you never know where things are going these days." His tone was bitter. Too bitter for such a young man. Victor looked on, saddened by the whole event. He moved in closer to the supine body and knelt down to look at the man's still-open eyes.

At first he was simply going to close them and leave, but then a wave of calm and clarity came over him. He had remained where he was to learn about the people in his kind brother's former realm. With Ramsey in place, there would be no peace. None for Capricorn and Sagittarius. Victor placed two hands on the man's chest and closed his eyes. In his mind's eye, he saw the man's still heart and empty lungs. He peered deeper and deeper until he found the only cell activity still producing cytoplasm at an incredible rate in the man's lungs, liver, and pancreas. As he watched he felt his hands warm. The more his hands warmed, the more the cytoplasm division slowed. Eventually it stopped and then began to melt away. This continued until he saw no more of the malady. Moving out of the cellular level, he put his hands on the man's heart and head. Instead of heat, he felt a low electrical current running through his hands.

Unaware of time, he felt the man move and his heart beat. His head felt warm and then Victor heard the man breathe, slowly, consistently, and without interruption. Victor took his hands off the man. He looked at his peaceful face. His eyelids fluttered and he looked up at Victor. There were tears in the man's eyes. Victor was confused.

"Is something wrong?"

"No. I had a terrible dream that I died and left Margaret here alone. Hey, Vic? How are you doing? What's going on? Did I say something in my sleep?"

"No, Lazarus. You looked uncomfortable and I thought I would check on you."

"Thank you, Vic. That's very kind," Lazarus said. With that, the man turned to embrace his still sleeping child and returned to his sleep. Victor watched and felt a quiet joy. He stood and turned to see what Gabriel, Raphael, and the soldiers were doing.

When he turned he saw that an entire crowd stood ten feet back looking at him, slack-jawed and wide-eyed. There was no noise except for the low-pitched hum of a bioscanner running and street sounds.

"Well? What did you expect? Raise a man from the dead with just a touch and you're bound to be seen as unusual. I would say our cover is blown," Rose said.

"Hmm," was Victor's acknowledgment.

"Vic? How did you do that?" Raphael asked.

"Lieutenant? We got to keep this on the down low. If Central Command hears about this..." an older, bearded soldier started.

The lieutenant looked at him sharply.

"You think so, Sergeant! Set up the jamming device now," the lieutenant ordered.

"Mark! John!" the lieutenant said. He raised his voice for effect. It worked.

"Yes, sir!" two soldiers responded.

"Cover our exits and make sure the curious are not around! Bart—what's your medical opinion?"

"I'd say it's really messed up," the medical soldier said, still slack-jawed.

"Bart—wake up and look at your readings. Mathew—keep the jammer going and make sure Private Iscariot is deep in the back of the roller going through the ammunition and is seeing none of this. Andrew—take everyone else and tell them to forget what they saw," the lieutenant ordered. He kept his eyes on Victor. As the soldiers moved to carry out their tasks, the medical soldier read aloud her readings, as if that might explain the results.

"Sir…these readings are pinned in a way I've never seen before. But I got DNA markers…holy crap!"

"Stay focused, Bart. Is he who I think he is?"

The young woman looked at him first in dismay and then as if she understood something.

"No way! You believed he was here?"

"Bart! DNA markers now!"

"Prince Victor Venture IX. Royal family. MIA more than five years ago. On that Hell planet. Origins 001, old Sol System. He's heir to this world's crown, sir. Crap!"

"And he's a dead man as long as Prince Ramsey is here," the lieutenant said quietly. He moved slowly toward Victor, who felt a small smile forming on his face.

"My prince. You are in grave danger. We can hide you and get you off the planet. We must do this quietly. Prince Ramsey has spies everywhere. Private Iscariot is from his ranks and reports everything. We must go, Prince." The lieutenant was all business, adjusting his weapon and tactical gear. His team started to do the same thing.

"What is your name, Lieutenant?"

The young man looked baffled and confused.

"I know I am in danger, but this is all part of the plan. What is your name, Lieutenant?"

"Lieutenant Peter Stone, sir," he said and gave a bow of his head. Victor watched Bart do the same thing.

"All right, Peter. I am Prince Victor, and this is all part of my plan. I will need a royal guard while I am here. You and your team are it, except for that Iscariot person. Agreed?"

"Yes, Prince," he said.

"Now, what I am going to say next may be confusing, but all is accounted for and this is part of a greater plan. Are you listening, Lieutenant?"

"Yes, Prince Victor."

"*So...this is the time. It starts,*" Rose said. Victor nodded his head and went on.

"Please finish giving out supplies. Once that's complete, make sure that Private Iscariot understands who I am so she can betray us all. Have your sergeant call in who you have found and make sure there is plenty of media coverage about you bringing me in. Also, please let my friends here know who I am. Let them know that my time with them was humbling. I will do my best to follow my brother Jason's footsteps, and I have them to thank."

"I will do this without reservation. But my prince, your brother Prince Ramsey may kill you outright. He sees conspiracies everywhere. Your actual presence here might push him to extreme action. I am...concerned for you, my prince." For such young man, Stone looked too old for his age. Command and the times must have weighed heavily on him.

Victor's smile broadened. He placed his hand on the lieutenant's shoulder as he had before. Royalty never touched anyone who was not a royal. Such an act was unheard of. The lieutenant did not shy away from the touch but remained still as a rock.

"I appreciate your concern. As you can see, I have some powers that no one, royalty included, has. Wouldn't you agree?"

Victor was surprised to see him smile. When he did, the worry lines vanished.

"That is very true, my prince."

"Sir? Will...will you save us? Save us all?" Bart asked. Her expression was a mix of worry and hope, fear and joy.

Victor felt very small. He placed his arm on her shoulder as he spoke.

"We will save one another. There will come a time of

great terror and trepidation, but you will not have to fear. If we stand together, we are strong. Those who divide us will fall. I promise you that a great storm comes. Thunder, lightning, fire, and brimstone. It will be cleansing. And when it's all over, the faithful, kind souls that preserved hope when darkness fell will be remembered and embraced by a new kingdom. Jason's new world order is upon us. That I promise you," he said.

Victor watched her eyes move from fear to hope to wild enthusiasm.

"Yes, my prince!"

There was a moment more of silence. Shouts of recognition and joy were heard from the cluster of civilians he'd lived with for thirty-nine days. He caught the waves of Raphael, Gabriel, and Michael. The lieutenant and other soldiers were busy with the next steps. Victor took a moment to review with Rose.

"Nice speech. I especially liked the 'faithful will be remembered and embraced by the new kingdom.' Excellent. Now…will our team back home know what to do?"

"You know, I think that will be more theater than a bloodbath. We'll see," he said.

"I hope you're right, Prince. I'd hate to disappoint these soldiers."

Victor nodded his head. He folded his hands behind his back and watched everyone.

"Me, too, Rose. Me, too."

Victor watched as the soldiers moved to give out all of their supplies. Their speed looked driven by mission rather than fear. That's when he saw Raphael and Gabriel gently guiding Ruth toward him.

"Raphael? Is something wrong with Ruth?"

"Vic…I mean, Prince Victor…"

"No, Raphael. You and everyone here are to call me Vic just as you have."

"See! I told you he'd be all right with Vic. So Vic? Can you help Ruth? She hears the voices," Gabriel asked.

"Can you make them go away, please? Or at least make them kinder," she asked. Her eyes were filled with tears and she held on to him with both hands.

Victor held her close and put her head on his shoulder. Not knowing what to do, he simply held her. She wept and wept but stayed where he held her. He wondered if he could make the voices go away.

CHAPTER 26
BREAKING NEWS

Therefore any cruelty has to be executed at once, so that the less it is tasted, the less it offends; while benefits must be dispensed little by little, so that they will be savored all the more. — Niccolò Machiavelli, *The Prince*

"Lieutenant Stone! Lieutenant! Please? Just a moment, sir."

The shaking of the video camera finally stopped as a young lieutenant turned to face the reporters and videography staff that were in hot pursuit. It looked to be early morning in a town center with a series of four large military trucks lined up in a row. Soldiers were seen handing out various supplies that were readily identifiable as food, water, linen, clothes, and temporary shelter. One of the soldiers stuck out, as he was bald and wearing a simple dark green flight suit with clothing underneath, while the others wore black battlefield dress uniforms with tactical vests. Upon closer inspection, there were no weapons on their persons to speak of.

"Lieutenant? Is it true that this is your fourth stop of the night? Where did you get these supplies?" a young female reporter asked.

"The Royal Food Dispensary and Distribution Center. Our leader saw it on the way to the hospital and decided that it made sense to get food and supplies if we were handing out medicine as well," he said.

"Lieutenant? Aren't you afraid of court martial or even death? Are you and your team being forced to do this?" another reporter asked. The tone was that of concern.

"No," he said calmly. "We are doing this on our own free will." It was easy to see a smile form on his face.

"Is it true that your leader is Prince Victor Venture IX?"

"All right, everyone. We established that hours ago with bioreading scans and I'm sure you figured out the time-space space distortion . The Origins planet, Earth, was abandoned and quarantined for a reason. Unpredictable time distortions are something you don't want to deal with," he explained.

"Well, he certainly lacks hair and the royal garb we have become accustomed to. A simple olive-green flight suit with a sweater underneath? In this heat?"

"It's a dry heat," the lieutenant offered. There was laughter.

"Seriously, why no weapons, Lieutenant? You left one of your privates—a Private Judas Iscariot—with all your weapons and ammunition at the first site you reportedly hit. Why did you do that?"

"Private Iscariot is a loyal supporter of Prince Ramsey and the Capricorn Sector government. Her politics and philosophical viewpoints do not align with mine and those of my command structure, my crew, and Prince Victor Venture."

"Is it true that he brought a man back to life after thirty minutes?" A shout came from the back.

"Yes."

"The prince helped a crazy woman regain her sanity?"

"Yes. She was deprived of her medicine when the crown shut down the hospital. Prince Victor helped her, too."

"But Lieutenant, there have been several attempts to catch you already, and you have managed to not only break in and secure much-needed supplies for the civilian population but to do it without hindrance, without witnesses, and without being caught. How is that possible?" the original female reporter asked. The camera shifted to a serious-looking soldier coming up from behind the lieutenant.

"Lieutenant? We got five aerial assault vehicles and three platoons coming in from all sides," a bearded older man said. His rank designated him as a sergeant. The camera remained on their faces to see if fear, anxiety, or anger would seize them. Instead, there was calm and peace.

"Well, civilians, this concludes our interview. We will talk again very soon. Now if you would please move to the sides of the road and clear the street, it will allow the incoming troops to set up barriers, take up a defensive perimeter, and allow for clear lines of fire," the lieutenant said.

"How do you know that?" another reporter asked.

The lieutenant chuckled and pointed to his sergeant to answer the question.

"That's what we would do to detain and/or capture enemy combatants," the sergeant explained.

"But you have no weapons. You have given out much-needed food and supplies. How can you be enemy combatants?"

The lieutenant turned to the female reporter who had asked the majority of the questions. His smile was sincere and his eyes warm. Even though he was young, his crow's- feet and smile lines implied wisdom from experience.

"Grace, we're not enemy combatants. We represent new ideas and beliefs that put citizens first. That makes us very dangerous," he said. With that, he and his sergeant turned.

As they walked away, two loud rumbles of thunder came from the east. The camera was shaking again and the reporter, Grace, continued to report on the situation. After some movements and false starts, it looked like the camera found an ideal place to allow a panoramic view of the now empty street and the men they had just interviewed now lining up in two columns. The camera took in three rotor aircraft that were clearly circling the area to ensure safety and to provide suppression support. In the distance more thunder rolled in. What made the thunder confusing was that the early morning was crystal clear, without any clouds. All the soldiers looked up as the younger, bald man in the plain jumpsuit seemed to be speaking to them. The camera angle shot toward the other end of the road, where a series of wheeled armored vehicles came to a sudden stop several meters away from the lined-up soldiers. The road that was perpendicular was populated in the same fashion.

"Citizens. It is obvious that Lieutenant Peter Stone and his men are outnumbered and completely surrounded. The younger man who is reportedly Prince Victor Venture IX seems to be talking to them. He might be giving them instruction to surrender…" Grace said. She was interrupted by a loudspeaker.

"Lieutenant Stone? This is Colonel Herod Mortis of His Majesty's royal guard. I hereby command you to walk to us with your hands up and no sudden movement. You are to leave the nonmilitary citizen there. You have one minute to comply."

More thunder rolled through. It was louder than before.

"This has been a crazy night. Rumors of Prince Victor appearing on Prince Jason's world to take the crown seem true. There was a series of successful raids on royal and military bases to steal food and supplies and give them to the citizens. And with no weapons in hand, surrounded by Prince Ramsey's troops, it seems as if this miracle is coming to an end," Grace reported offscreenoff-screen. Another set of low, rumbling thunder rolled above them.

"And to top things off, we have rolling thunder on a crystal clear day with no humidity, and the rainy season is still several months away…wait…they are moving," Grace added.

The camera panned to the left and saw the column of

soldiers, including the bald young man, walking with their hands up to the armed blockade. Thunder rolled on but it seemed as if it was just two meters above their heads.

"Wow! That's unbelievable! Did you hear that? It's right on top of us."

Without warning, a fast-growing, blinding light expanded from above. There were shouts and yells as the light intensified and a loud, long rumble of thunder seemed to shake the camera. It was hard to say if the light dissipated quicker for hominids' eyes or if the camera lens was somehow affected. Through the thunder, yells, and shouts, there were calls for help as a temporary blindness gripped everyone near the thunder. More time passed, punctuated by crashes and explosions. The light was clear and the thunder rolled on but was much farther away.

"Holy shit! Darren? You getting this?" Grace said.

To the camera's right and on the opposite side of the street, all the soldiers who'd had guns on the lieutenant and his cadre were beginning to move off of the ground, rubbing their eyes and ears. The aircraft that had been above them were now grounded, as if they had lost power or their bearings. Two looked as if they were burning. One exploded before the camera lens. Shouts and military vernacular were heard from all around them. While the whole scene seemed to be recovering from the thunder and lightning and a possible power surge, the column of men and the prince were gone. There were more shouts from soldiers calling for any signs of the cornered troops.

Grace came in front of the camera. She spoke rapidly as if she was sure her transmission was about to end. There were a number of soldiers moving toward the other reporters and camera staff, ordering them to turn off all recording devices.

"Citizens—what I believe you just witnessed was an escape of Lieutenant Peter Stone, his soldiers, and Prince

Victor Venture IX, right in plain view. Surrounded on land and from the air with superior, well-armed troops, this unarmed troop of…of missionaries provided much-needed supplies and then disappeared. Stay tuned. There is more to come. This is Grace Honorer of…"

The transmission ended. The room fell dark.

#

"Lights," Admiral Virgil said.

The lights flickered on in the large conference room. The admiral walked to the front of the line of occupied chairs while the star charts rematerialized on the wall behind her.

"Well. As you can see, our prince has made both an impression and the news. We are green to launch in five minutes. All hands—to battle stations," Virgil said calmly. A siren sounded and she and the crew of the *Harbinger* moved out the various doors. It didn't take long for Captain Marcia Devin and Lieutenant Dias to catch up with her. She caught Dias's new rank insignia and glanced at her own new captain bars.

They walked in silence for a few moments, dodging the other crew members as they headed to preassigned posts. Devin looked at her hands and felt her face. It was a growing ritual since the removal of all her scars, pains, and injuries from the beam on the planet several months earlier. In times when she felt there was an impending conflict, she looked at her hands and felt her face in case an injury was to follow.

"So…are you used to the new bars, Admiral?" she heard Dias ask.

Without hesitation, Virgil answered, "Yes. Much better than commander, and, I must say, better than vice admiral. If we live, I wonder what other promotions await us?"

"Yup. If we live. For all the talk, planning, and training

for the last forty days and nights, I have only seen twenty-eight, maybe thirty ships of our allies. We are going up against at least two hundred battleships, and fifteen are as large as or larger than the *Vega*. And that's just the Sagittarius Sector occupation group. We're not even talking about Sagittarius Sector's defense fleet, King Talus's fleet, or Capricorn Sector's fleet," Devin said. She was walking behind the admiral and noticed that her boots were particularly shiny and her skirt was slightly shorter than expected. Somehow she carried it off.

"Luciel has made it clear that there will be more than enough of Sol System's ships to launch this two-pronged attack on Sagittarius and Capricorn Sectors. Further, the Xenons are on their way to King Talus's home world," Virgil said.

"And that's twenty ships. As advanced as they are, that's a task force."

"Still, I have faith in the prince and Luciel. The other commanders—Asbel of Earth's Eagle fleet, Aurora of Mars's Hawk fleet and the Origin Xenons' Venusian Raven fleet—all seem competent," Virgil started.

"The Raven fleet will only be used as a rear guard. I do like these Earthers' thinking," Dias said.

"And very large, those Earth giants. I liked them better when they were hairy and stayed in the mist with their spears. Now? Hairless, towering over Xenons, and all of them having those wolves for pets? They're just scary," Devin said.

"And their ships would have to be huge! I mean, we've been kept outside of the system, but I think we would have seen a fleet of both size and numbers by now," Dias added.

"And did you see their weapons? The majority of their assault rifles and ordnance is based on gas-powered projectiles. Some explode on impact while others simply rip the skin apart. Just to round out the barbaric weaponry, they all have a series of edged weapons," Devin said more to herself than her companions. It was an effort to understand how such a high-tech civilization still used low-tech cylindrical, pointed bullets, swords, and knives in the age of photon weaponry.

All three were just outside the bridge's hatch when Virgil came to a stop and addressed the two soldiers.

"All right, you two. Once we're on the bridge, I want nothing but wild-ass support and conviction. We're the most seasoned ones in there, and I know that five of them have updated their last will and testament. They need us to be strong, and I need you to help me do it."

Devin felt her gaze hit the floor. She felt bad for being negative, no matter how accurate their assessment.

"Sorry, Admiral. We sometimes forget our role," Devin said. A moment of silence passed.

"I know the odds are stiff, but there's something about Prince Victor and this place. This Origins Sector is strange, but you've seen the inhabitants. They weren't there months ago when we were here before. It's amazing that they are here. It's amazing we've gotten this far. So just hold on and let's see what happens," Virgil said. While her voice was firm there was compassion. Feeling dressed down, Devin moved from one foot to the other. The admiral turned around and adjusted her tunic and dress before entering the bridge.

"Anyway, if we go in with what we have now, we'll be dead in seconds. So either way we win—victory or a swift death," Virgil added. Matter-of-fact, focused on the next step, Virgil chuckled as the hatch opened. Dias snorted and Devin kept herself from laughing.

As soon as they entered the bridge, a series of visuals was up on the screen: Luciel, the female Earther who led the Origins Sector fleets, was standing with similar-looking crew members in a darkly lit bridge. They wore full black compressed body armor that enhanced every curve of both genders' athletic bodies while various cartridges, sidearms, and sheathed knives were well placed for ease of access. Their pale, flawless skin and heads were the only things not covered, giving them a specter-like impression.

"We are prepared for launching our expedition. We will have the majority of our forces head to Capricorn Sector under my command. They will be primarily the Venusian Xenons. They will be familiar with them. You have two-thirds of the Earthers' Eagles and the Martians' Hawks. We will appear from nowhere at Capricorn. They will have no warning. However, they will warn Sagittarius of your arrival. What is your strategy, Admiral?"

"It all depends, Luciel. How many ships are we talking about?" Virgil said. She moved to her chair and sat down. Devin looked at Luciel and was surprised by what she saw—a broad smile with white teeth.

"Admiral, you have well over five thousand warships. Eagles are manned by Asbel. You know them as species AB180. Their ships are massive, to hold their kind. Their ships carry the symbol of the ancient bird of prey, the eagle. They will appear from the sun's zenith in ten seconds. Aurora will command the Martians' Hawks. They carry my species. The ships will be dark, with blood-red piping among their wings. They will appear from the sun's nadir. The Eagles carry troops and landing craft while the Hawks are smaller, swift, and heavily armed for atmospheric combat in addition to space. Good luck, Admiral."

Devin looked at Dias. She was not surprised to see the intersex's eyes as big as saucers.

"Thank you, Luciel. Our strategy is simple. You gave them a warning. We will offer those who wish to surrender a sector to do so. Good luck and see you on the other side," Virgil replied.

Luciel's image faded out and was immediately replaced

by an image of the Origins' sun. Devin and the entire bridge group held their breath as they watched dozens after dozens of ships emerge from the top and bottom of the medium-size yellow sun. As the ships approached, they grew in size and number. After three minutes, the star field and solar system behind them were no longer visible, obscured by ships. With the exceptions of the ship's engines, air recycling, and workstations, the bridge was unusually quiet as the fleet gathered together. The Eagles were massive and the painted gray, white, and black feathers made them look as if they were alive. The Hawks were black with dark red piping; they were harder to see in the backdrop of space. They looked like old female images of death. When Devin saw the *Harbinger* for the first time, she had not been impressed with the more than twenty-year-old decommissioned warship. But now? Unbelievable!

Two images displayed below the armada.

"Asbel! Aurora! It's nice to see your fleets after so much time and speculation," Virgil said as casually as if she were getting a dress altered.

"It is great to be a part of this venture. Speaking of which, how is our prince doing?" Asbel said. His large jaw, body, and pale, hairless skull made him look intimidating. More intimidating than when his kind were covered with hair and hunted with their spears. To his left were two relatively small creatures called wolves. Similar to Luciel, he and his crew sported low-tech weaponry, from firearms to swords.

"He is causing havoc. Giving away food and supplies. Giving the population hope and frightening the establishment."

"Excellent! For little creatures your kind has skills," Asbel said with a smile.

"If it wasn't for him and our species, you would still be hunting in the mist with all your hair and rocks," Aurora said with a laugh. She looked nearly identical to Luciel, but she was definitely the more liberal with her humor.

"You could do better to find other friends, Admiral Virgil. Aurora—just make sure your people provide in-atmosphere cover when we land," he said.

"Will do. Admiral? Is the word given? It is a three-day flight and Luciel is on her way," Aurora said.

"In sixty seconds, on my mark. Good luck. When they see my ship, they will come at us with everything. Take care," she said. Both images nodded and then flickered out. Impossibly, more ships seemed to be filling the ranks.

"You know, I actually feel bad for the kingdom," Dias said.

"I have never seen such an armada. It's off the charts," Devin said. By now she was feeling that she had control over her slack jaw.

"Don't feel too bad for the royals. Oceania, Pax, Ploutonion, and all the other planets have suffered under their yoke. No. They will have no sympathy from me," Admiral Jana Virgil said. Devin looked at Dias again. It was rare to hear the admiral be so dark.

"Helm—take us out," she said.

CHAPTER 27
DEVELOPING STORY

He who becomes a Prince through the favour of the people should always keep on good terms with them; which it is easy for him to do, since all they ask is not to be oppressed. — Niccolò Machiavelli, *The Prince*

"...Again, if you are just joining us, a series of cataclysmic events has occurred throughout the entire Capricorn Sector and all the realms and outposts of Prince Ramsey's purview. This overwhelming attack came without warning and from nowhere. The attackers are unknown. The larger species are said to be species AB180, relegated to the Hell planet in Origins Sector. They appear to occupy the larger ships and are accompanied by large, four-footed, furry creatures with large teeth. They too reportedly come from the Hell planet and are classified as W428. They are outfitted with cameras, audiovisual, and sensor mounts that appear to guide species AB180. The smaller species is very similar to us and occupies the smaller black ships. Both ships have the shape of mythological birds of prey, and the two hominid species are without hair. While the larger species is primarily dark, the smaller species appears pale with larger eyes. But the largest group attacking appears to be smaller versions of the Xenon species. They reportedly come from a planet called Venus in the Origins Sector. While they share the same physical appearance as far as limbs and body type, they are pale, hairless, and attired like the others.

"The realm's Sector Defense Ministry has issued a total disaster distress beacon. All citizens are to remain in place and are not to be on the public ways. The following is an audiovisual summary of the last eighty-two minutes. Please note that these visuals are graphic, intense, and simply frightening to comprehend."

The camera panned from the newscaster to the large segmented screen behind him. There were time indexes indicating the chronology of the rapidly evolving events: large, winged alien spaceships ramming and cutting capital ships in two with little to no damage. As one large group of royal ships fired upon and hit multiple alien craft, several more attacking ships came in from all sides, swamping the entire battle group. After two passes, only wreckage and destruction were left in its place.

Other images on different planets showed hundreds of armored vehicles, infantry, and heavy weapons on tractor vehicles and aircraft swooping in headlong to meet the opposing alien combatants. Time-lapse footage of merely eight minutes showed an advancing alien force of two hominid species and a ferocious four-footed carnivore species as they carefully marched through dead bodies, soldiers, and destroyed materiel. At the battlefront were brief glimpses of Venusian Xenon troops firing weapons. Squadrons of both space and atmospheric aircraft flew into the alien aircraft. In seconds, images captured only the alien aircraft—winged black ships and larger gray ships with birds of prey painted on them.

More images, both still and moving, of lesser quality also showed up on the screen, as if taken from the social media devices that had been banished more than thirty years ago. Startling images of all were less about battlefront destruction but rather a simple image of royal ministers and Princess Carol, consort wife of Prince Ramsey, kneeling before a pale, hairless female clad in black. Surrounding the kneeling group were all three alien species and their wolves. They all were hairless save the wolves. As all the images flickered by, audio from the battlefront and throughout the sector came through:

21.21 minutes: "…listening outposts along the Capricorn Sector have gone silent. All diagnostics indicate that this is not a communication grid error. There have been some unsubstantiated reports of unidentified spacecraft by the thousands sweeping in and obliterating their orbital defenses…"

34.31 minutes: "We have confirmed a massive fleet of unknown origin has appeared from three different sectors within Capricorn. Outer planets are reporting a large occupation force of four species. Two of hominid descent, one Xenon, and another of four-footed, carnivore origins. In regards to the hominids, one species is physically larger than the other. Both hominid groups are hairless. All Capricorn Sector fleets are en route to engage the force while they are stalled at the sector's perimeter with their occupation efforts. The Xenon consul meeting with King Talus and Queen Vega report that a science officer, Theta, of Sagittarius private vessel *Harbinger*, claims that these species are from the Hell planet, once known as Earth. He also reports that they are under the control of Prince Victor Venture IX, who was rescued by former Vice Admiral Jana Virgil and Captain Marcia Devin. Both of these soldiers were demoted for not following orders during the Oceania protests…please wait. Transmission from our loca—"

01.01 minutes: "…Mayday, Mayday, Mayday…Lieutenant Desire Oval reporting from the battleship *Ramsey III*…our entire battle group—eight battleships, twelve destroyers, two supercarriers, and fifty-three heavy cruisers…we're…we've been routed from our defensive position. We're outnumbered four to one by superior fighting vessels. Tactics and weapons I've never seen…"

22.22 minutes: "…we are in full retreat! All ground command structure is gone. We're all retreating. These things' weapons and strategy are nothing I've ever seen! Their assault rifles are nonphoton, a type of lead projectile that can rip skin and muscles apart without cauterization! The larger ships drop out of nowhere and then the smaller black ships suppress all attacks. When these bigger ships deploy ground troops, they launch and support the smaller ships by targeting armored vehicles and heavy weapons…we have no defenses! We're doomed! Fall back! Keep shooting! Fall back…"

12.12 minutes: "…to repeat, we have seen these aliens smash through all defense perimeters established by the realm. These creatures, however, have not targeted the civilian population as far as we can tell from our location. Other sectors and reporters have told us the same. Who or whatever these aliens are, the civilian population, businesses, and entire cities and provinces that do not have a strong military or royal connection have been overlooked entirely…"

12.12 minutes: "…Aurelio Spenser of the Capital Royal News. I have interviewed a captain of the invading force. She wants me to relay the following to the civilians of the Capricorn Sector: 'To the civilians of this sector—do not attempt to interfere with events that are affecting your government. The kingdom as you know it is ended. We are from Sol System. It is what your kind calls Origins Sector. We come from the three planets there, one of which, Earth, you call Hell. You will await direct news from our field commander shortly, at which point a number of locations— food dispensaries, hospitals, all businesses related to food, shelter, and supplies—will be listed for you to receive everything needed without hindrance or cost. It will be all yours. There will be order. There will be calm. There will be peace and eventually, there will be self-governance.' There you have it…"

52.52 minutes: "…all analysis indicates that these invading forces' speed is based on their intimate knowledge of all orbital defenses in the sector, as well as their seeking out all military targets and leaving civilian assets alone. With no need to support or suppress some entire planets with little or minimal military presence, they are able to focus entirely on the offensive…this…lightning war…"

33.33 minutes: "…all social media jamming devices have gone off-line…all social media jamming devices have gone off-line…citizens are now able to utilize social media unhindered. The Royal Media and Communication Control Center has been overrun by the invaders. The aliens have shut down all jamming devices used to scramble planet-wide social media networks. For the first time in thirty-three years, all citizens within the Capricorn system are free to use any and all social media without hindrance and without fear of imprisonment…"

50.50 minutes: "My name is Luciel. I am a human from planet Earth. Species AB180 are Rephaims. There are descendants of Xenons within our ranks who come from Sol System. We have watched and waited. We are here. Before me lies your chief of defense, his directors of campaigns and royal expeditions, and your Princess Carol, spouse of Prince Ramsey. They have surrendered unconditionally to spare their lives. I am here to liberate you citizens from the yoke of your kingdom. We are not associated with the Xenons. We follow the leadership of Prince Victor Venture IX. We know him as Lucifer One. It is his will that the royal family relinquish their realms, that a temporary government be established and a new order be begun to allow for the civilians to self-govern. It is called a republic. It is his wish that the Xenons come to oversee this new form of government. As to Prince Ramsey— this is your only warning. Step down and allow your brother to reclaim what Prince Jason left for him. This is your only warning."

11.11 minutes: "…King Talus has launched his royal guard fleet to protect the Sagittarius Sector. It is reported that as Capricorn Sector is lost to this invading fleet just short of two hours since the invasion, the king and Queen Vega have decided to assist the still standing fleet at Sagittarius, as this sector is probably the next target…"

1:01.10 minutes: "…is Grace Honorer reporting from the royal capital of planet Ploutonion. After three days of dodging and evading capture, Prince Victor Venture and his eleven soldiers are reportedly on the move to confront Prince Ramsey. The efforts of Colonel Herod Mortis of His Majesty's royal guard to capture this renegade platoon have been met with spectacular and mysterious failures. With the royal court completely fortified with troops and armament, it is unclear what the outcome will be…wait a minute…there is news coming in from the court even as we speak. No, wait. News from the court and from Sagittarius outer defense grid…

"Citizens of Sagittarius Sector, we will bring you more news on Capricorn Sector as soon as it becomes available. Now to recap the top news, or rather the only news in Sagittarius Sector, we have been invaded by a superior, massive fleet that has targeted all of the realm's military and defense networks while leaving the civilian population unharmed. In addition to our in-the-field reporters, a number of citizens have been flooding our lines with pictures, videos, and even some interactions with the invaders. Again, the aliens have not approached civilian targets. If you are just joining us, we will review what we've learned over the last ninety-three minutes with the following reports throughout the entire sector, with more news to come from Capricorn Sector as well. The following is a summary of events starting with the first indication of an attack…"

43.43 minutes: "…listening outposts along the Capricorn Sector have gone silent. All diagnostics indicate that this is not a communication grid error. There have been some unsubstantiated reports of unidentified spacecraft by the thousands sweeping in and obliterating their orbital defenses…"

58.58 minutes: "We have confirmed a massive fleet of unknown origin has appeared from three different sectors within Capricorn. Outer planets are reporting a large occupation force of four species. Two of hominid…"

CHAPTER 28
A BLAST FROM THE PAST

You ought never to suffer your designs to be crossed in order to avoid war, since war is not so to be avoided, but is only deferred to your disadvantage. — Niccolò Machiavelli, *The Prince*

"Prince! It's happening!" the sergeant said. His dark eyes and beard enhanced his strong voice. But the zeal and energy he exuded were that of a child on a day of feasting.

The group was having a very simple dinner in the home of a widow who had been surprisingly open with her disdain for Prince Ramsey and longed for the day he would be overthrown. As soon she learned that this military group had gone rogue, and saw them walking through the alleyways, she immediately called them in for food, rest, water, and time.

After three days of running amok, Colonel Mortis was becoming more aggressive. Orders had been issued to shoot on sight. Their disappearing in front of cameras and a series of audiovisual devices was news as big as that of the collapse of Capricorn Sector's defense line. Their last strike had been on the Royal Media and Communication Control Center. During Prince Jason's reign, he had allowed ownership of civilian media devices to flourish as a means of creating loyalty to the realm and autonomy, but upon his arrival, Prince Ramsey erected a planetary jamming system of all of these devices just as he did in his own domain for decades. It ensured isolation

and lack of connectedness. Victor was getting a tutorial from
Private Mark Merak of how wind could affect a photon shot
when Sergeant Luke Josephs burst in.

"Calm yourself, Sergeant," Lieutenant Stone said. All the
members were up on their feet and gathering around the
sergeant. He focused on his breathing and nodded in
agreement. It took him just a minute to settle down.

"I was scanning the old café area. It was filled with
civilians. They were all on their media tablets. Your reporter
got the news out that the jamming devices were all down. And
with Sagittarius's social media back online, I guess people
found their old stuff and checked. It's all working now," the
sergeant said.

"So? That's great, but what's the big deal?" Bart asked.

"Stick with first aid, Bart," the lieutenant said.
"Tactically, we can get the word out about the prince and the
forces. Remember how difficult it was when Prince Ramsey
took over? First thing his forces did—we did—was take out all
civilian planetary communication. Isolate and then give them
only one source of information—you now have a population
immobilized, learning only the things you want them to."

"Now it will be really difficult to get all of it back offline
without there being some fallout. Prince Jason was quite
liberal with this media. He was ahead of his time," the sergeant
added.

As the soldiers talked and speculated about how fast
things were moving, Rose was thinking way ahead.

*"Prince? What would you think if you and these soldiers
went out there and jumped on this planetary social media to
tell everyone who you are and what's to come? This would
undermine the autocracy and support Prince Jason's legacy of
a republic."*

Victor turned away so he could talk to her. It was easy to
do as all of them were engaged in what targets should be hit

next.

"Hmm. It might make sense. But we can't just send them out to talk about me. Need some kind of doctrine. Something or things that can appeal to the individual and ideals for a society. Some of that old stuff from Earth…you remember those manuscripts? One was a religious text that had a list of rules for people's behaviors?"

"The Bible? I was hoping you'd say Shakespeare, but his stuff is all dark. Great insights on hominid behaviors, but nothing real uplifting."

"And there was one document that was about a great republic and it actually worked for centuries. It was not an oligarchy nor parliamentary. Definitely not royalty. It was really out-there thinking…"

"The United States Constitution? Are you suffering from heatstroke?"

"No, I'm freezing. You remembered that one, too," Victor said excitedly.

"I remembered it because of all the things that stood out on Earth, that form of government was the craziest."

"Ah, come on, Rose."

"Seriously, Prince? 'We the People of the United States, in order to form a more perfect Union…' You mean that? The one government that has all those checks and balances between the legislative, judicial, and…what was it? Executive power? It's amazing that system worked at all, let alone how long it lasted. That won't work here. It barely worked there. It only worked once on Earth!"

"Rose. I know it's a long shot. But think about it. You have a premade document that outlines the ideal of a government that doesn't allow my family to seize power and do what they want, and you have those commandments that dictate ideals for individual behaviors. Prince Jason was working on that. This sector was getting ready for this kind of leap. That's why he was stopped," Victor said. He felt his words and breath come up short at the thought that his brother had been killed for trying to lead his people down a more equitable path.

"Business, trade, and commerce were booming, and poverty and crime were decreasing profoundly under his reign. Then Ramsey came and the very things these citizens were craving were taken away. They are ready, Rose. They just need leaders with a vision and a map. We can give them a map. We can come up with the leaders."

Rose was quiet. Her lack of immediate response typically meant that she was seriously weighing the pros and cons of an outlandish plan.

"And you think that if these eleven soldiers go out with these ideals written down and start preaching to the masses…"

"Yes. It will go everywhere. The ideals and lofty nature of these principles will not only catch on here, but everywhere," he said with zeal.

"Hmm. All right. But I want to add another set from the Bible," Rose said.

"Oh? What?"

"I want to add Ecclesiastes 3, from the King James Version of the Bible: 'To everything there is a season, and a time to every purpose under the heaven: A time to be born, and a time to die; a time to plant, and a time to pluck up that which is planted…'"

"That's kind of odd. Why that one?"

"Because it addresses the fact that hominid behaviors and makeup can be contrary. That there are 'times for war and a time for peace,' or in our case, a time to rebel and a time to comply."

Victor took a moment to recall the verse in its entirety. His smile broadened.

"Wow. You are pretty smart there, Rose. Good addition."

"All right. So we got three manuscripts that are relatively short, eleven soldiers to get the word out, and then you can hide out."

"It might make sense for these soldiers to tell the world what they have seen and done, and it will give me time to see my brother, not hide."

"All right, *that's not the plan I was thinking,*" she said.

"Rose, Luciel has already crushed Capricorn Sector. I'm betting it's just a matter of time until Admiral Virgil and the others get here—as in, about a day. If these men and women can tell their story, move around, that will distract Ramsey and I can get close to him."

"And do what? Kill him? I know we both killed thousands on the Vega, *but that was from afar in a blind rage. Do you think you can commit fratricide up close and personal? Kill your brother? Are you Cain to his Abel?"*

"More Abel if he had learned what Cain was going to do," Victor responded. He was surprised by Rose's lack of immediate response. Usually she was faster, but that was only when she was convinced she was right.

"Well, maybe…still, to kill a family member, even in self-defense, might leave a pretty big mark on your psyche."

Victor paused to make sure he understood. "You're worried about my mental health as the Sagittarius Sector's freedom hangs in the balance?"

"Yes. You are the only one I care about."

Victor looked down at his boots. He felt embarrassed and smiled at her consideration.

"Like a sister, Prince. I wouldn't think of competing with Ms. Large Mammary Glands. And I would suggest returning to Earth to age another ten years before you consummate that relationship. She'll hurt you. But we'll talk about that later. All right. I agree it makes sense. I would suggest that you send the soldiers out in pairs and divide them in different directions to

get the word out. That will make it harder to find them and allow them to contact more people. It will also distract that Herod character."

Victor chuckled. While he had an enhanced seventeen-year-old body and the mind of a very old scholar from a dead though still powerful world, he agreed that his body and mind were probably not ready for a woman like Regina Devin.

"Well, if necessary, Mary will be the regent and Regina her guardian. Mary's installation does not require I be wed to her guardian."

"Ah, Prince? When was the last time you checked on royal right of accession? When we have time we should probably check Sagittarius's regional law."

A burst of sweat erupted from his head, along with the sudden fear that there was some terrible loophole that would require him to have Regina as a consort.

"Damn," he said.

"The disadvantages of having such a daring plan are the risks associated with it. But one cluster at a time, O magnificent prince. I bet that hiding out idea is sounding a whole lot more attractive now."

"Nice, Rose. Real nice."

"So to get back on track, I'd split them up and send them out as quickly as possible," she said in all seriousness.

"All right...time to change the world through social media."

CHAPTER 29
WE THE PEOPLE OF THE SAGITTARIUS SECTOR

For however strong you may be in respect of your army, it is essential that in entering a new Province you should have the good will of its inhabitants. — Niccolò Machiavelli, *The Prince*

"I have never read anything like this before. I never thought I would see something like this. And this is being transmitted from where?" Devin asked. She was still reading the reams of transmissions that were flooding interstellar communication.

"This is all coming from Ploutonion?" Regina asked as well.

"That's where it all started. First it was returning civilian social media, and they got it from eleven soldiers who have been helping the prince steal and distribute resources, supplies, food, and medicines. They had it all written down and now it's all over the Sagittarius Sector, and there's a whole lot of downloading that going on in the other sectors. The Xenons are clearly impressed and say they know the source," Dias added. She too was reading the material. While the bridge of the *Harbinger* was small and not well lit, it was next to impossible to find anyone not at their posts reading the material.

"Check this out," Admiral Virgil said. "'All civilians accused of all crimes shall receive a trial by a jury of their peers with the sole exception of cases of impeachment.' And here's another—'In order to ensure a well-regulated citizen soldier, all civilians have the right to bear arms that may not be revoked, infringed, or minimized' This is unbelievable. These principles undermine the entire charter and covenant between the royals and their subjects. Conscription, the need to be tried for all crimes…this is just unbelievable."

Devin looked at the admiral, surprised at how stunned she was. She was right, of course, but then, all of the principles were giving civilians more rights, breaking up the consolidation of ruling power, and invoking a checks-and-balances system by a system of laws and judges.

"There's this part where any leader, I think the king and queen, too, can be impeached and removed from office. There's a system to get rid of leaders," Dias said.

"Then there's this short, half-page thing called *The Nature of All Civilians*," Regina said. She had been leaning against a console, engrossed in a separate document that outlined individual principles of behaviors. She and Mary had spent several hours a day preparing for their presentation to the public, if that became necessary. But when word of a new charter emerged from Sagittarius Sector, she was roped in like everyone else.

"First he gives Ten Principles for Civilian Interactions, and they are pretty high up there, and then he gives circumstances for when some of these same principles may be rescinded. Take this one—'To everything there is a reason, a time to every purpose under the stars. A time to kill, and a time to heal; a time to plant and a time to harvest; a time to weep and a time to laugh; a time to mourn and a time to dance…' Wow! And then there's this part: '…a time to keep silent and a time to speak; a time to love and a time to hate; a time of war and a time of peace.' What does this all mean?"

"It speaks volumes and it's poetic," Virgil said.

"He's talking about the duality of our species. We should hold ourselves to higher principles, but at the same time there are circumstances that require us to act differently, even as to be forbidden to kill and then to have a circumstance when killing is allowed, maybe even necessary," Dias said.

Devin found herself staring at her subordinate just like everyone else, marveling at her precise and clearly formulated interpretation of the documents. The silence was deafening. Dias finally looked up and saw the bridge's reaction.

"Well, I actually listened to how the team that got all this going understood it. It was that lieutenant, Peter Stone, and four others—Sergeant Luke Josephs, Private Mark Merak, Lance Corporal Matthew Paige, and Private John Marshall—that said the same thing. For soldiers, they're pretty articulate," she explained.

"So is he implying that monogamy is the preferred way? I mean, what about us who want more than one partner? It would help with managing the home, business, and, ah, other desires," Regina said quietly.

"So that's why you went right to the individual behavior one. Worried that he's narrowing the field?" Devin chuckled.

"Shut up, Marcia. Some of us can get more than one partner at a time," Regina said. She adjusted her corset and continued reading. Devin admired her quick retort and read more about the limitations of power and the safeguards against corruption. *This is incredible, impressive, and idealistic.*

"Well, the scholars and politicians will be interpreting these documents for years," Virgil said with a suppressed smile.

"The applications and execution of the larger document will require assistance from the Xenons. This is just what they have been asking us to do for decades," Dias said.

"Before we start creating election centers, we need to convince Prince Ramsey and his military to leave," Virgil said.

She was now sitting in her command chair and surrendered her tablet to a crew member. The recently promoted Captain Mason Martinez called for Virgil's attention.

"Admiral? We just confirmed an audio communiqué from Captain Robert Dyson of the *Frozen Lake*. It took about ten minutes, but it's authentic," he said.

"Now that is a name I haven't heard in years, Captain. What does he say? I'm sure he is his terse self," Virgil said with a broad smile.

Devin realized she was nodding in approval and smiling. Regina shot her a look indicating she had no clue who Dyson was. It was Dias that gave her the intel.

"*Admiral* Robert Dyson was the only one to refuse to reduce Vice Admiral Virgil over the Oceania incident. He then left fleet command and took a heavy cruiser warship rather than the top-of-the-line capital-class fleet carrier. We think he would have resigned his post and left if it wasn't for his staff and crew. They're family to him. The royal family would have eaten them all alive."

Regina acknowledged she understood. "I get the family thing and crew thing," she said. She smiled at Devin. Marcia was often amazed by how she and Regina could be teasing each other one minute and then be nice to each other in the next.

"All right, Captain, put it on audio and make sure you share it with Asbel and Aurora," Virgil said.

"Will do, Admiral. Just so you know, the audio came over conventional carrier wave and is probably three days old. There's a lot of interference, most likely jamming from the source," Martinez explained. He nodded to a young crew woman at the communication-research console.

"*...attack vectors cut off all civilian refugees. Capricorn warships have surrounded the convoy and have refused to accept surrender...The* Arcadia *and* Pristine *are gone...*"

The static male voice cut out abruptly. There were reverberations of salvos striking a ship's hull that was devoid of shielding. Devin felt her chest tighten and looked at Virgil's back. The admiral looked at Martinez, who had the audio replaying. He had replayed it three times. A clear audiovisual signal came in from Aurora's ship—she had also heard the cryptic message.

"Admiral? I would like to dispatch three squadrons to the audio source's location. We will be passing over the location in three minutes. Due to the size of the fleet, we cannot all slow to a stop nor would it be wise to have the *Harbinger* fall out of the lead. Do you agree?"

"Agreed. And thank you," Virgil said.

"No problem. The last three squadrons will fall out of rank. Two squads of Ravens and a squad of Eagles. They will report their findings directly to you."

"Thank you, Aurora," she said.

The bridge was unusually silent once Aurora's image faded off the main screen.

"Dyson is a good leader and able soldier," Martinez said finally.

"The *Frozen Lake* is a solid warship, but it's like our lady, just short of decommissioning," Dias added.

"Captain?" the young communication crewman said. His voice was high, indicating either his youth, anxiety, or both.

"Jacobs?"

"Sir, I just looked up the names *Arcadia* and *Pristine* in the royal fleet, and there are no listings. I expanded the search and came up with two passenger liners that bear those names. Both are about twenty-eight decks and can hold four thousand passengers each," he said.

"Any weapons?" Martinez asked.

The crewman looked down and read a bit more. The bridge air-conditioning turned on and the electronic sounds from various instruments were the only sounds on the bridge while those who were not monitoring their stations listened to their own thoughts and fears.

"The standard repelling crews against intruders. There are some armed patrol teams on each vessel."

Martinez nodded. Devin looked at her hands, as if their perfect skin would somehow help her feel less anxious about the ships' fate. Her stomach was all knots. She felt her cousin's supportive hand on her shoulder from behind.

"That was Dyson's voice. If he was protecting those ships, he wouldn't leave without exacting retribution, even if it meant his own ship's demise," Martinez said quietly.

"Yes," Virgil said. Her still profile gave the impression of a boulder. And while her voice was steady and soft, its message was foreboding. "You're right, Captain. He would not let an attack of this savagery go unanswered. If he was successful either way, he will not be forgotten. If his success is due to self-sacrifice, and the royals are involved, we will be the instrument of their destruction."

"Yes, Admiral," Martinez said.

CHAPTER 30
SOS

It is double pleasure to deceive the deceiver. — Niccolò Machiavelli, *The Prince*

"*You know, you're a bit too natural in this environment, Prince. If only your corporal was a major, you'd be all set as far as moving around unhindered. I'm glad you're not on this team, though,*" Rose said softly.

Victor nodded his head slightly as he moved from one surveillance monitor and media station to another. His uniform was ill-fitting, but that was easily explainable as weight loss while his lack of hair was readily interpreted as intersex. The cavernous command and control center occupied a reinforced armed compound right in the center of the capital's central plaza, in the middle of a recently converted military base. There were rows after rows of small monitors, with only half the staff in place required to operate them. The majority were out looking for his renegade soldiers, whose media blitz of republic and freedom was causing havoc and desertion in droves. Nearly all the exterior walls were floor-to-ceiling screens with varying visuals of Capricorn vessels being crushed by the invading force's fleet. Other images gave way to visions of the massive invading squadron ships, giving the appearance of dark, predatory birds from an ancient past swarming over nearly every inhabited world in the sector wherever royal outposts and bases were positioned. *Eagles,*

Ravens, and Hawks, he remembered.

"*Still, I am glad that young man decided to join the sergeant and the others. I'd like to think he changed sides at the right time,*" Rose added.

Victor nodded again. Over the past three days, civilians and military had been leaving both the cities and the planet when possible. With the fall of the Capricorn Sector to the Fleet from Hell, as the invaders were now called, obtaining a young man's uniform and papers merely required asking for them. Victor had gained access to the base by escorting Colonel Herod Mortis and his troops to a high-level briefing. A preemptive electrical surge fried all retinal and handprint scans for about an hour. "*Timing is everything,*" Rose had said at the time. By the time he made it into the bunker system, it was easy to blend in, as everyone was more focused on events just outside their door. He had arrived right when word of an escaping armada had arrived—it had been engaged and destroyed.

Victor's level of shock was similar to that of a number of the support staff when they learned the "armada" had been a fleet of private ships, passenger liners, and other smaller refugee ships trying to escape from Ploutonion before the invasion. The captain of the only warship defending the refugees, *Frozen Lake*, had surrendered immediately, but his surrender had been refused, so the *Frozen Lake* had attacked the superior fleet, finally ramming into a capital ship three times its size. In its own destruction, it destroyed a superior vessel and three smaller ships.

Victor was angered and saddened at the same time. He made sure to remember the captain's name. In his republic, this captain and crew would be revered.

Victor heard his brother's loud voice booming from the elevated control room that surveyed the command and control center. He heard it both in anger and in elation. A furious shrill and profanity spilled out of the darkened chamber when social media and royal stations distributed articles and principles of freedom, civilian and individuals' rights, privileges, and responsibilities, and a new form of government called a republic. It was then that he heard his own name venomously spewed out with a serious of demeaning, colorful metaphors.

When the *Frozen Lake* and the escaping civilian ships were destroyed, he then heard Prince Ramsey Venture the Elder cry out in joy and clap his hands together, as if it were a sporting event. It was then that his brother emerged for all to see. Looking at the short, round, pale prince, surrounded by his taller consorts and bodyguards, angered Victor to no end. Rose's attempt to engage him in a game of chess was well timed. His emotions stirred very quickly and he felt electrical impulses tingling his fingers. He promised himself that should the time come to face his brother, he would not look upon him for fear of what rage might come forth. The power he unleashed on Pax was fresh in his memory even though it was several weeks ago.

Days later, he was still at his bank of monitors, with two of them modified to emit a repeating coded message that he was sure anyone from Earth's past would clearly understand. With a series of dots and dashes to get the attention of the fleet via SOS, international Morse code, and another set to indicate "yes" and "no," he was sure that its brevity and carrier wave would be overlooked among the expected audiovisual communication.

"You are a cunning little spy, Prince. First the electrical surge to knock out scanning devices and now you fashioned an old transmitter with just a tap of your hand. I assume you plan to implement at the first sign of the Earth Origin System fleet's arrival?"

Victor nodded again.

"It's pretty amazing how these original Earthers came up

with this tapping Morse code. Its simplicity and efficiency are excellent for covert operations behind enemy lines. At some point I'd like to research how this was used," Rose said.

The prince nodded again and checked his makeshift transmitter just as a loud klaxon came on and a series of wall monitors shifted perspectives to Sagittarius Sector space, which appeared empty. After just a moment of silence, an old-style heavy cruiser appeared, alone and small. Victor smiled at the *Harbinger.* She was not the prettiest of design, but he knew her crew and was very happy to see them. After almost fifty days behind enemy lines, he was glad to have company.

"Now, that's a sight for sore eyes. Well, Prince, this is it."

"It sure is," he said quietly. He poised his finger on the button that was now a tapping device. As he tapped out a series of three dashes, three dots, and three dashes on the carrier wave, he saw one of the large panels come to life with a standing image of Admiral Jana Virgil. She looked regal but at the same time, she appeared either tired or angry. It was hard to tell while she remained silent. It was only after she spoke that her voice revealed resolve and conviction.

"To the royal fleet of Sagittarius Sector. You have but one chance to surrender. That is one more chance than you gave Captain Robert Dyson and the Frozen Lake *crew. For those who wish to surrender, you must start your trajectory to the fifth moon of the second planet before my transmission ends. Any ships standing in between military bases and the royal family will be obliterated. All civilians—please remain secured in place and do not attempt to intervene. We do not wish you harm. For the misled who stand and fight on behalf of the royal family, your demise will be brief and merciful..."*

The transmission suddenly cut off as if it was either an accident or something had gone wrong. From his perspective, Victor would have sworn she was not finished. He looked down at his monitor and saw that his transmission was going out.

"Well, that was short and to the point. I hope they're getting our SOS," Rose said.

"Me, too," Victor uttered.

CHAPTER 31
A DIAMOND IN THE ROUGH

He who wishes to be obeyed must know how to command. —
Niccolò Machiavelli

"Captain? I am guessing that your abruptly terminating
my message was for a reason," Devin heard Virgil say. She
was still hearing the admiral's warning as if it were a repeating
afterimage or recording when she saw Captain Martinez
unceremoniously cut Virgil off in mid-speech. To Devin's
surprise, the admiral was not perturbed as much as she was
surprised. Images of the debris field where Captain Dyson and
crew of *Frozen Lake* had made their last stand against a
superior force were still fresh in their memories. The scouts
from their battle groups had located and transmitted the black
box information of the ship's records and its last engagement.
It was disturbing and it hardened the resolve of everyone on
the *Harbinger*. Devin pushed the images out of her mind and
focused on the present.

"The Earthers say that it's an old-style communication
code used prior to computer and artificial intelligence. Simple
to use if you have the code. And since there is only one person
who was on Earth that would know it on Ploutonion or
anywhere in our sectors, I am guessing that it is Prince Victor,"
Captain Martinez explained.

"So these dashes and dots stand for letters?"

"Yes. Apparently it is repeating 'SOS,' which means

'save our ship.' It's a distress signal."

"Can we narrow the focus and locate its source?" Virgil asked.

"Yes, but we need to get closer. We're too far out. We can communicate with who's sending it, though. Jacobs has downloaded the code to the computer for transmission and interpretation. I recommend 'yes' and 'no' questions."

The bridge was quiet. Virgil called Devin and Martinez closer to the computer interface.

"Are you ready, people?" she asked. Both acknowledged yes. She waited a minute to pull her questions together and then nodded when she was ready. Martinez flipped a switch and the green light for the interface came on.

"Are you Prince Venture?" A series of dots and dashes blurted out faster than expected and was immediately translated by the computer.

"I am Victor. Lucifer One. Stop. Home in on my location as soon as you are in range. Stop. My brother is within twenty meters of my location. Stop. The base is heavily fortified. Stop. When you have my location, inform me by finishing your message you sent earlier. Stop. I will bring down the repulsion fields. Stop. Friendlies are also en route and won't survive. Stop. My status is not secure. Stop. Hurry. Stop."

Devin reminded herself to breathe. She had not thought that the prince would be able to send such a fully arranged code in dots and dashes, nullifying the need for yes or no questions. The expressions of everyone on the bridge were just as surprised. Virgil's astonishment mutated to a broad smile.

"He is a clever prince. If only all the royals were like him," Martinez said.

"If they all were, Pax, Oceania, and all of the kingdom would be at peace and prospering," Devin said. It came out more factual than bitter.

"Quite right, Captain," he responded.

"Message received and understood. ETA..." Virgil started and looked at Martinez, who in turn looked at the navigator/helmsman.

"Under five minutes," the woman said. To confirm, she shot a look at Jacobs, who was looking at another monitor and clarified the estimate.

"Four minutes, thirty-five seconds—mark."

"A little over four minutes. Hold on AJV out," Virgil said.

"Mark. Stop."

The transmission closed and Virgil was in her seat when the split screen showing two images came to life on the main viewer. Aurora appeared as she had before—pale, hairless face, clad in black, porcelain skin, and eyes sparkling a fiery red. Asbel also looked as he had before, but he was outfitted in a black exoskeleton, with even more tactical gear and weapons. More of his crew wore similar gear. The wolves were also modified in their own exogear, making them look far more dangerous than before, and yet all the additional accessories seemed devoid of technology such as light-emitting diodes that would indicate onboard electronics. Devin looked on with envious eyes as she listed off her own gear that Dias and her team were assembling. As primitive as her allies' gear looked, in the right hands, they could be very dangerous. *Wish we had gear like that.*

"Asbel? I thought you were the shipmaster? Looks like you're heading on the first wave," Virgil said. Aurora rolled her eyes as if she already knew the answer. It was obvious that Asbel and his crew were glad she'd asked.

"My first and second officer can handle the ship and the attacks from above. I plan to hit the surface where Lucifer is. I have waited my whole life for this. I will not be deprived of such an honor." As he spoke he checked his wolf's gear and then patted the creature.

"Please excuse our Rephaim allies. They are the more martial of the Sol System. While they give the impression of beasts, they are remarkably skilled, strategically brilliant, and tactically cunning," Aurora explained.

"Why, Aurora, that's the nicest thing I have ever heard you say to anyone. I am impressed," Asbel said with a toothy grin. The laugh from his crew came through loud and clear.

"Yes…well, I am the nice one. Be careful down there, Asbel. Luciel will not be pleased with me should harm come to you. She has lost one percent of her fleet and crew. She is not pleased with those losses and prefers to lose no more," she explained.

"Oh? And here I was thinking I was special."

"You are, Asbel. I said take care from me and my crew," she said. Her smile was smooth, showing perfect white teeth.

"Captain," Jacobs from communication said. "Long-range shows that a series of Sagittarius ships are fighting their way to the moon of the fifth planet."

"Looks like the royal family's fleet does not want their ranks to thin. I will take care of those ships and ensure safe passage," Aurora said. Her smiling face changed within seconds. Her eyes narrowed to slits and her jawline clenched. Devin marveled at how a perfect doll-like creature could become so menacing within milliseconds.

"Be well, Aurora. See you on the other side," Asbel said.

"Good luck to us all," Virgil added. Aurora's image faded out, leaving just Asbel.

"Admiral? We are within thirty seconds of our mark and both navigator and communication have a location of the prince," Captain Martinez said.

"We got that, Admiral," Asbel said. "Let them know that judgment day has arrived."

"Will do, Asbel. Good luck. The prince's guards and new regent will be there shortly," Virgil said. She pointed to Devin and gave her the thumbs-up as Asbel's image faded. Devin felt adrenaline flowing through her body. She nodded and moved to the hatch.

"And be careful, Marcia. You don't have wolves, advanced exoskeletons, or alien ships to protect you. I want you, your crew, and your charges back in one piece," Virgil said.

"Will do, Admiral." Devin gave her a smile and moved through the open bridge hatch to the corridor.

"So we are finally here," she said to herself. The *Harbinger*'s crew were moving rapidly throughout the ship. She made good time down to the launch bay, where *Nightfall*'s second in command, Jackson, waved her rapidly to the ramp. Dias, Ross, Athena, and Mayer had their hands full with assault rifles, heavy ordnance, and all sorts of edged weapons when the ship's klaxon sounded and Captain Martinez made his announcement.

"To arms crew! Contact with combatants in one minute. *Nightfall*—you are clear for emergency launch in thirty seconds. Once clear, drop three hundred meters directly below us and hold course. Hawks will be swooping in above you in the hundreds at the fifty-second mark. Eagles will come in to your flank with more Hawks aft. Prince Victor's coordinates will be sent to you in two minutes. Captain out. Good luck."

Devin broke into a dead run. The emergency decompression lights for the launch bay were flashing and she heard the telltale hiss of air and pressure leaving the large area. By the time she was on the ramp, it was closing and Regina was heading to the bridge with Jackson.

"All right, everyone, grab a seat or hand rails. We drop in ten," Mary said. Her voice was calm and steady. For a teenaged girl, she was the epitome of a veteran pilot. Regina, Jackson, and Devin held onto the grips while everyone else was strapped into their seats. When the countdown hit zero mark, Devin wished she had sat down, as her stomach launched into her throat and she felt wobbly on her feet.

"I hate it when she's that calm," Jackson said. He was using two hands to hold on. Devin looked at him, confused. Regina filled in the gaps.

"We only use our best pilot when we go in hot. The landing zone is contested even though the repulsion fields are now down."

"The prince did it? He got them down?" Devin asked.

"Sure did, but their defense came up fast and their ground troops are in place though they are engaged," Franklin added.

"We got boots on the ground?"

"No. Remember that Lieutenant Peter Stone, Sergeant Josephs, and his platoon? They hit the east side of their installation. It won't take long for them to be targeted and taken out no matter how fast they are. If we don't get there in under five minutes, we'll be landing at a grave site," Regina said.

Devin felt her stomach settle back and gravity returned to her feet. The ship's intercom came to life again.

"We just missed the first two waves of Hawks. We'll have an escort of Eagles in ten. I need gunners at port and starboard. I need the captain for coordinates and first officer for targeting. Whatever Prince Victor did, it worked. It might be temporary, but we're going in," Mary said calmly.

"Damn it. I really hate it. I've never heard her this calm," Franklin said.

"Marcia? Look at me," Regina said. "Be careful. It's going to be hot and it's going to be crazy down there. Watch yourself."

"Will do," Devin said. Suddenly she noticed as Regina moved through the gangway to the bridge that her cousin's outfit was a sleek, flat, black material, not showing any cleavage at all. She was nearly covered up, attired similarly to the Earthers. Devin almost said something until she felt someone pulling her in the other direction. Dias was handing her her tactical gear and weapons as she spoke.

"We're going to have to clear the ramp in less than a minute, and then figure out which group is Stone's."

"Tell me something I don't know," Devin shot back. She really didn't expect a response.

"I'm pregnant. Mayer's the father. Wish us luck," Dias said. Her tone was matter-of-fact.

Devin felt as if the wind had been knocked out of her.

"Are you kidding?"

"Nope. Snap up, Captain. We got to go. A clean dispersal. Mayer and I got flanks. Athena and Nova got point, and you got our six. Here's the images of the good guys we're trying to hook up with. And keep your helmet on. There's a lot of flak flying around down there." Dias moved off to check the other members of her team as Devin slowly regrouped.

"Unbelievable."

CHAPTER 32
SHOCK AND AWE

Never was anything great achieved without danger. — Niccolò Machiavelli

"Turn that witch off!"

The command and control crew kept their heads down as the superior officer continued to scream. Victor kept focusing on his monitor as he searched for the power coupling junction somewhere in the cavernous war room. Colonel Mortis was infuriated at Admiral Virgil's demand for an immediate, unconditional surrender. After a series of expletives and colorful metaphors, he cut the transmission with that order.

Since Victor's SOS, the massive control room had come alive with staff scurrying back and forth from audiovisual and visual devices to monitors of all kinds to make sure that what they were seeing was real. With no time to spare, he only stole a glance at five Earth ships converging simultaneously on a royal destroyer. They were more maneuverable and easily avoided being hit. They also launched chemical-based missiles in addition to standard laser and photon-based weapons. These additional—albeit primitive—weapons of mass destruction were effective in wreaking havoc on ships tailored for energy-based battles. The sheer numbers of the invading ships were also impressive, according to reports of the larger ships' landing troops and vehicles, while the smaller ships provided significant air support.

Victor concentrated on the repulsion field generator and multiple control junctions that might be able to disrupt the connection and bring down the field. Once he exhausted all of his leads, he came across one file of schematics that required retinal identification to unlock. Without hesitation, he let the scan run its course and was rewarded with the file opening up.

"You probably got ten minutes before the central computers and peripherals confirm you're a royal and enemy of state."

"I know, but I had to get to this file and I think it was a good find," Victor mumbled.

"Honestly, Prince, couldn't we just leave? I mean, the repulsion shield will eventually fail once the power is eliminated," Rose said.

"If we wait, the battle will be prolonged. If we clear a path for a frontal attack on the head of the snake, it will hasten the results." His voice was low as his hands toggled layer after layer of schematic diagrams, getting closer and closer to his goal.

"I get it, Prince, but once we find the couplings, we'll have to arc them to short out the power for ten minutes, provided the backups aren't updated. And while you are powerful, if you touch them, you will die. If by some miracle you live, it won't take them long to figure out what happened and they'll find you."

"Yes," Victor said calmly as he checked and rechecked a promising location. He looked up briefly to make sure he had the right location as well as to mnemonically memorize the entrance hatch's lock code. He also swore he heard Rose sigh before she spoke again.

"All right. Let me reiterate. You are in the planet's command and control center and it is under attack. We are more than likely twenty meters from your beloved brother, who will be happy to use you as a bargaining chip and then kill

you, or just kill you outright. We are surrounded and help is a quick two-kilometer run in any direction."

Victor nodded to himself and turned off his monitor. He adjusted his ill-fitting uniform and marched to the farthest wall where the last floor-to-ceiling images were listing engaged ships and ground forces. As he walked by stations of operators and troops looking at the monitors, he casually picked up an unattended standard rifle. He glanced upward and caught blurred images of wolves and the large Earthers he remembered as hairy and primitive in the mist. To his and everyone's surprise, the Earthers' preferred weapons were shooting ballistic, chemical-powered projectiles that made loud popping sounds. Their effect on flesh was to rip and tear it apart rather than lacerate it cleanly, as the photon-based weapon commonly used throughout the kingdom did. For his own mission he was glad to have a photon-based rifle.

"Ah, with respect, Prince, the door is in the other direction," Rose said.

"Good to know. We are heading to junction F thirty-two behind panel five D. There are exposed couplings that will serve our purpose."

"Oh, the young and the crazed. All right... I see that you have something to cut through their protective sheaths, but once exposed, how are you going to arc them? You can't touch them or use your body to get near it."

Victor removed a small wall panel and found a heavy metal hatch with just enough room for him to get through. He tapped in the twelve-digit combination and felt the lock release. He opened the small hatch with ease even though it was very heavy. He smiled as he felt it. From the small opening he saw a series of pipes, couplings, switches, and lots of circuits. He closed the hatch and took a brief look to see if there were exposed hinges in place to let the door swing. He smiled again at his luck. Curiously, nearly all the various dials, knobs, buttons, and switches had labels, with the exception of two couplings, six inches in diameter, that were hardly noticeable and easy to overlook. The schematics were clear that in case the command and control center was captured by enemy forces, the royal elite squad would gain entry here and use two specific and elegant tools to shut down the repulsion field by disrupting its energy source.

"Intruder alert! Intruder alert! Monitor RSV thirty-three has been accessed by unauthorized personnel," a muffled warning from the other side of the wall blared repeatedly.

"*Well, I guess your retinal scan has finally been identified as a bad royal,*" Rose remarked. Victor chuckled at the use of "bad royal" and the thought that many citizens saw the royal family as bad royals.

"It took them five minutes, but I needed to gain access to that top-tier file," Victor said calmly. He took aim at two heavily insulated conduits and started part one of the operation by severing the couplings with a sustained cutting laser blast.

"*All right, Prince, you will be through both of them in less than a minute. They will be exposed, but you won't be able to touch them at all.*"

"What is the probable composition of that hatch we used to get in here?" Victor asked. He maintained focus on his cutting and waited for her speculation. It took her longer than he'd expected.

"*Well, well, well. We are a devious one. Low technology, but it is effective. Where a safe power coupling cutter and insulated arc grips would be the preferred choice for such an operation, you're going in with a laser rifle to cut and a metal bridge to arc an overload. Crude but effective. There's only one thing...*"

Victor stopped his cutting as he watched the couplings' final covering melt and smoke. He was sure he felt heat filling the room with various photons and electrical power now leaking from the cut. He turned his attention back on the hatch he'd come in through and started cutting the hinges.

"As soon as I shove the metal between the coupling's contacts, it will arc. Even if I release in time, the shock will be—well, it will be…"

"Damaging? Deadly? Electrocution or evaporation? Since no one in their right mind would ever do such a thing, we have no idea what will happen." Her voice was noticeably somber.

The hatch hinges fell away and Victor tossed the weapon aside and squatted down to pull the hatch free. His plan was to move the plate and push it between the couplings in one continuous movement.

"Well, Rose, in case we don't make it, it was great living with you," he said. While elated at his ingenuity of his plan, he was greatly saddened at losing Rose. His own demise didn't seem to bother him, but he felt bad that he was to end her life along with his. He had a choice. She did not.

"It's been quite an adventure, Prince Victor. If there's another side, I hope to see you there."

By now Victor was right beside the hot, exposed coupling. It was throwing off enough heat that he was drenched through his uniform. Two laser shots just missed his head. He turned to see one soldier making her way through the hatch while another was trying to get a clear shot. He turned and took a deep breath.

"For freedom," Rose said.

"For the lives of others," Victor responded. He pushed the heavy plate right between the exposed conduits and retracted his grip as quickly as he could. While he was sure he let it go, the ensuing arc released both electrical and photon discharges, knocking him off his feet. Darkness closed all around him as visions of the first time he was shocked—in his transparent tube on Earth—came to mind. He felt as if he was floating until he felt his body abruptly stop as if it hit a wall, the floor, or both. He thought he could speak, but he felt exhausted and found himself floating again. Floating into darkness.

CHAPTER 33
STANDOFF

If an injury has to be done to a man it should be so severe that his vengeance need not be feared. — Niccolò Machiavelli, *The Prince*

"I don't need you and Mary here, Regina! I need air support, armor, and ground support in Dias's sector first and then mine! The LZ is too hot! Don't attempt," Devin shouted into her headset. She, Sergeant Luke Joseph, and about fifteen soldiers were keeping Prince Ramsey's troops bottled up at the east gate until reinforcements came. All had seemed well until she and Lieutenant Stone had divided up their forces to intercept a squad of soldiers leaving the northwest gate with a VIP. It was after they were reduced to fifty that more of Ramsey's troops flooded their area. Now at fifteen, all injured, she looked at the dead and dying around her. She glanced at her bleeding arm, side, and thigh. Her once perfect skin now had its first new set of scars. She had little time to be sad. She looked at the battlefield and sighed. A beautiful, clear day and a warm breeze made for a dichotomous backdrop to the destruction. When her headgear crackled to life, she hoped it was reinforcements and not her cousin and the suicidal young pilot coming in a descent ship behind their lines. She was still trying to hear what Regina was saying when Sergeant Joseph spoke up.

"Beta squad is down to ten. Their targets and VIP got

through. The LT and the others have to hold ground to keep the wounded safe. If you want him back, he and three others will come back."

Devin's thoughts immediately went out to Dias and Mayer, who had jumped into that group before there was time for her to find a reason to keep Dias with her. Their proximity to Lieutenant Stone's position and the chance to capture Prince Ramsey was too high to let slip, so she'd let Dias and the others go.

"Negative. Hold ground and wait for support," Devin said immediately. The roar of *Nightfall*'s drop ship was so loud she was sure that it was on a crash course. It came in so low that it clipped a number of structures and surrounding trees before coming into a tight 180-degree turn and then making a rapid descent.

"I hope to shit they brought weapons and reinforcements," Joseph said. Two laser shots erupted above the broken structure he was using for cover.

"Nope. And where the hell is air support? They were here ten minutes ago," Devin yelled back. She looked high up in the sky and saw bright flashes even in the height of daylight. She returned to her situation, assessed that her partial structure was not stable, and decided to take a chance. She broke cover to join Joseph's position just as her shattered pillar gave way to heavier blasts from the enemy.

"That was close, Captain. Not your first day in the field, I see," the sergeant chuckled. While her team fired on the enemy's position, the response in return fire was much greater. And then as suddenly as it had increased, it stopped. Devin and Joseph looked at each other to see if the other knew what was happening. Athena broke cover, squinted her eyes, and pulled back.

"They got the prince," she said quietly as she replaced a depleted energy cell in her assault rifle.

"What? No way," Sergeant Joseph said. He checked his energy level and looked around the corner. Without hesitation he changed cells and gave a report.

"Eight to nine combatants flanking twelve in the middle. Looks like Colonel Mortis is breaking cover with two privates, holding up the prince. He looks as if he might be unconscious, or worse. He's injured. Could be burns," he said. He pulled into cover and gave a stern look.

Devin found herself oddly calm and taken with the sergeant's look of concern. Prince Victor had been on the planet for weeks, and he had inspired veterans and citizens alike to stand by him. She ripped her empty cell from its chamber, replaced it, and adjusted her scope to see for herself. As she cleared her cover, she scoped the area Athena and Joseph indicated. The assessment was accurate. Her heart jumped when she saw Prince Victor was not only nonresponsive and being held up by two soldiers, but it did look like the skin on his hands and part of his face was burned and the back of his head was bloodied. She pulled back and found herself suddenly angered at his condition.

"I swear if they tortured him…" Athena started.

"Get in line, Private. I got bids on making Colonel Mortis my personal hand puppet if he did anything to Prince Victor," the sergeant snarled out. Devin started to come up with a plan but was interrupted by Private Merak.

"Captain? Sergeant? You hear that?"

Devin watched and listened. She expected to hear something ominous, like the high-pitched screech of a massive explosive or the high-pitched shriek of the gas-injected Earth missiles she had heard of late.

"I don't hear shit, Merak," Private Nova said.

"That's what I mean! There's no noise. No sounds, nothing," he went on.

Devin nodded and then turned to look back at the east

gate, where the prince was being held captive in plain view. She was sure that at any moment Ramsey's soldiers would either send a courier demanding Devin and her men surrender or just execute him.

"That's not going to happen," she uttered. As the wind shifted from head-on to behind them, she continued her observations even as a familiar sound howled in the distance. She pulled back behind cover and then heard two more howls on her flanks.

"What is that? Is it those things I've seen pictures of?" Josephs asked.

"Captain? Those howls? It's wolves, right?" Athena asked.

"Captain? Sergeant? We got friendlies coming in from the flanks and rear. It's the big Earthers with some smaller ones, too," Nova said.

Devin looked back to confirm the report and then her attention went skyward as a series of thunderclaps erupted from behind them in a clear, cloudless day. She looked back to see the vegetation, trees, and underbrush come alive with large Earthers, all tall and heavily armed in their black exoskeleton tactical suits and gear. Their primitive weapons were all poised. A meter taller than she and her team, their pale, hairless bodies with varying colored eyes made them look like the ancient death wraiths she had heard of as a child. With the rear and flanks clearly covered, Devin switched her sights back to the prince. It was easy to see that the combatants were getting spooked. She zeroed in on the leader of the group and took pleasure as his arrogant smile vanished. She watched him stare at her suddenly heavily reinforced position. More thunderclaps boomed to her right and the shattered remains of the broken wall gave way as a bolt of lightning blew it apart.

"What the hell! What are your allies using?" Josephs asked. The wall's debris was still falling from the sky when

Shipmaster Asbel and his foot soldiers appeared at Devin's side.

"It is not us this time. I am pleased you held these villains in place until our arrival."

"What took you so long?"

"A heavily armed detachment of King Talus's fleet arrived unannounced. I was impressed with their efforts," he said. His pale skin, toothy appearance, and dark eyes made him look menacing.

"Should I be worried about an aerial assault?" Devin asked, her attention now back on the motionless prince.

"Only if you count mangled metal, debris, and burning wreckage falling from space. They came in with thirty-three ships and two were allowed to escape to bear witness to the defeat," he said quietly.

Devin kept her eyes on the colonel. He was redeploying his troops in a defensive line. Another series of thunderclaps exploded and heavy clouds raced in.

"So if you're not the one with the thunder and lightning, who the hell is?" Josephs said. It was obvious that he did not like mysteries.

Devin jumped back from her scope as three large wolves jumped on the colonel, who had moved to point out possible targets for ordnance. The ferocious creatures were swift and complete, pulling the screaming leader away from his troops as they looked on in shock. Finally two raised their weapons, but nothing happened. As they looked at their weapons to see what had happened, both soldiers fell back violently, as if struck by a death blow. Devin turned to ask what their resources were and if they had weapons that could end the standoff. Asbel finished talking to someone on his own headset.

"Their leader has been taken out by our pets," Asbel said without emotion. The distant scream of a man was cut short as if to highlight the point. "Our long-range snipers are in position and two combatants have been neutralized," he continued.

"With respect, my large devilish friend, where's the air support?" Josephs asked.

"Your kin, captain of *Nightfall*, made it clear that we needed to keep all air and mechanized armor—anything with an engine, chemical, or otherwise—at least a kilometer from this position. That's why we took so long. We had to hump it a kilometer to get here," Asbel responded, and then he turned back to his headset, giving orders. He made a face and then tapped the headgear before he resorted to hand signals to his other troops.

Devin felt her eyebrows knit as she immediately looked down at her recently charged power cell. She looked closely at it and then she stood up, clear of cover, and tried to shoot her weapon into the ground. There was only a click but no blast.

"Unbelievable," she said aloud.

"Get down, Captain," Josephs and Asbel said at the same time.

"Not again," Athena said. She too got up, checked her power cells, and shook her head.

Ross was next.

"Mine's dead, too. Just like last time. Crazy, huh?" Ross added.

Josephs looked at all of them and then checked his own weapon. He looked just as confused as Devin had been when all of their weapons lost power on Earth, when they'd seen the full-grown prince for the first time and then the cylindrical metal first aid things. Asbel looked at Devin for a response.

"All of our power cells for our weapons are drained," she said. Devin slung her defunct assault weapon and pulled out her combat knife. Asbel nodded and gave hand signals after finding his headset was not functioning. A series of whistles sprang up as choruses from all around as both Earthers and wolves broke cover and moved in unison toward the encampment with weapons all pointed ahead. One of Asbel's lieutenants came up from behind.

"Sir? Our optics and communication are down. Permission to test weapons."

Asbel nodded as he took in the entire fire zone. Devin followed his gaze and knew he was figuring on moving in on the dug-in troops.

"Six warning shots above the combatants' heads. Three from distance and three short-range," he ordered. Two more whistles came up. One full minute later, six shots rang out in the silent field between both camps.

"Well. That's interesting. The Earthers, with their primitive weapons, are operational and state-of-the-art right now," Josephs commented. Even as he spoke, Devin scanned her enlarged force and noticed that the smaller Earthers were present as well. They stayed in groups of five while the larger-framed Earthers moved in threes.

"We got your back, Captain. However, if our prince is dead, there will be no prisoners taken," Asbel hissed out. Devin nodded in agreement. As they closed in on the enemy soldiers, Devin looked several meters to her right to see Mary walking with Regina behind her. Devin could see that Mary was determined to reach Prince Victor as soon as possible. Devin would have waved her off due to the danger of combat, but Mary's hands and shoulders were aglow with brilliant red and white light. She was also surrounded by wolves, and bands of large and small Earthers, all heavily armed, and all clad in formfitting black tactical apparel and gear. Devin picked up her pace to catch up with Regina.

"Mary says he's alive but unresponsive," Regina whispered.

"How does she know?" Devin asked.

"She says she feels him."

"Oh. That figures."

Mary stopped in front of the soldiers that still trained their nonfunctioning weapons at her.

"Your weapons are useless. Ours are not. Drop your weapons, form a single line, and put your hands on your heads," she said. Her voice was older, imperious, and with no hint of fear.

"We are Prince Ramsey's royal guard," a sergeant started to say.

A bolt of lightning flew from Mary's extended hand and snatched the offending soldier off the ground and then tossed him several meters against a wall, where he was impaled on exposed metal support rods. Devin was surprised at how casually Mary took a life, without reservation.

"I will not ask again," she said quietly.

"I would do it. She will kill you all," Asbel added. The sounds of multiple manual weapons cocking, along with the wolves' growls and howls, supported the recommendations. Devin waited and then she saw Mary's hands glowing brighter, white, blue, and red at the same time.

"Prince Ramsey's guards—stand up and drop your weapons. Get your feet on the line and put your hands on your heads," a young, nervous voice shouted from their ranks. The soldiers moved quickly and left their weapons where they were and formed a single line. They stood like stones with hands on their heads.

Devin, Josephs, and Regina were at Prince Victor's side. It took little time to determine that he was not dead, but he was unresponsive. His hairless, light brown body had first- and possible second-degree burns along both hands and arms, part of his chest, his neck, and the left side of his face. He had two large gashes on his head and there was blood coming from his mouth. Still, he had a pulse and was breathing.

"Damn it," Josephs said.

"We have to get him back to *Nightfall*," Regina said. Both she and Athena went to pick him up. Devin turned to see Mary watching the silent soldiers. Asbel and the Earthers stood right behind her. By the time she too was behind her, she heard Mary ask a question in a deep, dark voice that left no doubt as to the gravity of their situation. The growling wolves with flesh and blood still dripping from their teeth punctuated the deadly atmosphere.

"I will ask this question once: Where is Prince Ramsey?"

CHAPTER 34
HEAD TOWARD THE LIGHT

The best fortress which a prince can possess is the affection of his people. — Niccolò Machiavelli, *The Prince*

"So this is where?" Victor said again. The floor and air were warm, but it was hard to see anything in the darkness. He had no idea where he was and how he'd gotten to this dark place, but at least the throbbing headache, burning fire in all of his nerves, and ache in his muscles were all gone. It was clear to him that he was moving around by his own will, but he couldn't feel his legs or his weight on his feet. Nonetheless, he sensed that there was more to this opaque, empty space. He moved in nearly a direct line for what seemed to be a long time until he saw a faint, shimmering light. As it was the only visible thing, he moved toward it.

"Well, finally this is something. I wonder what it is?" Not sure how he was moving, he continued in the same direction. As the light grew, he waved his hands in front of his eyes to see if they were injured. When nothing appeared, he closed his eyes and reopened them. The only difference was the presence of the dim light growing as he got closer.

"Hmm. Is this death? Is this it? I mean, I thought it would be more than this. Maybe this is hell? Dark, empty, void of company…"

"*Not so fast, Prince,*" an all too familiar voice said. He felt his face crinkle up in a happy expression.

"Rose! It's great to hear you."

"I'm happy to be here in light of that massive jolt you took! I'm also surprised that I made it here, wherever here is," Rose said.

"I know. I can't see a thing except for that faint light up ahead," Victor said.

"Me, too. I have no idea where we are, but as soon as I saw the light, I moved toward it. You think it's our final place? I've always wondered what death would be like. I didn't think it was a place, though I'll be happy to see for myself."

"I was hoping not to see it for a long time."

"After all we've been through, you actually thought you'd live longer than you had? Dropped into Hell as a boy and then living in a hostile environment for years, you thought you were going to live a long time? I'm surprised you lived this long. Thrilled, but surprised. You're not offended, are you?"

It looked to Victor as if the light was slowly getting larger.

"Offended by you? Never, Rose. I'm glad you're here. Seems like we're meant to be in the adventure together. Hard to think of you not being here."

"That's sweet. It is possible that the overload might have burned me out, but it has become clear to me that my presence is now deeply embedded into your cortex and limbic system. If I die it probably means you're dead, too."

"You figured this out now?" His tone must have made clear how surprised he was, as Rose's response was immediate.

"Yeah, I know, right? I always thought that I occupied a small area of your brain, but since my arrival here in this void, I've been able to see that my artificial intelligence has expanded from the original placement site and has attached to nearly every part of your cortex and limbic system."

"So you figured all of this out here?"

"Sure did. I think this place is somewhere between consciousness and unconsciousness, like hidden neural pathways. I think that we're in some kind of coma."

"A coma, huh? Well, I guess that's better than being dead. I was pretty sure that arc was going to kill us. Well, I'm glad we have each other to keep us company. Any idea what that light up ahead is?"

"None, but we have some time to go see. By the way, if we ever do make it out of here, and if Devin, Admiral Virgil, Luciel, and Miss Large Mammary Glands make it, what are you going to do about Prince Ramsey?"

"Banish him. I will banish him and his consort to Earth." Victor was surprised at how quickly the answer came to him. He also immediately thought of their children and other royals making reparations by spending their time rebuilding the planet Pax. He figured that while they were less guilty of their parents' and relatives' crimes, they should be allowed to put their powers to the good of the people. But for his brother and his betrothed, and his father and mother, banishment to a hell he'd endured seemed fitting, with one noticeable difference—there would be no chance of rescue or escape.

"Well, that sounds fitting, final, and well thought out. How did you come to that decision?"

"I don't know. I think that this place helps figure things out. I had no idea before we got here, but when you asked, the answer came without hesitation."

"That's funny. Same thing with me. Somehow I know the answers to a lot of things. I had no idea how much I had grown into your neural net until I got here. Maybe this place isn't too bad."

"Maybe not."

"So you would banish them to Earth? Prince Ramsey and all the others?"

"Yes. Princess Carol, his wife, and our parents, King

Talus and Queen Vega. All the others that were against Jason will suffer the same fate." Even though his voice was even, there was anger and an ache in his heart. He felt it as if it were a physical pain.

"So they will all go to Hell, where they must have abandoned all hope."

"Yes. What was that old Earth piece of literature about ruling in hell is better than being in paradise?"

"'Better to reign in Hell than serve in Heaven.' John Milton wrote it millennia ago. Still appropriate, I'd say. You are quite the philosophical pragmatist. You solved the problem of not killing your family and punishing them by taking away the thing they value the most—their power over their subjects. Pretty powerful justice."

"I suppose we should first confirm that we are alive and not dead."

"Probably. I bet we're alive. So the whole family goes to our old hangout?"

"Yup. They can rule over the wastelands of my former home under the watchful eyes of the Red Cross and the Earthers. Walk the desolate lands and fend for their lives with more resources to start than we had. They'll have one another, at least. Maybe it will build character? Maybe some good will come of them?"

"Now that is hell. Now what was that… 'Hell is others'? Something like that. Pretty apt here, I would say. By the way, is that light getting brighter?"

Victor, who had been lost in thoughts and discussion, shifted his focus and saw that Rose was right. While not profoundly larger or brighter, it was steady and expanding.

"I think you are right. I wonder what it is?"

"Me, too."

Victor swore he could feel the corners of his mouth crinkling upward in the form of a smile.

"Just like old times," he said.

"*You know? I was just thinking that,*" Rose said.

CHAPTER 35
THIS STORY SHALL THE GOOD MAN TEACH HIS SON

Tardiness often robs us opportunity, and the dispatch of our forces. — Niccolò Machiavelli

"I'm so sorry, Dias," Devin kept repeating. The emergency medical evacuation center was filled mostly with combatants who had offered resistance to the invasion. Once Prince Ramsey and his fleeing troops had been tracked and captured, Devin found her way to the medevac center where Lieutenant Stone and his few remaining soldiers stood guard over the dead and the wounded. His vacant look and downcast stare indicated how he and his team had hung on to life after trying to thwart Prince Ramsey's escape.

Devin's gaze caught the handful of identification tags Stone held. With Earthers surrounding the survivors, it was easy to see that many of the soldiers sent to guard the escape route had now departed. Lieutenant Dias was semiconscious but well aware that her paramour, Mayer, was gone. Putting rank and war aside, Devin hugged her as Dias lay prone, silently weeping at her loss. Dias had also lost her entire right leg below the knee. In addition, her hands were burned and her face scarred. *The scars will heal and she'll get a prosthetic. But the loss of Mayer...*

"I should have been there," Devin said quietly to Dias.

"You found our prince and got the intel on Prince Ramsey," she muttered.

"Too much, Dias. The cost is too much." Devin was not one to cry, let alone allow emotions to emerge in a fire zone, but seeing her lieutenant battered and nearly half of her team gone was too much. She allowed just a few tears and held on to Dias to comfort her friend.

"The baby is still alive, Marcia. At least that's something I can hold onto. At least that's a part of Charles that lives," she said weakly. As Dias spoke, Devin lowered her back to the cot and watched her fall into a sedated slumber. She looked on and was able to block out all the sounds, smells, and voices of organized chaos all around her. Devin was looking down at her friend when she heard Captain Stone's tired, grave voice.

"She and her squads held ground. We were outnumbered and outgunned, but they managed to hold on to delay their escape anyway," he said.

Devin nodded. She had been to the battlefield. There was a large contingent of the enemy still dead on the field. And while Stone and Dias held a chokehold on the exit, the superior-sized force had only one way to go, and that was through their defenses.

"Even as she pulled her team out, they kept at her. Private Mayer protected her when she went down…"

"Stone. I…know. I get it. We all lost good people today," Devin said.

Stone fell silent. It was plain to see that he was not only saddened by the loss of his troops, but angry that he had few injuries and nothing to show for it. Almost nothing to show for it. Devin looked closely at him and found something that might make him feel something had gone right.

"Captain? Asbel and Aurora say that Prince Ramsey sustained a narrow-focused laser shot that cleanly severed his ear. Two more inches over and the shot would have been a kill," Devin said, her eyes narrowed as she watched his response.

"I missed. Privates James and Thomas took out his immediate guards. They boxed him in and managed to get close, too. If I was just a little closer, I would have had him. Maybe his troops would have given up if he was dead," he said. His voice was sad and frustrated at the same time. He gazed at his own set of military identification tags. Troops he knew, just like the ones she knew in her command. Devin felt for the soldier. It was easy to see that he not only thought of his team but was a thinker. If it was her, she was sure she would think and feel the same way.

She was about to say more when Aurora appeared with Regina by her side. It was odd seeing her cousin in similar garb as the Earthers, looking just as imperious. The other Earthers, both average-sized and large with the interspersed wolves, were all about ensuring a secure zone for their own wounded.

"It's bad, isn't it, Marcia?" Regina said as she stepped ahead and hugged her. The triage center fell quiet and the world seemed just a little bit safer as she embraced her cousin.

"Bad. Many good people are gone. Dias and the baby are alive…"

"What! Dias is pregnant?" The shock was evident.

"I didn't know until we were heading in. She covered the back door, which became the primary route of escape."

"That low-down, slack-jawed maggot, arrogant, fat son of a…"

"It's all right, Regina. How's the prince?"

She sensed Captain Stone moving in closer and the chatter around the medevac hushed all at once, both Earthers and the warring factions. Regina shook her head as if to clear her thoughts and pulled away from Marcia's hug. She did her best to focus on something constructive. Devin was very impressed with her younger cousin's ability to shift gears. Her years as captain and guiding her team had surely created her leadership abilities and strong character. It was easy to see that Regina was aware that all ears were bent to hear what she had to say.

"Prince Ramsey of Capricorn is in custody. He is on an Earth ship heading to Admiral Virgil. *Our* prince is alive and recovering from his sabotage that lowered the repulsion field. He is in a medically induced coma so he can heal. All medical indicators are positive. He will recover. He should be dead, though, based on what he did, but he's recovering."

Regina turned to Captain Stone and handed him a folded letter.

"Captain Stone, Admiral Virgil would like you and your team to come back with us to her ship. Based on multiple reports of your keeping our prince safe and your heroics for his flag and cause, she is sure Prince Victor will want you by his side when he awakes."

"Yes, ma'am," Stone said. He didn't even look at his orders. Regina turned but was stopped by Stone's question.

"Ma'am? I was the master of arms on the *Frozen Lake* under Captain Dyson. Is it true what they say?"

Devin watched Regina's eyes narrow and her jaw tighten.

"Yes," Aurora said before Regina could respond. Similar to others of her kind, her pale, hairless skin, black uniform, and sharp auburn-colored eyes enhanced what she said, as if she were a stone speaking.

"*Frozen Lake*, captain, and crew lost their lives in the protection of innocent civilians. We narrowed and identified the engine trail signatures of the offending ships. *Frozen Lake*'s logs displayed the names of the attacking ships. They were immediately destroyed upon entering this system. It won't bring their lives back, but their souls may rest a bit better. I am sorry for your loss, both on the field and in space."

"You knew Captain Robert Dyson?" Stone asked. Devin could easily understand why the captain would be surprised that an invading alien force would know of a shipmaster, no matter how well known he might have been.

"Admiral Virgil and the ship's flight recordings supplied the critical information. Data seized from the Capricorn home world's main military computers gave more background. Similar to your prince, our Lucifer One, he and his crew believed in fairness and fidelity to others," Aurora said. Her motionlessness was in great contrast to her passionate response. *They are all stoic. Just like the Xenons.*

Stone nodded. Devin moved closer to her cousin to speak for just their small grouping to hear.

"How is Mary?"

"She's prepping the descent ship. I want to get back to *Nightfall*. That's why I'm here. I want to evac all our wounded. Aurora will make sure we get on our way. The Xenon fleet has also arrived, and Luciel is negotiating a joint provisional government for both sectors until each is able to form elections," Regina said.

"Elections? Really? That could be a while."

"I know, right. Looks like the documents the prince had Captain Stone and his team disperse really took off and have captured the hearts and minds of the citizens. And while the Xenons are cryptic about their feelings, they are more than willing to work with these Earthers to maintain security while the sectors get their houses in order postroyals. I guess the Xenons are used to long-term projects."

"Let's hope they have better luck than they did on Earth," Devin said as she remembered confronting Theta on the Earth-Xenon connection.

"Yes. The Xenons were partially successful. They transplanted the survivors out here. Not bad, really, for the most part," Aurora said, her mouth hinting at a smile.

"For the most part," Regina repeated. Devin caught the surprised look on Captain Stone's face. It was clear he was aware that there was an inside joke going on that he was not privy to. Devin smiled but then looked back at her sedated lieutenant, injured and alone.

"Dias and everyone is coming with us?" she asked.

"We don't leave anyone behind," Regina said as she followed her cousin's gaze.

CHAPTER 36
THIS JUST IN...

The main foundations of every state, new states as well as ancient or composite ones, are good laws and good arms - you cannot have good laws without good arms, and where there are good arms, good laws inevitably follow. — Niccolò Machiavelli, *The Prince*

"Just to recap: We know that Prince Victor Venture IX, Prince Jason's younger brother and heir to the Sagittarius Sector, has survived an electrocution incurred when he sabotaged the planet's command and control center. He is reported to have recovered and is resting. His acts allowed for soldiers loyal to him and these Earthers to find and capture Prince Ramsey of Capricorn Sector, who seized control of our sector when Prince Jason died," the newscaster reported.

As he spoke, images played of devastation in space with royal ships shattered and smashed, littering the star field, and then were replaced by shots of birdlike black and gray ships flying over columns of captured royal military while both soldiers loyal to Prince Victor and Earthers with their wolves corralled them into makeshift detention camps. Images of war shifted back to the tired-looking newscaster, who shifted from one table to another before continuing his extended report. Images of a blue-and-white planet enshrouded by a sparkling green field came on-screen. A subtitle indicated the planet's names as Hades, Hell Planet, Earth, and Third Planet of

Origins Sector.

"While this flash onslaught and lightning war appears to have subsided, the Xenon fleet has arrived. Their intentions were made clear by a spokesman, Theta, who reports they are familiar with these Earthers and the documents of governing that Lieutenant Stone and his soldiers released on behalf of Prince Victor. These principles and articles of governing are surprising in both their breadth of freedom and the responsibilities given to civilians. Three scholars from the planet Pax, the planetary teaching and learning center that was nearly destroyed several months ago by Prince Ramsey, report that they, too, have some surviving ancient documents on this form of governing. Our report is that Admiral Jana Virgil has asked for a contingent of Xenons to assist in Prince Victor's efforts to rebuild the university planet. Please refer to the three tabs displayed below for Admiral Jana Virgil's service record. Presently, she is the highest-ranking military official of this sector and supreme commander of the invading forces."

The newscaster shifted to yet another tablet and squinted his eyes to see something.

"In response to this invasion and the fall of Capricorn and Sagittarius Sectors, King Talus gave the following interstellar announcement:

"'I do not recognize the authority of the rebel leader Jana Virgil, and refuse to accept defeat. I will not stand by idly as my rebellious, traitorous son Victor plays out his temper tantrum. I demand he release the rightful leader of Capricorn and Sagittarius. I insist that Victor release Prince Ramsey and Princess Carol and return them to power. I demand the Xenons insist these Earther bastards leave our sectors in peace. Upon my royal name, I will make these freakish creatures from Origins Sector wish they never left their hellish corner of their pathetic solar system!'"

The voice of the king, though older, was strong. His

anger, hatred, and desire for revenge were not missed by the newscaster as his expression went from serious to surprised. It took him mere seconds to shift to a more neutral stance.

The newscaster continued, "Prince Victor gave a systems-wide response."

The image shifted to a young, dark, hairless man whose skin had obviously been recently burned, scarred, and pitted. Still, his arms folded over his chest and his dark eyes were piercing and his voice calm. He stood solidly in the middle of the screen in a black uniform fitted with knives and Earth weapons. Right behind him were two similarly attired women—one was very young, hairless, with perfect skin, and another, standing close to the younger woman, was older, with dark hair and perfect skin. Behind them stood the familiar faces of Lieutenant Peter Stone, Sergeant Luke Josephs, and Admiral Jana Virgil. There were other soldiers loyal to Prince Victor, as well as four Xenons and several Earthers—the smaller ones and the larger-framed ones with their wolves.

"On behalf of my royal family, I apologize to the citizens of Capricorn and Sagittarius," Victor said. "In an effort to right the wrongs of tyranny and abuse of power, I have released my armies from Hell to topple this form of government. Absolute power corrupts absolutely. As a result, the hard work ahead is to build a confederation where the power lies within the citizens' hands. I turn to the wisdom of the Xenons and leaders like Admiral Jana Virgil, Captain Marcia Devin, Lieutenant Peter Stone, and others for the long-term task of creating this new form of government, with its safeguards and commerce. For military support, safety, and sector security, I turn to my Earthers—Luciel, Asbel, and Aurora.

"In regards to my father's demands, the answer is no. Should you wish to pick up your son, my brother Ramsey, and his consort, Carol, send one ship under the symbol of peace to Origins Sector, Earth, and start your search. Both Ramsey and

Carol will be given provisions and the freedom to walk the planet. Further, stay away from planet Pax. I will rebuild the knowledge your son tried to completely destroy.

"Citizens of Capricorn and Sagittarius, creating a new way of life will be a long process. It will take years to fully realize your rights and full freedom. The infrastructure of food and medicine distribution that Prince Jason fostered will be expanded. But to have more, you must invest yourselves, your time and energy. Freedom is not free. Your contribution will be needed to provide solutions to problems, constructive ideas to criticism, actions to thoughts. It will be difficult. But I know that when the tenth anniversary of this people's movement comes, you will look to the other sectors and be happy you are here, and hopeful that your cousins across the stars will join you in your prosperity and freedom. I will be with you, Prince Victor Venture IX, ambassador of Capricorn and Sagittarius Sectors to Origins Sector. Thank you."

The newscaster nodded and turned to another person, a female in scholar's robes.

"Well, there you have it. A declaration of independence, and an outline of the tasks ahead. To comment further on Prince Victor's speech, especially the telling part where he referred to himself as ambassador rather than prince or even king of the sectors, is scholar Melinda Benton Job, specialist and expert in political science and history of the university planet Pax, to elaborate more on this historic occasion…"

CHAPTER 37
BETTER TO REIGN IN HELL THAN SERVE IN HEAVEN

A prince is also esteemed when he is a true friend and a true enemy. — Niccolò Machiavelli, *The Prince*

"It's very pretty, actually," Victor said. He followed the ridgeline that led to his former home on Earth, where he'd spent much of his childhood. Earth was still a harsh place, with its strong gravity, bright, hot sun, dry wind, and multiple predators. While species AB180 was now the large spartan fighters of the planet, the Rephaims, other hominids, had taken their place in the wild. They were smaller, faster, and cunning, but nonetheless hostile. They were mostly in the old cities that had been abandoned hundreds and thousands of years ago. The wolves had been domesticated by the Rephaims, leaving a large feline, saber-toothed smilondon species as a top predator.

"All these changes in months," he said.

"Once again it's that time-space anomaly that's led to all these changes. From our perspective, it's been months. For witnesses here, it's been generations."

"Those settlements over there are new."

"Based on what I was able to get from Luciel and Asbel, they are only two hundred years old." Victor nodded in full appreciation of how the living structures were embedded in the mountainside, shielding them from the sun and elements while taking advantage of geothermal air-conditioning. For the first time in months, he actually felt warm. Even with significant

activity behind him—the movement of soldiers transporting supplies and personnel from *Nightfall*'s drop ship—he looked across the vista and wondered what it might be like to return to his lodge and forget about heading back into space.

"Is it true the Earthers left my shelter as a museum?"

"More as a living shrine. Reportedly their youth are taken there to show them what it was like for you. They also show them the laboratory in the underground facility where both you and their different species were created. New data show that the original Earthers called the project of repopulating this planet the Lucifer Project, hence your name, Lucifer One. You're kind of a big thing here. Sure you want to leave?"

"Don't start, Rose."

"I'm just saying."

Victor heard the distant, distinct sounds of chains moving closer. He moved his scarred hands from across his healing chest to his sides as he remained looking out. The warm wind felt good, except the newly forming epidermal skin was sensitive to the light and wind. Without looking behind him, he could hear the activity slow to a stop. The sun of the Origins Sector was bright yellow. When he returned to Earth, he felt the planet's gravity pull at him, as it had the first time he landed when he was twelve. What was different this time was that he had been there before and it took him less than twenty minutes to acclimate. The others were taking much longer.

"Prince Victor," Captain Devin said. "Prince Ramsey and his wife, Princess Carol, wait to hear from you…" She was interrupted by a very angry voice.

"Look at me, Victor! I am the eldest! How dare you treat me like a common criminal? I am not an animal to be chained," Ramsey said with vehemence.

Victor found himself nodding as if he were agreeing.

"Well. I guess he thinks he's still in charge," Rose said.

The silence was thick except for the sound of the wind

and the periodic cry of a bird of prey. Victor could tell that his prisoners were less than two meters away. He could hear their breathing along with that of the soldiers who surrounded them. Focusing on the small bands of mist below the ridgeline, he tilted his head slightly so that he might be heard while his back was turned.

"As you are family, I give you the gift of all that you see. More than that, I give you two weeks' supplies and your spouse for company—much more than I had when I arrived here."

"You will not leave me here! I demand you release me and relinquish all you have taken from me," Ramsey hissed out.

"No, my brother. I give you a new life. I will not take your life as you took Jason's. I will not return to you what was not yours to start," Victor stated.

"What do you want? Do you want me to submit to you? To bend my knee and serve you?"

"'Better to reign in Hell than serve in Heaven.' I know you would never serve me. I would not ask. Here is your new kingdom," Victor said as he stretched out his hands to the wastelands. The wind died down suddenly and the warm breeze vanished.

"What did I do to deserve this?" he heard a weak voice cry out. "What of my children? Heirs to the sectors," Princess Carol asked.

"Clemency for all of them. They are on planet Pax to assist with rebuilding there. And as for you, you are here because you shared his power with zeal. You enjoyed it. And when my brother was killed by your husband, you did nothing. My father and mother did nothing. They will join you here as well someday," Victor said calmly. His attention was caught by a brief movement of a large-toothed smilondon that emerged from the mist and then returned. *Impressive. It's fast, too.*

"But I am not trained for this," she said through sobs.

"Neither was I, and I was twelve, with far less than you will have."

"Just kill us then, you miserable little boy! Look at me, or are you too frightened?" Ramsey said.

Victor let silence sit in the air again. He unfolded his arms and looked at his scars.

"No, brother. I am different from you. I will not kill my brother. I will not look at you, either. You are nothing to me. Your punishment is banishment."

"My father will come for me and he will bring his entire fleet," Ramsey started.

"No, he will not. If he brings one ship under a flag of peace, he will be allowed to look for you both and bring you to their home. I would not hold my breath, Ramsey. Do you really think that a king who would allow his younger son to be killed in his sleep and his other son murdered by his own brother would risk his own safety to find you?" Victor asked. When no answer came, he nodded his head.

"Not to worry, though, Ramsey. Both King Talus and Queen Vega will join you. It will be years for you and Carol before I find them, but they will join you here. Granted, the time-space distortion might make it a generation or so from now, but that is the price for being evil."

"Who do you think you are? How could you do this to your very family? How could you turn on the very blood you came from? Why would you do this?" Carol said.

"You could have had everything! All you needed to do was to go to our father. Instead, you destroyed our way of life by leading an invading force to our very homes! Is this the tragedy you want?" Ramsey's voice was defiant and angry.

Their questions triggered memories of old stories of men and women enduring great hardships and surviving. Empty of anger, hubris, or revenge, Victor focused on his thoughts instead of his brother's rage. A flash of poetry or some archaic literature he swore must have come from his time in the transparent chamber below flooded his thoughts. The words formed before his eyes as he spoke.

"'The real tragedy of life is not being limited to one talent, but in failing to use that one talent.'"

The pause was palpable until Victor sighed and spoke again.

"You and my family had a chance to be benevolent, just, and kind. You let it go. Jason was the shining example of all these and more, but you snuffed the flame of hope out. And why? Power. I can only hope that my talents approach my brother Jason's. But to be clear, I will use my talents."

"There is nothing here. This planet is a wasteland. And these Earthers will not embrace us. We will be alone," Carol sobbed.

"You will survive, and may even grow. This place molded me. 'Solitude is the nurse of enthusiasm, and enthusiasm is the true parent of genius.' You're lucky to be here," Victor said quietly.

The wind picked up from the west, reviving a hot, dry breeze. Victor realized that no one spoke in addition to all hominid sounds behind him. A smilondon's distant roar came from the east and another predator responded with a howl from the west. Without looking back, he spoke one last time to his brother and his spouse.

"Good-bye and good luck, Ramsey and Carol. Master of the guard?"

"Yes, Prince Victor," Devin said.

Victor took one last look around the land that was once his home and sighed.

"Release the prisoners to their new domain. The Earthers will make sure not to interfere with them and let them live their rest of their lives alone."

"Yes, my prince."

"Thank you," Victor said and walked away without once looking back at his brother and sister-in-law.

"Don't you walk away from me! I'm your older brother! Obey me!"

Victor walked away without hesitation to the descent ship while looking up at the clear sky. The wind blew and the howls of the predators echoed in the distance. He wished he had time to see the old ruins and the new hominid species, but he knew that time was slipping away in space, as time experienced on Earth was slow but invariably faster than elsewhere.

"*He's a real class act, Prince,*" Rose said. Exasperation was evident in her voice.

"He really has no idea how lucky he and his spouse are. They can now spend all their time exploring the secrets of this world."

"*I don't think they see it that way. They want the power. The food, feast, adulation, sex, and influence. By the way, you were quite the orator there. Milton, E. W. Howe and Isaac D'Israeli from Earth? What fine choices. Of all the things to say, how did you think of them? You know no one understands you.*"

"They just came to me. I wish I could say I was original, but all seemed apt. You are so right about me and Ramsey. I see it so differently. I would love to stay here and find the secrets of this place."

"*I know. You miss this place, don't you, Prince?*"

"It shows?"

"*Sure does. Anything would be better than going back to find your parents and other siblings, who have wreaked havoc on our known galaxy. And rebuilding another form of government? Not easy. Nothing wrong with just walking away, you know. You did liberate two sectors and free the civilians from the yoke of oppression, and started a path to self-determining government, as difficult as that will be. You're entitled to walk away, and no one would think less of you."*

As Victor's feet hit the metal ramp leading to the descent ship's interior, he immediately flashed to what he thought his former mentor, Bishop Brent Miles of Pax, would say about Rose's thoughts.

"Maybe. But what would Bishop Miles say we should do?"

It was rare that Rose delayed, but since Miles was in essence her creator, he could understand her taking time to be thoughtful.

"He'd say there's no end to ensuring freedom of thinking."

As Victor passed by several empty seats and locked-down crates, he heard music coming from the cockpit. He smiled at the thought of Mary still finding enjoyment in flying ships with music blaring.

"Well, I guess we have to keep going," he said.

"When you put it like that, I guess you're right."

CHAPTER 38
SECOND STAR TO THE RIGHT

It is not titles that make men illustrious, but men who make titles illustrious. — Niccolò Machiavelli, *Discourses on Livy*

"No way! He didn't even look back at them? After all he's been through, he didn't even look at him? Didn't even take a moment to relish in the glory?" Regina asked. Devin was still smiling when she told her cousin how the prince had just walked away from his brother and Carol. Regina's jaw was slackened and her eyes blinked rapidly.

"You look just like you did when you were seventeen when I told you Gavin Marcus wanted to ask you out."

"Well, that was big news back then, but this? Wow! You were gone for days, too. Crazy that it was only two hours for you," Regina said. Both women walked along the narrow corridor of the *Nightfall*, which was filled with more personnel than usual. The ship's engines were louder and the vibration more noticeable, but overall Devin was glad to be with her cousin. She was also getting used to her cousin's change in wardrobe to basic black without cleavage and skin showing. While her figure was clearly enhanced by the material like all the other Earthers, her long hair made her stand out.

"So we're heading back to Sagittarius Sector to rendezvous with Admiral Virgil and the *Harbinger*. Dias and the others are doing well, fortunately," Regina reported. Devin visibly sighed and breathed for the first time in days. She hated leaving Dias and her injured team behind, but upon waking from his coma, the prince had insisted on bringing his kin to Earth.

"It would have been so much easier to just kill this Ramsey," Regina muttered.

"Maybe. But I think the prince prefers that Ramsey not be seen as a martyr. I guess he also doesn't want to kill his own brother. He's kind of good that way. He must be adopted."

"I would have thought that, too. Mercy for his nieces and nephews, an opportunity to rebuild Pax, and letting his brother live…"

"Well, to live on Earth with its crazy gravity and time-space distortion thing is not exactly a great deal if you ask me," Devin said.

"Maybe the experience will make Ramsey a better person," Regina commented as she opened the heavy hatch leading to the launch bay near the engine room. Devin tilted her head and thought back to what Prince Victor had said about solitude, talents, and being better to rule in hell. She was surprised at how young the prince was and yet how mature, even wise he had become in the short time she had known him. She was still thinking when she heard muffled music behind the descent ship's cargo bay door. She looked at the heavy reinforced doors and then back at Regina. Her cousin had been pretty tight-lipped about why they'd come to the launch bay. With so much on her mind, she hadn't pressed much to find out.

"Really? Is she playing that loud music and dancing again? She's going to go deaf," Devin warned.

Regina smiled and seemed to take her time in responding, as if she were looking for the words.

"More like *they* will go deaf," she corrected as she pressed the hatch release to open the doors. As soon as they opened, festive, loud music with heavy drums and string instruments flowed out. Devin covered her ears and looked in to see a strange sight. As expected, Mary was dancing with multiple crew members. In addition, there were a number of Earthers of both species—average height and large size—also dancing as well as playing the music. Still outfitted in their battle garb, the black-attired, hairless, pale bodies all glistened with sweat as they played and jumped around with *Nightfall*'s crew and various ground troops. The smell of cooked meat and perfume filled the air. And while many were dancing, gyrating, drinking, and eating, there were a handful of interspecies couples and triads kissing in the shadows.

"This is unbelievable! How long has this party been going on?" Devin shouted.

"As soon as you got back, the prince asked me if he could have guests from Earth and the other planets here to have a party and celebrate with our crew. Since we're in the Origins Sector surrounded by Earth ships, I thought now would be a good time. The Earthers brought the food, drink, and music. They do know how to party," Regina explained.

"Earth's history during times of war and peace always had music," Devin heard from behind her. She turned rapidly to see Prince Victor standing with his arms folded over his chest, watching the same events. Even though he had scars and his skin was much lighter, even pinkish where it was healing, he looked both youthful and mature. *A leader*, Devin thought.

The music was still blaring and the gyrations and movements were quickening.

"Prince Victor? Have you come to watch?" Regina asked. There was a sly smile on her face.

"No. I have come to partake," he said. His eyes were alight with fire and he moved slightly to catch the beat. Devin's look of surprise was not missed. Royals never were among the people, let alone to celebrate and dance among the troops.

"Earthers have a different history steeped in tradition, pomp, and circumstance. It also has a history of celebration once an ordeal has passed so as to rejuvenate for the next one. A strong bond among soldiers and leaders makes for a formidable foe. If we are to fight together and live together, then we should rejoice together," he said.

Something in the crowd caught his eyes and made him smile. He pointed to a couple kissing in the shadows. Right next to them were two triads of males and females, Earthers and Sagittarius soldiers, doing the same thing.

"Wow," was all Devin could muster.

"So I take it there's more to come," Regina said in a loud voice to be heard.

Devin watched the prince look at her and nod.

"More to come, Captains. There are ten other sectors, and four of them are clamorous for the rights that we set free in Sagittarius and Capricorn Sectors. The Xenons are dug in to help with reconstructing a new government based on a form of governing that worked only once on Earth, and there's the little thing with my parents still out there and not happy with me. There is more to come. But until then, Captains, it is time to celebrate," he said as he held both hands out in the direction of the party. Regina nodded in approval and moved as if she were escaping a burning building.

"For prince and cause," she said as she moved directly to the table of meat and drinks.

"Captain? Just a word of warning," the prince said before she moved too far from earshot. The loud music made it very difficult.

"Yes, my prince?"

"Be wary of the drinks called scotch and whiskey. I tried them earlier and they make our drinks pale in effect. I had simply two sips of each and once you get beyond the taste, the aftereffects are stunning," he said.

Devin was still taking in the advice when her cousin came back to grab her. It was as if they were teens again back home on the farm.

"Hey, Marcia? Aurora and Asbel are doing some kind of drinking game in the corner. Wow! And they want us to try the drinks they brought—some things called rum, whiskey, and scotch. Sounds interesting," she said as she led her away.

Devin looked back to see the prince still smiling. He waved and walked toward Mary, who was dancing with great skill and enthusiasm. For the first time in a long time, she felt happy, almost carefree. While there were many things to consider, plan, and worry about, she felt she could just relax and enjoy the moment.

The prince is right. Enjoy the moment. Who knows when we'll be able to celebrate again, she thought. Without much hesitation, she took a mug from Asbel and joined her cousin and Aurora in a large gulp of liquid fire. After the initial burn, Devin nodded in approval.

"This stuff is really good," Regina said with her arm wrapped around Devin's waist.

"It sure is," she responded. Her smile felt genuine and relaxed. It had been a long time.

ABOUT THE AUTHOR

In addition to the award-winning Birds of Flight series—*Albatross*, *Raven*, *Eagle*, *Falcon*, and *Flight of the Black Swan*—J. M. Erickson has written the critically acclaimed science fiction novellas *Future Prometheus I & II* and *Intelligent Design: Revelations*. Erickson holds a BA in psychology and sociology from Boston College and a master's degree in psychiatric social work from Simmons School of Social Work. He is senior instructor of psychology and counseling at Cambridge College and senior therapist in a clinical group practice in the Merrimack Valley, Massachusetts, USA.

A NOTE FROM THE AUTHOR

If you enjoyed this book, please feel free to let your friends know about it. I would also appreciate it if you could leave a review. For more information on my other stories, please feel free to stop by my websites.

Websites

www.jmericksonindiewriter.com

www.jmericksonindiewriter.net